Lucy J.

THE LIFE AND TIMES
OF AN EARLY FEMINIST

JAN SPARKMAN

Jan Sparkman

10-1-2016

Books by Jan Sparkman

Fiction
Window to Home
Silk and Steel: Stories of Strong Women
A Memory of Summer

Poetry
The Porch Poems

Nonfiction
Our Fathers before Us: A Family Journal
Years of Grace, Years of Light
One Vision, Many Hands

Library of Congress Control Number:		2011901248
ISBN:	Hardcover	978-1-4568-5853-7
	Softcover	978-1-4568-5852-0
	Ebook	978-1-4568-5854-4

Black and white artwork by Trey Harris.

This book was printed in the United States of America.

To order additional copies of this book, contact:
Xlibris Corporation
1-888-795-4274
www.Xlibris.com
Orders@Xlibris.com
92509

To the two living great-granddaughters of
Lucy J. Williams:

Kathleen McTeer
Carol Sue McTeer Nellessen

And to Lucy's great-great-granddaughter:

Tricia Nellessen Fowler

With gratitude for her tremendous
support for this project

Preface

This book is a fictionalized account of the life of Lucy Jackson Moore Williams taken from extant county and state records and newspaper files in Kentucky, New Mexico, California, and Nebraska, as well as family history data supplied by her descendants.

At a time when women—especially rural women—were expected to stay home and raise children, to defer all important decisions to the appropriate male, Lucy J. Williams strode forth from poverty and loss to influence her world on her own terms. That world was not wide, but it was clearly defined. To step outside its narrow boundaries was, at the very least, to invite the scorn of all the men and many of the women among whom she lived. Lucy would not find fame in her day, but her legacy of wisdom and determination still endures, and those qualities are the essence of her story.

I became fascinated with Lucy Jackson Williams when I ran across accounts of her actions in old local newspapers. The more I found out about her, the more I wanted to tell her story. But despite all the information I gathered from census reports, county archives, old newspapers, and other sources, the story I began to write seemed as dry and inanimate as the dusty books and papers from which I'd resurrected it. How could I infuse it with the character and personality of Lucy herself? I considered different formats, finally deciding on fiction because, in a fictional format, I could use dialogue and imagination to bring Lucy to life. This device allowed me to fill in gaps where no historical record existed, but the story, as written, is much more true than fabricated. The majority of the characters appearing here were real people who have been placed in their proper historical time and setting. However, except in the case of documented words or deeds, they speak and act at the discretion of the author.

Born in Laurel County, Kentucky, in 1857, Lucy Jackson Moore lived with her parents, Campbell and Mariah Moore, until she married Henry Jarvis

Williams in 1881. Some records indicate that she taught school for a few years before her marriage, but this cannot be verified.

Henry was poor but ambitious. By the time he was twenty-five, he had established himself in the mercantile business in London, the county seat of Laurel County. His death from typhoid just before his thirtieth birthday cut short what would surely have been a successful career and, according to family history, left Lucy with little more than her daughter and a son about to be born.

All quotes from newspapers are verbatim as found in the old publications. They tell much of Lucy's story, as well as the history of London, Kentucky, when Lucy lived there. Less information was available for the western component of the book, but what is written here is based on research of census, court and newspaper records of New Mexico and California for the period of Lucy's residence in those places. This research was done on-site and online.

Names are spelled as found in the old records. For instance: Faris/Farris. Though these families were related to each other, those who lived in the town of London seemed to use the "Faris" spelling while those in the rural areas of the county used "Farris." Sometimes, the two spellings were used interchangeably within the same resource.

Lucy's friendship with Poca Ewell FitzGerald is based on letters from Lucy's daughter, Lillian, to Poca's brother, Logan, in the 1960s in which Lillian says in part: *Your sister Polka* (sic) *and mother were great friends. She would come over to visit Mother in the evenings . . . such peals of laughter emanated from that back room . . .*

Pocahontas Ewell was a real person, but I confess to having made up her personality. Once I knew that she and Lucy were friends—that they laughed together—I saw Poca as providing a foil to the serious nature of Lucy's character and wrote her in that role. She threatened to take over the narrative, at times, but I came to love her and to wish I had known her better.

For those readers who know London, the railroad may seem out of place here. That is because, in Lucy's time and prior to its relocation in the second decade of the 1900s, the railroad ran where lies the present Mill Street.

I was euphoric when, in the course of my research, I discovered that Henry Jarvis Williams was a brother to my own grandfather, making Lucy my great-aunt! Why had I never heard of this woman? Why had I had to discover her by chance? The answer lies in the passage of time and my own lack of interest in family background at a time when older family members were still alive and could have given me information. Thank goodness that so many records of Lucy's life still exist despite everything.

And thank goodness for the Internet, which helped me locate Lucy's great-great-granddaughter, Tricia Nellessen Fowler, who provided family stories, old newspaper clippings, letters, and wonderful photographs. I feel blessed to have discovered a relationship with a woman I never knew but came to admire so much and also to have actually met and become friends with the last of that woman's descendants. We are, after all, cousins.

Jan Sparkman
December 2010

Prologue

CATALINA ISLAND, CALIFORNIA

APRIL 18, 1925

Today, I have been thinking of London. Not the huge English city across the ocean, but the tiny village in Laurel County, Kentucky, where I lived for so many years.

When I first moved to London after my marriage, it was a town of fewer than 250 residents, most of them children. John Jackson and his son, Jarvis, had donated land for the town back in 1826 and built the first courthouse and jail. Settlement was slow, for the rugged terrain was unattractive to early settlers who passed it by for flatter, more easily cultivated areas to the north.

London's Main Street spanned the famous Wilderness Road, thoroughfare for immigrant families, as well as for farmers driving their hogs and cattle to the Bluegrass markets, and salesmen (called drummers back then) heading to the state's mountainous eastern region to sell their wares.

Jarvis Jackson was greatly revered in Laurel County. He was once a member of Kentucky's legislature, and he fought long and hard to realize his dream of a railroad through the area. Many of the Swiss immigrants who founded a colony west of London in 1881 bought their land from him. I never knew him because by the time I moved to London, he was old and near death. I got the impression that he was an opportunist, but a benevolent one. Many boy babies born in Laurel County after 1825 were named for Jarvis Jackson, including my husband, Henry Jarvis Williams.

Levi Jackson, to whom I was related on my mother's side (and from whom I got my middle name), also played a part in the history of London, but he and Jarvis Jackson were no kin despite what most people believed.

11

I don't wish to go back to Laurel County, for all those I knew and loved there have moved away or died, but I still feel a deep connection to the place. It is not only where I grew up, married, had my children—it is also where Henry died and where I was forced to come to terms with life on my own. It was there that I had the first glimmer of what I could become.

It was not easy. Survival for a widow in the 1880s generally took one of two forms: remarriage or some sort of dissipation. I was not inclined to take either route. I intended to care for my family through honest work and to encourage other women in similar circumstances to do the same. My zeal for this in those early days made me unpopular with all the men and many of the women until I learned the value of proper timing.

I sometimes ask myself: What if I had taken the path of least resistance as I was expected to do? Would I have seen my children educated? Would I have run a successful business, traveled, come here to this island? What if I had not made up my mind to do as I pleased that long-ago night?

Chapter One

LONDON, KENTUCKY

Lucy tried to marshal her thoughts as she made her way to the stables with Lillian's small hand clinging to hers. She would have to be careful. Jake was not used to opposition, especially from a woman. Her body dragged with the weight of the child she carried inside her. A child who would have no father, no home, not even a horse and buggy if Jake had anything to say about it. *Just keep that in mind,* she said to herself.

What did they expect of her? Not once in the week since Henry died had she been allowed to ask any of the questions that were swirling about in her head. At first she had been too numb to care, had even let Bettie talk her into staying at her house "just till things get settled," but when the first wave of pain and confusion wore off and she'd said she wanted to go home, Bettie had been evasive.

"You might as well stay here with me till the baby comes," she said. "A woman about to deliver doesn't need to be alone. And I paid Lutie Butler to go in and clean up. After all, Henry laid there sick for a month."

"My house wasn't dirty, Bettie," Lucy said. "But thank you for your concern. I'll see Lutie gets paid."

"No need," said Bettie, looking away.

Henry and Bettie's husband, John, had been partners in Faris and Williams, London's largest mercantile establishment. When John died, Bettie promoted her cousin Jake to run her share of the business. At the time, Lucy had said that if it was her, she'd run the business herself, but Bettie was shocked at that idea.

"It's not seemly for a woman to be in trade," she said. "Why, I'd be the talk of the town. And the men wouldn't buy from me."

But she worked behind the scenes. No sooner was John in his grave than she took the account books home to see who owed what. Henry was livid.

"Does she think I'm stealing from her?" he raged. "John would be mortified if he knew. He'd not like her letting Jake run things, either. I don't trust that man, but Bettie . . ."

Lucy tried to soothe him, but inside she was glad that Jake Baugh had not charmed Henry the way he'd charmed Bettie and half the town.

Jake had been the soul of concern during Henry's illness, however, coming by each evening to keep him up to date on things at the store.

"Maybe I was wrong about Jake," Henry said. "I never thought he'd take hold like this in an emergency."

But Lucy had seen the gleam of avarice in Jake's eyes. It should have come as no surprise to her to find that he had somehow managed to wrest Henry's share of the business away without her knowledge, but it did—for the simple reason that Jake could not have done it without Bettie's help—Bettie, who had been her friend and ally when she'd come to London as a new bride.

When she found out that Henry's share of the store did not come to her at his death, but to Jake, Bettie's new partner, the sense of betrayal was so overwhelming that Lucy was physically ill. She looked to Bettie for denial but saw only confirmation on her face.

"But of course you can live with us," Bettie said, looking at Jake. "Until you remarry."

Lucy felt anger rise like hot liquid in her throat. Was that all that was left to her now, a choice between starvation and a loveless life with the town's neediest widower or bachelor? She knew she should be angry with Henry for not leaving his affairs in better order, but Henry hadn't meant to die when he had just started to be successful.

It was obvious that Bettie expected words of appreciation from her for the offer of a roof over her head, even a temporary one, but Lucy could not bring herself to say them.

"I'll manage," she said, trying to keep her voice from shaking. "I can take the buggy and go to Zack and Kate's until the baby comes, then I'll think of something."

Bettie would not meet her eyes.

"What is it?" Lucy asked after a moment.

"It's just that, well, the buggy belongs to us too . . . Henry . . ."

Lucy left her standing there, sputtering. Now she was on her way to seize at least some of her property from Jake—by force, if necessary. The idea of a woman in her condition taking on a man of Jake's strength was laughable, of course. Still, she kept walking.

Jake watched her approach, his shape outlined in the doorway by the light of the barn lantern. Lucy took a fresh grip on Lillian's hand. "Shush," she said when the child began to talk, and Lillian grew quiet.

"Jake, I've come for my horse and the buggy," Lucy said when they stood face-to-face. "By some trick you've got everything Henry worked for, but a woman's got to have a way to get around. So I'm taking it. Don't try to stop me."

She pushed past Jake and went to the stall where stood Prince, the chestnut stallion Henry had given her as a wedding gift. He nickered at her approach, and she spoke to him softly as she led him out. Maybe the buggy belonged to the business, but Prince was hers. His strong warm body gave her courage.

Without looking at Jake, she gathered up the harness and moved toward the wide back door of the barn, and the buggy parked just outside. She put Lillian into it and began to hook Prince to the shaft. When she'd finished, she heaved her heavy body up onto the narrow seat and clicked the reins.

Jake did not try to stop her, but as she drove past, she heard him say, "You can borrow the buggy, Lucy, till you find yourself a man and settle down again."

Chapter Two

Like a hunted animal, Lucy felt an urgency to hide, to find cover for herself and Lillian while she waited for the birth of this next child. She had meant to go to Kate's, but it was late and she could not face the ten-mile journey to her sister's home at Raccoon. She would go to Henry's parents for the night. They were only two miles away in the little mining village of Pittsburg.

The barking of Benny, the old foxhound, brought Till and Sally to the door. Seeing the buggy, Till came down the ragged path toward her, the pain of losing his son still fresh on his face.

"Lucy," he said in his taciturn way. "Get down and stay a spell."

"I was afraid you'd be in bed," she said, handing Lillian into his arms before stepping carefully to the ground.

Sally had followed Till and said, "We would've been in a mighty few minutes, but something just told me we ought to stay up for a bit."

If she had not been so exhausted, Lucy would have smiled at her mother-in-law's claim to second sight. Conversations with Sally were always peppered with pronouncements of things to come that only she was privy to. Sometimes, God got credit for these epiphanies, but more often than not, it was the ubiquitous "something" that told her of coming events.

For the first time, Lucy wished that she believed in such things. Maybe Sally could tell her what she and her children were going to do now that Henry was gone and Jake had taken everything else.

Till and Sally's home was little more than a cabin. By putting beds in the loft and adding a lean-to at the back, they had managed to accommodate Till's children plus four sons and two daughters they had parented together. One girl and one boy had died as infants, and of the remaining daughter and three sons, only the boys were still at home. These children were only slightly older than Lillian, and she loved them. On this night, however, only one-year-old

Edward was at home, Charles and Sidney being away at their sister's house, and so Lilliam was disappointed.

There was nothing of grace or beauty about her in-laws' house, but it was clean. Henry, with his aristocratic good looks and his ambition, had never seemed to fit in here. He'd left as soon as he could, anxious to prove himself. Lucy felt the familiar surge of rage at the unfairness of his death.

Till and Sally made them welcome. They did not ask why she had come, but Lucy told them.

"That's not right, Lucy." Till shook his head. "Henry wouldn't have done you that way. There's some mistake."

She felt a moment of hope. Maybe there was something she could do to challenge Jake and Bettie. If only she were not so tired.

Sally saw her fatigue and said, "We can't solve this tonight. Lucy needs some rest. Everything will look better in the daylight."

She put them to bed in the lean-to, empty now of daughters. Lucy was glad to stretch out and comforted by Lillian's peaceful breathing beside her, but she could not sleep. She felt Henry's presence in the old cabin and was overcome with grief for him.

They had grown up together. Henry had been her champion in the squabbles that arose among the neighborhood children until, at eighteen, he'd moved into London to board with Bettie and John Faris and to clerk at Faris General Store. On his visits to Pittsburg, he talked to Lucy about his dreams of one day owning the store. "I'm saving my money, and when I get enough, we'll get married," he said. "I'm going to make something of myself, Lucy. You'll see."

That was good news to her since she had loved him for years but had not known how he felt about her. She settled down to wait for him, passing the time by helping her parents on the farm and sewing for neighbors. She liked best to trim hats, and it was not long until the women in the community were calling on her whenever their head wear needed refurbishing.

Henry rose from clerk to sales manager to partner, and in 1881, they were married. On their wedding day, Henry presented her with Prince. After the ceremony at her parents' home, he hooked Prince to his buggy, and they drove off toward town and the house Henry had built for them there. First he drove the length of Main Street so she could see the town, and there was his store, with the Faris and Williams sign on it. Lucy had thought she would burst with pride and happiness.

Henry had purchased a lot on Long Street and built a house and stable on it. He told Lucy she could fix up the house to suit herself, so she spent the first months of their marriage making curtains for the kitchen and bedrooms and drapes for the big bay window in the living room. She covered the wood floors with braided rugs, and when spring came, she set out shrubs and planted flowers around the yard.

Lucy had waited eight years for Henry to be ready to marry. During that time, he had become a prominent citizen of London. She was startled, and a little frightened, to find herself invited to community gatherings and expected to entertain from time to time. Neighbor women were forever dropping in so that she had to stop whatever she was doing and provide refreshment and the latest gossip. Lucy had nothing to tell, but she tried to make these women welcome as best she could. They were London's elite, according to Bettie, who had taken it upon herself to educate Lucy.

"Your husband is an important man," she said. "A woman's place is to support her husband at all times. That thought must be uppermost in your mind. What you do or don't do reflects on him and, in a sense, on the store."

Lucy felt a pang of anger. "I'm sure Henry won't ask me to do anything I don't want to," she said.

Bettie gave her a look. "You have a lot to learn, my dear," she said. "I hope you aren't one of those modern women who insists on having her own opinion."

Lucy was, but she knew better than to say so to Bettie Faris, with her splendid house and lofty social status.

"You must help Henry become a success," Bettie said.

Henry didn't need any help as far as Lucy could see. He worked as hard as John and a lot harder than Jake, who had come out of nowhere the year before and who depended on his ingratiating ways to get him by.

At home, Henry was affectionate and always ready to listen to her, but Lucy noticed that when he was around his partner, he grew stiff and formal and often seemed to want her to stay in the background. She let it go because she needed time to consider how best to handle it.

She was excited when she became pregnant, but Bettie was full of dire predictions. Having a first child at twenty-four could be dangerous, she said. Every time they were together, Lucy had to listen to Bettie's accounts of women who had died in childbirth after hours of suffering. She spoke as if she'd experienced it firsthand though she and John had no children. Lucy tried not to let it worry her.

As it turned out, Lillian's birth was fast with no complications. Afterward, Bettie said, in Henry's presence, "Are you sure you haven't done this before, Lucy?" She laughed, to take the edge off her words. It went right over Henry's head, though. His mind was all on his beautiful daughter. He loved Lillian with a passion that was beautiful to see and spent all his free time with her, holding her, singing to her, playing with her. Now that he was gone, Lucy prayed that having known such a love would give her daughter special strength for a future without him.

When Lucy became pregnant again early in 1884, she worried that Henry would not want to share himself with another child, but he was ecstatic.

"Maybe this one will be a boy," Lucy said.

"It doesn't matter," Henry replied. "What could be better than having another girl like our Lillian?"

That was a sweet time. At night, they lay in each other's arms and talked about their dreams for Lillian and the child to come.

"I regret I don't have an education," Henry said. "I can manage without it now that I've got the store, but our little ones, they'll need that. Times are changing, Lucy."

Indeed they were. In February came the first case of typhoid, sometimes called malarial fever. Lucy wrote to Frankfort for information on the disease, but little was available. She guarded Lillian closely, taking care to keep her away from any house where there was sickness.

Bettie wasn't worried. "It's a disease of the lower classes," she said.

Henry didn't seem concerned, either. He was busy helping John and Jake add a storage room to the Faris and Williams building. The job was complicated by the need to dam a small creek at the back of the store to keep the new addition from being flooded during the spring rains. It was messy work. Jake didn't like doing it and appealed to Bettie, who managed to keep him busy on other projects.

John left Henry to mind the store and did most of the work on the dam himself. The weather was warm for the time of year, so he was able to finish the job without undue delays.

"John's worked himself to death on that dam," Bettie said at the end of that week. "He was sick all night, and I think he's got a fever."

A chill ran down Lucy's spine. "Bettie, you have to get a doctor right now," she said.

"If he's not better in a day or two, I will. But I think he's just worn-out."

It was soon obvious that John had typhoid. Bettie was so ashamed of it that she didn't tell anyone for more than a week. The doctor came after dark.

No one really seemed to know how a person got the disease. Dr. Bryant told Bettie it had probably been contacted from the creek water, but he couldn't explain to Bettie's satisfaction how that could happen.

"It's not because we're dirty," Bettie said over and over.

Lucy felt obligated to help in the sickroom, but she sent Lillian to Kate's at Raccoon where, so far, no cases of typhoid had been reported.

John died a week later. While Bettie grieved, Henry and Jake ran the store. Henry did most of the work.

That summer saw many more deaths from the disease. Both "good" families and "bad" suffered. Lucy lived in fear. Just in case it did come from dirt, she washed hers and Lillian's hands often. And she insisted that Henry wash his hands too when he was home, but of course, he was at the store most of the time. In addition to the sadness Henry felt over John's death, he now had full responsibility for the business, and he took that very seriously.

The town fathers debated the typhoid issue at length. On the advice of local doctors, they shut down the public well and decreed that children should not wade in the creek. But the weather was hot and the children loved to play in the cool water, so the ban was ineffective. Lucy often filled a galvanized washtub with water from her well for Lillian to play in on hot summer days. Not until later did she understand that that source of water could be contaminated too. So little was known about such things.

In the first week of August, Henry came home discouraged with the store and Bettie's partnership. "I think she'd like to get rid of me and make Jake her partner," he said.

Lucy could see the worry in his eyes. "I'm sure she's thinking no such thing," she said, hoping to comfort him. "She's still trying to get over John's death."

"Yes, but she's giving Jake more and more authority."

"Well, they're family. I guess that's natural."

"I suppose so. But he's making decisions I ought to make since I'm a partner. Today, I asked him to dredge around the dam and he refused. Water seeped under the back door."

Lucy leaned against him and felt his concern in the tenseness of his body. "You can hire someone to do it, can't you?" she said. "Some youngster looking to make a few cents?"

"Oh, I just did it myself. It was easier. And I'm sure that's what Jake had in mind all along."

He stretched out on the floor to play with Lillian, who was making a castle with the blocks he'd whittled for her. Lucy watched them, feeling restless. If only Henry would let her work in the store, she could keep an eye on Jake. So what if Bettie was embarrassed? She started to mention it to Henry, but just then, he looked up and said, "Come on, Lucy, we need someone to help us build this tower."

"If I got down on the floor, I might never get up again," she said, patting her burgeoning stomach.

"Never again?" said Lillian, and Henry and Lucy laughed together.

The next Saturday, Henry came down with typhoid, and four weeks later, he was dead.

Till and Sally were solicitous of Lucy and Lillian the next morning. Had they slept well? What would they like to eat? Lucy mustered all her energy to appear grateful for their kindness. The cold numbness of those first few days after Henry's death had settled into her heart again, and even Lillian's smile could not thaw it.

When they had eaten and done up the dishes, Till and Sally sat down at the kitchen table and looked at Lucy expectantly. She wondered what they wanted. Did they think she had come to stay?

"Thank you for last night," she said to them. "I'm rested now, so I can go on to Kate's. I'll stay there until the baby comes, and then I'll see what to do next."

Till's eyes filled with tears. "You know we've not got much, Lucy, but you're welcome to any of it."

"I appreciate that, Till, but everything will work out. As soon as I'm able to go about again, I'll make a way for the children and me."

"Henry set great store by you, you know," said Sally. "In his whole life, he never wanted anyone else. He told me years ago."

Lucy was deeply touched, but she was not surprised that Henry had first spoken of his love for her to Sally. Even though she was his stepmother, having married Till after the death of his first wife when Henry and his siblings were young, Sally was the only mother Henry could remember. It was obvious that she was devastated by his death.

"The two of you meant everything to him," she said.

The kitchen was quiet. Lillian, who had been cuddling one of Sally's kittens on the rug in front of the stove, noticed the silence. She put the kitten down and came to stand at Lucy's knee. "Where's my daddy?" she said. "I want my daddy."

A hello at the gate kept all of them from dissolving into tears. When she saw who it was, Lucy gave a little scream.

"Pa! Oh, Pa." She ran toward him as fast as her heavy body would move.

He took her in his arms. "How's my girl? How's my girl?" he kept saying. "I came as soon as I could." Campbell and Mariah Moore, thinking their daughters safely married, had bought a small farm in Nebraska the previous year.

"Where's Ma? Didn't she come?"

"She wanted to, Lucy, but she's not been well. She sent you her love."

With her father's arrival, Lucy knew her first moment of peace since Henry's illness began. He could go with her to Kate's, and there she could rest with family around her until the baby came. For a few weeks, at least, she would have a source of strength to draw from while she figured out her life. But even in her relief, she knew that family could only go so far. In the long run, it was up to her.

From now on, her grief must be a private matter. Lillian needed her. The new baby would need her. She alone was responsible for her children, and she was determined not to fail them.

Chapter Three

When he heard that Henry's estate was not to come to Lucy, Campbell Moore wanted to go straight back to London to look into it.

"We can stay at your house," he said.

"Jake says the house doesn't belong to me," Lucy told him. "He says Henry had it mortgaged through the business. Bettie's got the keys."

Campbell shook his head. "What's happened to you, Lucy? It's not like you to take this without a fuss."

"I-I'm not, Pa. I'm not. But I'm so tired, and Henry's dead, and I don't know what I'm going to do." She couldn't stop the tears.

"It's all right, Lucy. You need some time. I know you're doing the best you can, but I'd feel better if we were in town near the doctor when the baby comes."

Lucy held back. "I'd rather go to Kate's."

He gave in. "Don't fret yourself," he said.

But as soon as she was settled on Kate's snug summer porch, Campbell announced that he was going back to town.

"Let it go, Pa," Lucy said.

"I don't know what you're talking about," he said.

"There's nothing you can do."

"We'll see," he said as he rode off.

Kate came to sit beside Lucy. She looked worn-out despite her good house, her hardworking husband, and her healthy children. She never had a moment for herself, of course. No wonder she was morose. Imagine having four like Lillian to care for!

"I'll never remarry," Lucy said to Kate.

Kate looked stunned. "Of course you will."

Lucy shook her head. "If I hadn't married Henry, I'd never have married at all. Now he's gone, there's no need to be married again."

"That's just foolish, Lucy. How will you feed your children? Where will you live? Who will take care of you?"

"I'll take care of myself."

Kate gave her a pitying look. "A woman alone? Think of your reputation."

"I'm not planning to do anything scandalous, Kate."

"Well, of course not, but that won't keep people from talking."

Lucy felt the narrowness of her life closing in. "Let them talk," she said, with more fervor than she felt.

A look of alarm came over Kate's face, but all she said was, "It's nothing you have to decide today, Lucy, but in good time . . ."

"Don't you ever wish for something more, Kate?"

"More? What else is there?"

"Oh, Kate, there's a whole world. Don't you ever wonder what you've missed?"

Kate shrugged. "I can't see the good of wondering. My life's set, here with Zack and the children."

"It's just . . . What did you think of doing before you married? Wasn't there anything?"

"I married young, Lucy. All I could think about was Zack. What about you? What did you dream of doing?"

Lucy thought about it. "I just wanted to do whatever I liked even if it wasn't considered proper. Men get to do that. Why don't women?"

"Well, women aren't men, Lucy. There are certain things they just can't do."

"Who says so?"

Kate looked uncomfortable. "People smarter than I am. I only know how to do what I'm doing. I don't have time to think about what I'd like to do if I didn't have kids . . ."

"I know, Kate." Lucy reached over and gave her sister's arm a pat. "Don't mind me. I didn't mean to upset you."

They rocked in silence. Then Kate said, "Lucy, do some women really choose their own lives?"

"I don't know any who do, but that's no reason they shouldn't be allowed to that I can see."

Kate shook her head. "It seems awful risky," she said. After a few minutes, she got up and went inside.

Lucy sat there, unable to get comfortable with the baby in her belly kicking every other minute. At least that would soon be over. She closed her eyes and made herself think about life without Henry. She thought of how he would never see his children grow up or know what they became. How he would never own the store outright as he had hoped to do. Sadness gripped her, and she felt the tears just under the surface. But she had cried enough. She left the porch to walk around the yard, her feet making swishing noises in the fallen leaves. She had been happy with Henry, but Henry was gone. It was time to dry her tears and decide where to go from here.

Henry Jarvis Williams Jr. was born on the morning of October 1, 1884, in Kate's big front bedroom. As his sister had, he came into the world with little fuss.

"He looks like my boys did," said Campbell, peering into the tiny face.

"Yes," Lucy said, sadness in her voice. "There's nothing of Henry in him."

"Well, not in his looks, maybe, but he'll take after his father in integrity, I'm sure of it." He touched the baby's cheek. "Bettie's in the parlor."

Lucy sighed and looked away.

"She feels bad about the way Jake treated you, Lucy. She wants to make up."

"I know, but nothing's changed. I still don't have Henry's share of the store."

Her father started to speak, but she waved him off. "I don't care. Really. It's enough that you were able to get the buggy back for me. We've got a little in savings. It'll tide me over until I find work, but I don't know what to say to Bettie."

"Why don't you and the little ones come back to Nebraska with me for a while? It would mean a lot to your Ma."

"I know, Pa. I'll come for a visit, maybe, when I'm stronger, but for now, I have to stay here."

"I don't see why."

"There are things I have to take care of, look into."

Kate came in with Bettie at her heels. Lucy took a deep breath and said, "Hello, Bettie."

The older woman ducked her head. "Good morning, Lucy," she murmured without looking at her.

"Pa tells me that he paid you for the buggy."

Bettie nodded. "I reckon Jake got some of his facts mixed up," she said after a moment. "Turns out Henry owned the house free and clear. I brought you the keys." She laid them on the bedside table.

Lucy felt relief sweep over her. She and her children were not homeless! The house Henry had built and she had furnished with such love was not lost to her. So what if she didn't own a portion of the store? They had a place to stay until she could think what to do. And they had a way to get around. It was a start.

Bettie stood beside the bed, waiting for Lucy to absolve her, but Lucy could not. "You had to know," she said.

"No . . . I mean, I thought . . ."

Lucy turned away. "Thank you for coming," she said. After a moment, she heard the sound of Bettie's retreating footsteps.

Chapter Four

Though her son's birth had been relatively easy, Lucy's health did not return as quickly as she had hoped. She was weak and tired, and her mind refused to think about the future. It was all she could do to rouse herself to feed little Henry. Lillian would come into the bedroom from time to time, and seeing her, Lucy would think, *I must get up*, but she could not force herself to do it. Fortunately, her daughter was happy to have her cousins to play with and did not seem to mind that her mother ignored her.

She lay like that for a week, letting Kate wait on her on top of everything else she had to do. Her father had gone to Tennessee to visit her brother, and Kate's husband, Zack, was feeling puny. Not that Zack or Campbell was much help in the house, anyway.

One morning, when Kate brought her breakfast, the weariness on her face made Lucy gasp. "What am I doing, lying here like a stone?" she said to herself, shame washing over her. Then and there, she got out of bed and prepared to take her children and go back to London. Kate made a feeble attempt to stop her by saying that a woman ought not get up and move around for at least two weeks after giving birth. Lucy said that was a luxury she could no longer afford, and she tried not to see the relief in Kate's eyes.

Making the decision seemed to give her the impetus she needed, and by the time she climbed into the buggy with Lillian on the seat beside her and the baby in a basket between them, she felt her strength begin to flow again.

Lillian was dejected at leaving her cousins, but her natural tendency to find enjoyment wherever she was returned quickly, and she kept up a steady conversation as they drove along.

"What are we going to call this baby, Mama?" she asked.

"Why, his name is Henry Jarvis, just like daddy's," Lucy said.

"But we can't call him daddy!"

Lucy laughed and it felt good. "You're right. That wouldn't do at all. I always called your daddy by his first name, Henry, though most everybody else called him Jarvis. Which name should we call your brother?"

Lillian thought about it. "Jarvis," she said.

"Yes. Let's call him Jarvis. That was the name of the man who settled the town of London," Lucy told her. "Jarvis Jackson. Your daddy was named for him, and now your brother is too."

But her daughter was tired of talk of names. "I saw a squirrel," she said. "Right over there on that limb. He had a nut in his mouth."

And so she chattered, and her chatter soothed the ragged edges of Lucy's soul.

They arrived in London in the late afternoon of that October day. Coming in from the north end of town, they could avoid passing the Faris and Williams store. Lucy wasn't ready to face the emptiness that seeing it would bring, and she had no desire to run into Bettie. She knew her erstwhile friend would not easily forgive what she considered Lucy's betrayal. What would the loss of Bettie's influence and approval mean for her future?

She turned on Seventh Street and proceeded past the Christian Church and across Broad to Long Street. The house Henry had built with such love stood the same, and its familiarity gave Lucy hope and a surge of energy. Who knew what she could do if she set her mind to it? But still she felt lost.

Her neighbor, Maggie Scoville, had seen her drive up, and by the time she had parked the buggy under the shed's overhang and was unhitching Prince, Maggie was there.

"Oh, Lucy," she said, "are you moving back? Bettie said you were."

"I never moved away, Maggie," Lucy replied as she took off Prince's harness and turned him into the fenced area behind the shed. "I just went to Kate's to have the baby."

"The baby!" Maggie exclaimed, as if she'd forgotten that Lucy had been pregnant though she'd seen her only a few weeks earlier at Henry's funeral.

Bettie had said it wasn't proper for a woman in Lucy's condition to go to a funeral. "As far gone as you are, you oughtn't to be out in public," she said. "It's not in good taste."

"Well, I'm going," Lucy had told her. "And that's all there is to it."

"It's clear you don't care what people think of you," Bettie said.

Lucy felt the anger at Bettie—at convention—pour over her again, and it took her a moment to realize that Maggie was speaking.

"Here," she said, "let me get a look. Is it a boy or a girl?"

Lucy lifted the basket down from the buggy's seat and pulled the blanket back. "This is Henry Jarvis Jr.," she said. The baby slept, dark lashes curled against the whiteness of his tiny face.

Maggie looked at him and shook her head. "Poor little thing," she said. "Without a father."

Lucy covered him again and reached to help Lillian down from the high seat. "He's got me, and he's got his sister," she said. "I reckon he'll do just fine."

"But how are you, Lucy? Seems like it's awful soon for you to be driving a buggy, much less climbing in and out of it."

Lucy sighed. Maggie and her husband had been good neighbors—good friends—and she knew that her neighbor was merely voicing the general opinion that women were fragile and needed someone to take care of them, that they could not raise children well alone. She probably didn't even realize how cutting her words were.

"Come on in, Maggie," Lucy said. "I'll make coffee."

Maggie surprised her by saying, "No. No, thank you, Lucy. I'm sure you're tired from your trip. I'll visit another time." She started back across the little meadow that separated their houses, then turned and said, "I've been putting your newspaper in behind the screen door on the back porch to keep it dry."

"Thank you, Maggie. That was good of you."

Lucy watched her go, relieved not to have to keep up appearances any longer. All she wanted was to get the children inside and fed so that she could sit at her own table and take stock of her life.

She found the packet of newspapers where Maggie had said they'd be. Sitting down at the kitchen table, she opened the first issue of the *Weekly Examiner*, a new local paper that Henry had subscribed to when the editor solicited him. She spread it out to look at the headlines, and there it was.

> Died: Of malarial fever at his residence in London, Ky., Henry Jarvis Williams who was a member of the mercantile firm of Faris and Williams, aged 29 years, ten months, and six days. Jarvis Williams, as he was familiarly called and known was born and raised in this (Laurel) county, his mother died when he was quite young, his father being in poor and humble circumstances and having to provide for a large family was unable to give Jarvis advantages which sometimes assist young men in starting in the world (as it is called). With nothing but good health and a will to work he started

out for himself. By untiring industry and energy he soon acquired a fair business education.

Being called upon by C. B. and J. H. Faris he was induced to enter their employ as a clerk in their store in this place where he remained some three years and then by mutual agreement became a partner in the business which has continued to the present time without the slightest interruption or unpleasant relations in the firm.

He was a man of indomitable energy and whatever he regarded to be right and proper to be done, however great the difficulties in the way the greater were his efforts and determination to succeed.

Strictly moral and temperate in his habits, truthful and honest in business, he had many friends who will long remember Jarvis Williams.

Having provided a neat and well-furnished home he leaves there to mourn his loss a beautiful wife and one child.

Funeral services at the Christian Church by Revs. Gill and Boreing of the Methodist Church, after which the burial took place on the hill overlooking the town.

Lucy smoothed the paper out and read the piece again. Whoever the writer was, he had captured the essence of her husband when he wrote that Henry was industrious, honest, energetic, temperate. And those kind words would live on. She could show them to her children when they were older. This is how your father was, she could say. A man to be proud of.

She folded the paper and put it away in the top drawer of her desk. "Oh, Henry," she whispered, "where do I go from here?" What was her most immediate concern? To feed and clothe her children, but beyond that, to see that they were not looked down on as poor orphans.

She went to her closet and took out the only black dress she owned and hung it to air on the porch. She had not intended to wear mourning (what difference did the color of one's dress make?), but now she saw that not to do so would disrespect Henry's memory and cause her children to be pitied. She would wear the traditional black for a time, but that would be her only concession to the mourning convention.

Chapter Five

Lucy could not afford to hide away in her home for the prescribed year or more as many women did. Her children had to eat, and that meant that she had to find work at once. The cash that Henry had left at his death would do little more than buy a month's supply of food and fuel.

She lay awake most of that first night at home trying to think what to do. Near dawn, she dozed off and dreamed that she was walking in a garden full of flowers of many different colors. Several of the blooms broke away from their stems and met in the center of the garden to form a wreath. A fair-haired woman in a dress of pale green came into the garden and sat down on a bench among the flowers. The wreath wafted over to where she sat and lit on her head. She took a small mirror out of her reticule and peered into it. "It is a beautiful bonnet," she said, and in the dream, Lucy saw that to the wreath had been added ribbons and woven straw and that the result was, indeed, a lovely hat.

She awoke to a sense of having solved a problem. She remembered how her mother's friends had called on her to trim their hats from time to time and how satisfied they had claimed to be with the finished product. Why could she not put that talent to work to support her children? She got out of bed, found pencil and paper, and began to make a list of what she would need.

By noon, she had emptied her closets of all but the most necessary clothing and had begun to take the remaining garments apart at the seams, removing any lace or ribbons. Then she separated everything into neat stacks by color and texture.

Of course, she was frequently interrupted in this by Lillian's voice asking questions and by the baby's need to be fed and changed. She had put her work aside to fix the noonday meal when there was a knock on the back door. Bettie stood there with a basket over her arm.

"I've brought you some food," she said without preamble. "I didn't think you'd have much on hand that was useful since you've been gone so long."

Lucy had plenty of vegetables and fruits that she had canned the previous summer, and there was cornmeal and flour for making bread, but the gallon jar of fresh milk would be welcome. She invited Bettie in and thanked her with as much sincerity as she could muster. If another neighbor had come with such an offering, Lucy would have accepted it as a common gesture of concern and sympathy for her loss, but she no longer trusted Bettie's motives.

Still, she set places for three and made coffee. Lillian was happy to see Bettie, and Lucy left the two of them to talk as she prepared the food. She was not surprised when, after they had eaten and Lillian had gone off to play, Bettie came to the point of her business.

"I see you're preparing your mourning clothes," she said. "I'm glad that you understand the value of observing the proprieties. I have a number of dresses, veils, and so forth that I'd be happy to lend you."

"Thank you, but I'll manage with what I've got," Lucy told her.

Bettie shook her head, motioning to the stacks of fabrics and trimming. "There's no need for you to spend a lot of time sewing when you're so busy with the baby and everything."

Lucy considered not telling her what she had decided to do, but it was inevitable that Bettie would find out.

"I'm not sewing for myself," Lucy said. "I'm planning to open a hat shop."

Bettie sat back in her chair with a gasp. "You're planning to go into business and Henry not dead three weeks? Lucy, it just isn't done!"

Lucy wanted to laugh. "Bettie, my children have to eat. I can't depend on you and other neighbors to keep food on my table. What did you think I would do?"

"But you must stay in mourning for a time, Lucy."

"Why?"

"Why? Because it's how things are. A woman of your status must wear black and not go out in public for at least six months, preferably a year, except for the most serious of reasons."

"My status? What does that mean? And what could be more serious than caring for my children? I'll wear my black dress when I go out for a while, out of respect for Henry, but I have to make a living."

"Your husband was an important man—or he would have been. As his widow, you can enjoy the status that his position brought as long as you maintain . . ."

"No one has to tell me about Henry's importance. I knew him better than anyone, and I know that he would say that making a life for our children is my first priority." Lucy didn't remind Bettie that, but for her, she would have owned a share of Faris and Williams and her future would not be so insecure.

"You'll be considered a . . . a . . ." Bettie couldn't go on.

Lucy's patience was at an end. "What would you suggest?" she asked and began to clear the table.

Bettie had her answer ready. "I will make you a small loan," she said, "to help you through the next six months, say, and by that time, you'll have had offers of marriage, I'm sure."

"No, thank you," Lucy said, trying not to shout. "I do not intend to take charity from you or anyone else, and as for remarriage, how can you even bring that up?"

She had nothing against marriage to the right person, under the right circumstances, in some far-off time that, at the moment, she could not even imagine. It was the unbecoming haste with which everyone seemed to think she should proceed that made her so angry.

"Well, I certainly did not mean to offend you, Lucy." Bettie compressed her lips in disapproval. "I was only trying to help."

"Thank you for the food," Lucy said, matching her tone. "It was very thoughtful of you. Now I really must get back to my work."

Bettie left in a huff after saying that she washed her hands of Lucy. Before the day was over, every woman in London would know that Lucy J. Williams did not intend to observe strict mourning, was not interested in remarrying, and—worst of all—meant to be so crass as to go into business.

Chapter Six

For a week, Lucy worked all day and far into the night making hats from her old dresses. Her father stopped by on his way back to Nebraska and helped her make signs announcing her business. They were tasteful signs, she thought, saying only that she invited the women of the community to inspect her collection of hats for sale or to bring in their old hats for retrimming. She hung the signs on the front porch and down by the gate, and from her window, she observed several women stop to read them as they passed, but no one except Henry's Aunt Margaret Moore and her daughter, Martha Alexander, who lived on the hill above the railroad, took advantage of her services. They brought in six of their hats to be trimmed and encouraged Lucy in her venture. As far as she could tell, they were not in the least judgmental of a woman's going into business for herself. Of course, they were family.

After her husband's death, Aunt Margaret had moved in with Martha, and the two of them were charter members of First Christian Church. Lucy had hoped that their sanctioning of her business would bring other women of that congregation to buy her hats, but none of those women, nor any others, came during that first week.

She asked Martha about it. They were sitting on the front porch after a rain shower. It was late October, and the smell of winter was in the air. Lucy needed a load of coal for the stove and another of wood for the fireplaces in order to keep her children warm in the months ahead, and money was running low.

"I know the women in town always buy new hats in the fall," she said to Martha. "Why won't they buy the ones I make?"

Martha sighed. "Most women do what their man tells them to, Lucy, and men don't like a woman in business."

"But can't they see that I have to support my children?"

"You know the answer to that. They expect you to marry again, and the sooner, the better."

Lucy jumped up and began to pace back and forth. "I will not marry just to satisfy those bigots."

Martha laughed. "Bravo," she said, but then she sobered. "But you do see how difficult it's going to be, don't you?"

Lucy sighed and sat back down. "Yes," she said, "but I'm strong and well, and I'm going to stay independent as long as I've got a ghost of a choice."

"I just wish . . ." Martha hesitated.

"What?"

"I hate to see you cut yourself off from everyone like this."

"You mean Bettie."

"She sure could oil the skids for you."

"Of course she could, if I do what she wants. She has no children to take care of, and she has income from the store though she doesn't want people to see her there. John's been gone eight months. She's not remarried, has she? Because she doesn't need to."

Martha sighed. "Can I give you some advice, Lucy? Be mad at Bettie all you want to, but keep it to yourself if you want people to take you and your business seriously."

After she thought it over, she could see sense in what Martha said. Bettie had been a pillar of the community long before Lucy came to London. It was all very well to say that she did not expect or want Bettie's help, but she was beginning to understand that refusing to deal with the anger over her former friend's actions would, in the end, defeat only herself.

To tell the truth, Lucy hadn't had much experience with anger, having been blessed with parents who were mild-mannered and forgiving and who taught their children to follow the same path. The rage she sometimes felt over the loss of Henry and the inflexible traditions under which she was expected to live were new and frightening experiences for her.

Campbell went back to Nebraska, and Lillian missed him even more than Lucy did. She followed her mother like a shadow as she did the housework and sewed on her hats. Lucy made her a rag doll by stuffing six old socks of various sizes with cotton and sewing them together to form a body with head, arms, and legs. She made the doll a dress with bits and pieces of leftover cloth and sewed on yarn for its hair. Lillian loved it. You would have thought she had been given the biggest and best doll available at Bettie's store. Her pleasure lifted Lucy's spirits.

One day, William Jackson, Lucy's cousin, came through town on his way to the mountains where he made a regular circuit every few months to sell his stock of farm and home supplies. William and Lucy had played together as children, and she was glad to see him.

"I'm real sorry about Henry, Lucy. I was down in Tennessee when it happened and couldn't get back," he said. "He was a good man, a good friend."

She nodded. "He thought a lot of you."

They sat at Lucy's table, drinking coffee. William looked around at the hats that hung from every doorknob and chair back. "You going into the hat business?" he asked, and she knew he meant it as a joke.

"Yes," she said.

It took him a minute to see that she was serious. "Have you sold many?" he asked.

"Not a one," she said. "But I will. Surely."

"I reckon. Women always need hats. That's the first thing the women in the mountains ask me about. Hats. Course I don't carry 'em, but they ask just the same."

Lucy's heart began to race. "What if I sent my hats with you to sell to these women?"

He thought it over and shook his head. "What do I know about hats, Lucy? They'd likely ask me questions I couldn't answer."

"What if I went along? Have you got room on your wagon?"

"I-I don't know . . ." She could almost see William rolling the idea around in his head. "Would you be taking the little ones?"

"I'd have to. But they won't be any trouble, I promise. I'll provide food and bedding for us and do all the cooking . . ."

"It'd be good to have the company," William said after a moment. "Gets right lonesome on the road. When could you leave?"

"Whenever you say. I've got three dozen hats made up. How many should I take?"

"Take 'em all if we can find space for 'em. I got to rest my horses and wait on a shipment of tools to come in on this afternoon's train. Then I'll go on out to my brother's and clean out the wagon, see how much room I can give you. Could you be ready to leave Friday morning?"

Lucy wished they could go then and there, but she knew that William had been on the road for weeks and needed to see his family. "Friday's fine," she said.

She spent the next three days packing up canned goods, warm clothing, and quilts—and all her hats. When she saw what a stack of boxes it made, she was afraid that William would say it was too much, but when he came back to town on Friday morning, he calmly loaded them onto the big covered wagon with its side racks. To Lucy's surprise, everything fit in, and there was room left over for Jarvis's sleeping basket and Lillian's doll.

She hadn't thought what to do about Prince, but as it happened, William had. "We're going right past Zack's place. Why don't you leave your horse there until you get back?"

It was the perfect solution. She could see Kate and let her know where she had gone. Then after she told Aunt Margaret and Martha, everyone who needed to know would know.

She should have realized that, in a small village like London, her departure in William's wagon with Prince tied behind would not go unnoticed, of course. One of the first people they saw as they pulled away from her house was Jake. He flagged them down, saying he wanted to see if William had a certain tool he was looking for, but Lucy knew better. He wanted to find out where she was going and why. She looked him in the eye, daring him to question her, but her heart sank at the rumors that she knew would soon be flying.

William waited for her to speak, and when she didn't, he said, "Lucy's my cousin. I'm giving her and the youngens a ride to the mountains."

Jake smirked. "Didn't know you had people in the mountains, Lucy."

"It's a business trip," she said and turned away.

William gave her a look. He and Martha had advised her to keep her reasons for going with him to herself until she saw how things went. But it was done. If she got jeered when she came back without selling any hats, she would have only herself to blame. The stunned expression on Jake's face at her declaration gave her a surge of satisfaction, though. She wondered if Henry would still love the woman she was becoming.

Chapter Seven

At Kate's, they were met at the gate with the news that Zack lay ill with typhoid.

"You can't come in," Kate said, and the hollowness in her voice told Lucy that she held out no hope for her husband's recovery.

Lucy was already out of the wagon, but she hesitated. Even if she were willing to expose herself to the disease, she couldn't take that chance with her children. She reached for Kate, but her sister backed away.

"It's not safe, Lucy," she said.

"But what will you do? I have to help, Kate."

"No. You've been through this. You know what it's like. I'll be all right. Zack's sister, Dora, took the children home with her, and Aunt Molly's here."

Molly Renfro was not their aunt, just a neighborhood friend who was always willing to help in times of trouble.

"But I can't leave you like this." Lucy looked at William as if he could give her answers.

He sighed. "I can look after the little ones for a day or two, I reckon. We were going to be sleeping in the wagon, anyhow."

She walked over to him and touched his arm. "I know it's a lot to ask," she said. "But Kate was there for me when Jarvis was born. I have to do what I can."

He nodded.

"I'll come regularly and feed the baby," Lucy said, "and fix you and Lillian something to eat."

"But what about you? Won't it be dangerous?"

"I took care of Henry without getting sick. I know what to do. And I won't go near Zack."

William moved the wagon into a grove of trees behind the barn. Lucy fed Jarvis and soothed Lillian's disappointment over not seeing her cousins as best she could. Then she left them and went to Kate.

While her sister and Molly cared for Zack, Lucy cooked up enough food to last for a few days and then cleaned Kate's sadly neglected house. From time to time, Kate would come out of the sickroom and say she shouldn't be doing it, but Lucy knew she was glad for the help.

Before bedtime, Lucy washed her hands with lye soap and went out to check on William and the children and to feed Jarvis again. Her son was doing well despite the hours he'd spent traveling in his three short weeks of life. He just slept and ate and slept again.

"How's Zack?" William asked.

"He'll not last much longer," she said. "Kate knows it, but she won't say so."

"Well, no, she wouldn't, I reckon."

"She doesn't say much of anything. And she eats nothing."

William patted her shoulder. "Lucy, you can't do no more than you're doing."

"Thank you for being so good about this. I know you need to be on the road."

"Long as the weather's good, a few days won't make that much difference," he said. "Just so we get to the mountains and back before the snow flies."

Zack died on the morning of the second day they were there. Kate came into the kitchen, her face ashen. "He's gone, Lucy," she said. "I reckon you know how it is."

Lucy stood there, feeling the agonizing loss of Henry all over again. She remembered a day last summer when Kate and Zack had come into town for supplies and had spent the afternoon at her house. The four of them—Zack and Kate and she and Henry—had sat on the back porch, talking and laughing, while the children played around them. Who would have thought that three months later, both Zack and Henry would be dead? *It's a good thing we can't see into the future,* Lucy thought. *It would be more than we could stand.*

As soon as Zack was buried, she and William went on with their trip. She promised Kate that she would come to see her as soon as they returned. Kate nodded but said nothing. She stood watching them drive off, her arms folded tightly across her bosom. That picture of her was stamped on Lucy's mind.

By this time, it was the last week of October. The weather was cool in the late evening and early morning, but the days warmed up to hot and the sky was as clearly blue as Lucy had ever seen. The trees were glorious in their fall dress. As William's wagon took them deep into the Kentucky mountains, the beautiful surroundings soothed Lucy's aching heart.

Everywhere they went, they were welcomed. William would stop at the schoolhouse in each community, and the crowds would gather. The men bought his hammers and nails, his rope, his blocks of salt, and the women his cooking pots and sewing thread.

At each stop, Lucy would take the hats from their boxes and display them along the back of the wagon and on a wooden hat tree that William had made for her. The first day, she was so nervous that her hands were clammy and she had to keep wiping them on her skirt.

At one stop, a woman of about Lucy's age approached the wagon and stopped in her tracks when she saw the array of hats. "Well, I'll be," she said in awed tones. Then she came forward and began to examine the hats one by one.

Lucy swallowed her nervousness and asked if she could help her.

"I ain't had a new hat in a coon's age," the woman said, reaching out a finger to stroke the velvet ribbon on one of Lucy's creations.

"Would you like to try it on?"

"Could I?" She seemed to hold her breath.

"Certainly," Lucy said, taking it down. She was glad she had remembered to bring along a small mirror. She handed it to the woman, who looked at herself, turning her head from side to side.

"It's the prettiest thing I ever saw," she said. "How much you asking for it?"

Pricing had been difficult. Lucy did not know what mountain women would be willing to pay for a hat; and William, so astute with his own goods, had no idea what hats were worth. In the end, she had based the price on what she thought the materials would have cost her if she'd had to purchase them at Bettie's store and added 10 percent. William said that was fair and left her room to bargain with her customers.

"Don't drop your price too soon," he'd said with a grin. "Give 'em a chance to think they put one over on you."

"That one's a dollar," Lucy told the woman.

She sighed. "Too steep for me," she said, placing the hat back on its peg.

Lucy's heart sank. "I do have a few hats that are only seventy-five cents," she said, pointing them out.

The other woman shook her head. "That's the one I want," she said.

Lucy was about to break William's rule and tell her she could have it for less when a man came over. He put his arm across the woman's shoulder and asked her if she saw anything she liked. When she showed him the hat she had looked at, he handed Lucy a dollar, saying to the woman, "I reckon that ain't too much if it'll bring a smile like that to your face."

After that, other women came. They talked about the first woman. "She ain't showed no interest in nothing since her youngen died," one of them told Lucy. "Her man had just about give up."

Lucy felt a lump in her throat, not only for the dead child and the woman's grief, but also for the blessing of a man who understood that a hat could never replace a child, but it could give a woman something else to think about once in a while.

As they drove from community to community, word that William's cousin had hats for sale preceded them. When they arrived, the women were waiting. Before long, she had sold every hat she'd brought and spent her time at the remaining stops taking orders for hats she would make when she got back to London. Lucy noticed that mountain women seemed to know their own minds—unlike so many of the women she knew back home. They had a strength and scrappiness that she admired.

But she was tired. Within the space of six weeks, she had lost her husband, given birth, made her hats, helped her sister through the death of her spouse, and taken a two-hundred-mile trip in a wagon with her children. She could not wait to get home.

Chapter Eight

For the next week, Lucy was ill with exhaustion. Martha, who had come as soon as she saw that Prince was back in his pasture, put her to bed and stayed with her. Lucy protested, but in the end, she allowed it. Common sense told her that she had endangered her physical health by the long wagon ride so soon after Jarvis's birth, not to mention what the grief and pain of the past two months had cost her. The future was not as bleak as it had been, thanks to the sale of her hats, but it was still tenuous and would be for some time to come. If she did not want to leave her children orphans, she would have to take better care of herself.

As her body rested over those next few days, her mind was busy with plans for the store she would open. Her home was not suitably located for business. Not the kind of business she envisioned. She needed a more visible venue for her hats, and she racked her brain for solutions. Renting a store would be expensive to start with, and there would be the cost of heating it and buying stock. She dreamed of a millinery establishment that would serve not only Laurel but also the surrounding counties as well. Ambitious dreams for a poor woman.

One day, there was a knock on the door, and she heard Martha telling someone that Lucy was indisposed and could not accept visitors. She heard the low rumble of a man's voice but could not catch his words.

She was dozing when Martha came in and pulled up a chair beside the bed. "You had a visitor," she said. "But I sent him away."

"Who was it?"

"Well," she said, eyes twinkling, "I guess you'll soon know. He left you a note."

"The postman?"

Martha laughed and shook her head. "No no." She handed Lucy an envelope. "Find out for yourself."

The envelope told her nothing, so when she opened the letter and saw Jake's signature at the bottom, she knew a moment of panic. Why would he write to her? Had he found a way to take her home, after all? She opened the folded note, and by the time she finished reading it, tears were running down her face.

Martha was alarmed. "What is it?"

"I'm laughing," Lucy said to reassure her. "It is just so funny."

Seeing that Martha still had no idea what she meant, Lucy turned back to the thin fragment of paper, saying, "Listen to this:"

> Lucy—I have decided that you and me will get married as soon as you are better. I know you need a man and I need someone to cook and wash for me. Since you already have a house, I can move in there after the preacher ties the knot. I've talked it over with Bettie and she is agreeable. She says someone needs to take you in hand. I expect to hear from you soonest. Jake

As she reread the note, Lucy grew less and less amused. How dare Jake and Bettie decide that she needed "to be taken in hand"! She was not surprised that Jake could be so crude, but how could Bettie be party to it? What had happened to the rational woman she had met when she first came to London? Jake seemed to have an evil hold over her.

"Bring me my writing tablet," she said to Martha. "I'll nip this foolishness in the bud right now."

"Good," said Martha, handing her paper and pen. "You write it, and I'll deliver it straight into that no-good Jake's hands."

After setting down the date and time at the top of the sheet, Lucy wrote,

> Mr. Baugh: I have no intention of marrying you, so please do not write to me again. Hire someone to do your cooking and your laundry and tell Bettie that I can take myself in hand quite as much as is necessary, so she need not fret herself about it. Lucy J. Williams

And when Martha had marched off to Bettie's store to give Jake her missive, Lucy went back to her napping and dreamed that she and Henry were riding Prince through a field of grain that was nearly over their heads.

On the first day she felt well enough, Lucy took the children and walked the three blocks to Main Street. Lillian skipped along beside her as she pushed Jarvis in the big English-style baby carriage that Henry had purchased for Lillian just after she was born. It was a crisp November morning, the air filled with wood smoke from many chimneys and the sounds of children off to school at Laurel Seminary. Men on horseback and on foot hastened off to their day's labors. Women hung their wash on clotheslines in their backyards.

Lucy nodded to those she met. Southern men were respectful of women in public, regardless of what they thought of them in private, so most of the men politely doffed their hats to her in response to her greeting. They all knew her—knew that she was newly widowed and financially desperate—but they offered no smiles or kind words. Their attitude made Lucy more determined than ever to make a place for herself without their help.

None of the women she saw that morning nodded or spoke, having no doubt been instructed by their husbands or Bettie to have nothing to do with her. *And sheep that they are, they follow orders,* Lucy said to herself.

She was furious to be taken for such a pariah, and she did not begin to understand it. How did she threaten these women? A mere two months ago—before Henry's death—she had been respected by all of them. Now because she had not hidden herself away but continued to go about in public with her children and (worst of all) had actually announced that she intended to go into business, she was shunned. But how could she have done otherwise?

Her objective on that morning was to visit Henry's relatives, James and Phoebe Dees. James, a brother to Henry's long-dead mother, had a store on Main Street and was highly respected in London. Lucy did not know them well, but they had made her a condolence call, and she felt that she might be allowed to call on them in return. She was family, for better or worse. To her relief, she and the children were invited in and treated cordially.

Phoebe was a small round woman with a cheerful smile. James was quiet, almost stoic. A bout with smallpox during the war had left him scarred about his face. He shook hands with Lucy and then excused himself, saying he had to get to the store.

Phoebe offered her coffee and poured milk for Lillian. Lucy could not refuse her hospitality even though, since Henry's death, she preferred that Lillian eat only at home so as not to expose her to the threat of disease that, she was convinced, lurked in many kitchens.

James and Phoebe lived in small attractive quarters behind their store. Adjacent to the store, on Main Street, was an empty building that James had once used for storage. It was sturdily constructed and seemed a likely place for a business.

"Would James be willing to rent me the old storage building?" Lucy asked.

Phoebe sighed. "Ah, law, Lucy, I wouldn't know about that."

"But you must have some idea if he would," Lucy persisted.

"Now, honey, I don't get into his business."

Lucy saw that Phoebe would not help. She stood, saying, "Then I wonder if I might go over to the store and ask him myself."

Phoebe sighed again but said, "I reckon it wouldn't do no harm to ask."

Lucy thanked her for the coffee and began to gather up the children.

"Why don't you just leave the little ones here with me," said Phoebe. "I—we, don't have no babies around much. I'm just aching to get my hands on that one."

So Lucy left Jarvis there but took Lillian with her.

At the store, she found James sitting on a high stool behind an ornate cash register. Lucy had heard about this newfangled device from Bettie, who was miffed that James should have one in his store before she had one at Faris Mercantile, especially now that she and Jake had added a whole new section to the store, making it the biggest in London.

James nodded to her as she came in. If he was surprised to see her, he didn't let on. The store was deep and cavernous, but as far as Lucy could tell, there were no other customers. She took a deep breath and prepared to make her request, but before she could get the words out, James said, "Lucy, I could make you a small loan, I reckon, if you're needing one."

She got that familiar flash of anger, and it showed in her face for James put up his hand and said, "Now don't get on your high horse. Isn't that why you came?"

Lucy breathed slowly to calm herself. "No, sir, it is not. I came to ask you to rent me the storage building for my business."

"Lucy . . ."

It was her turn to hold up a hand. "Hear me out. I've just returned from a trip to the mountains with my cousin . . ."

He nodded, so she knew he had heard about that.

"And I sold all my stock of hats and took orders for dozens more. I can fill those orders from my home, but that won't bring in the new orders it will take to feed my children. I need to be here on Main Street, where passersby can see me, examine my work."

James shook his head. "What makes you think the women around here will buy from you?"

Her heart sank. "To tell the truth, I don't know that they will. But I've got to make a living, and I'm good at what I do. I have to start somewhere."

"Not had no men wanting to marry?"

She turned her back on him and started to walk away.

"Now, Lucy," James said, and she heard the hint of shame in his voice, "it's just what most women would do in your place."

She turned back. "I'm not most women," she said. "My husband has been gone but a short time. I'm still grieving for him. I will not marry for convenience no matter how many men come around asking me. No woman should have to do that."

He shrugged. "It's the way of the world, Lucy."

She shook her head because she could not trust herself to speak.

"How much rent could you pay?" James's voice was resigned.

"Not much."

He thought it over. "I'll give you a six-month lease on the building for thirty dollars. If, after that time, you're still in business, I'll renew the lease and raise the payments. Could you manage that?"

"Would I have to pay the whole amount at once?"

He sighed. "I'm not in need of the money, Lucy. I reckon you could pay it by the month. But that old building needs a lot of fixing up. You'd have to do that yourself."

"I can. I will. Thank you, James."

She walked home on air, not even noticing who did and who did not speak to her. She had a store building. What did it matter that she did not yet have any customers?

Something else happened that morning that seemed insignificant at the time. James had for sale a beautiful upright piano, and it was displayed to best advantage just inside the front entrance to the store. While he and Lucy talked, she had been vaguely aware of someone's tapping out a tune, but she did not realize that it was Lillian until she finished her business with James and turned to go. So intent was her daughter in finding the right notes to her little song that she did not hear her name called. When Lucy touched her shoulder, Lillian looked up at her as if she were a stranger.

"Come, darling, don't leave fingerprints on the nice piano," Lucy said. "We must go and get your brother."

"I played a song," said Lillian, making no move to get up.

"Yes," Lucy said. "That was very nice. Now we must go."

"But I want to play the piano some more," Lillian protested.

"When you are older, perhaps you may take lessons," Lucy told her, but she knew it would be a long time before they could afford such luxuries. Still, she was amazed at Lillian's aptitude. Where had it come from? While Henry's family loved to sing, Lucy had never heard any of them play an instrument. She could not know then what an impact that few moments at the piano would have on her daughter's life.

Chapter Nine

But that was far in the future. First, she had to get James's storage building clean enough to move into. It was little more than a shed, about twelve feet wide and twenty feet deep with two good-sized windows in the front. Inside, she found a row of shelves across the back wall, a small heating stove, and several years of accumulated dust and debris. She saw that it would not be safe to keep the children with her as she worked, so she arranged for them to stay with Phoebe. As soon as they heard what she was doing, Martha and Aunt Margaret came to help. The realization that she was not as alone as she had thought gave Lucy courage, and she set about her task with enthusiasm.

The fire they tried to build in the old stove was a disaster. Goodness knows how long it had been since the chimney had been cleaned. They poked out as much of the soot as they could with a broom handle and then laid a fire of paper and twigs in the stove's round belly. No sooner had they lit the paper than smoke began to roll out of the stove door and into the room. They opened the door and the windows, but that just drew the smoke out into the street and caused a commotion. Someone yelled fire, and that brought James and others running with pails of water. James doused the tiny fire in the stove, and the smoke soon dissipated, but not before Lucy had heard the laughter from the crowd. Well, that was what she got for insisting on having a store on Main Street, she told herself. Right out in the open for everyone to see. She would just have to get used to it.

James didn't say a word about the commotion. Instead, he cleaned the flue for her, and after that, the stove worked fine.

There was no well on the property, so she and Martha had to carry water from Phoebe's. This wasn't too bad since Lucy had to go there frequently to nurse Jarvis, anyway. They rigged up a trough of sorts behind the shed and soon stockpiled enough water for their cleaning. Lucy had never minded hard work as long as it accomplished something useful, so the next few days were therapeutic for her despite the derision she saw in the eyes of those who came by to gawk. Once they had moved out the trash and washed everything down, she sent Martha and Aunt Margaret home.

"I don't know how to thank you," she said as they left.

"You've still got a lot of work here," Aunt Margaret said. "Are you sure you don't need us to stay and help?"

"No," said Lucy. "You've done more than enough. And I love you for it."

After they were gone, she looked around at this place she had rented—had tied herself to. She pictured the shelves filled with spools of lace and ribbon, with bolts of fabric, with "notions" that the women of London needed for their sewing. And she saw the front windows showcasing the hats she would create. London's economy had grown on the strength of coal mining and the coming of the railroad, and Lucy felt justified in imagining that women who might eventually admire her products in the window could also afford to come in and buy. Common sense said they could not go on hating her forever.

She worked until nearly dark that day before she picked up the children at Phoebe's and went home.

That night, the little storage building burned to the ground. Tired from her hard work, Lucy slept through the fire bells and did not know about it until James came to tell her the next morning. He blamed a faulty flue, but she wondered.

"I've come to give you back your payment," James said. "I'm right sorry, Lucy."

"It's not your fault, James," she said.

So after four days of hard labor, she was right back where she had started with no idea of what she would do next. But as she looked into the rosy faces of her children that morning, she realized that she was lucky. She still had her babies, and they were well. She had lost the store building, but not her hats or the materials to make them. If someone had burned the building (and there was no way to prove or disprove that), James was the one they had hurt, not her. She would just have to start over. It seemed that was all she had been doing for months.

Lucy was thankful for relatives like Aunt Margaret and Martha and the Deeses, but she needed customers who would support her business; she needed to make an effort to be a part of the community. Her mother had often quoted a text from Proverbs 18:24: "A man that hath friends must show himself friendly." Lucy took that to apply to women as well, so the next Sunday morning, she took the children to the First Christian Church where

Martha had said there was a Sunday school class just for women. It was the first time Lucy had been in a church since Henry's funeral, and she felt quite uncomfortable not just because it brought back sad memories, but because she knew she was being watched—measured—by those around her. She had just about decided that this would be her first and last visit when a young woman came up to her and held out her hand.

"Good morning," she said. "I'm Poca Ewell."

She ran the words together so that it came out *pocoyule*, and Lucy took that to be her first name.

"I'm Lucy J. Williams, Pocoyule," she said.

"Call me Poca," said the other woman, laughing. "Ewell is my last name."

Lucy was embarrassed and apologized, but Poca waived it off. "I've been wanting to meet you for ages," she said. "I hear you're opening a store."

"I was," Lucy said. "But now that the building has burned . . ."

"That was a shame," said Poca. "But it wasn't much of a building. You can find something better."

Lucy felt light-headed to have met a woman who seemed to accept her as she was. She invited Poca home for Sunday dinner, and she accepted. After they had eaten and Lucy had put the children down for their naps, she and Poca talked and talked. Poca said that she'd been away at school and had just returned home, and Lucy described how difficult it had been since Henry's death and why she could not just sit around waiting for life to improve.

"You should probably not be seen with me," she said to Poca, trying to make a joke of it.

"When you get to know me better, you'll see that I don't pay much attention to what people say," she answered. "And you shouldn't, either."

"I know you're right, but I just wish . . ."

"What?"

"I wish that women didn't have to consider traditions and rules and . . ."

"Who says they do?"

"Just about everyone."

"Then maybe it's up to you to change that."

"I? How can I change it?"

"By showing those women that they can speak and act for themselves, that they don't always have to do what their husbands dictate."

Lucy laughed. "That could get me killed."

Poca gave her a look. "Well, at least you'd be dying for a good cause," she said.

Poca was a breath of fresh air in Lucy's life. She inhaled Poca's robust enthusiasm, her cosmopolitan sparkle. She could not get enough of the tales of her travels, her studies, and though Poca seemed to revel in Lucy's fascination with her, she was easily bored. Lucy worried that she would not be able to hold Poca's attention for long, so she soaked up her ideas, her fervor while she could. Poca's friendship helped Lucy over that first hump of despair after the fire and opened her mind to a wider world.

Like Martha, Poca told Lucy to mend her fences with Bettie—not for Bettie's sake, but for her own.

"Bettie's not a bad person, you know," Poca said. "She's just bossy."

"Tell me something I didn't know," said Lucy. "From the moment I moved to London, Bettie's been trying to sort me out according to her own wishes. If Henry had lived . . ."

"What? He could have acted as buffer between you and Bettie?"

"Maybe. But what I meant was, if Henry had lived, he would have bought Bettie out and then she would have had no more influence over me."

"You don't know that. And anyway, it doesn't matter. Henry's gone and Bettie's got the store."

Sometimes, Poca could be brutal.

Lucy sighed. "Bettie won't be happy until I'm safely remarried," she said and told Poca about Jake's proposal and Bettie's comment.

Poca laughed, but then she said, "You know, there's another way to look at this."

"At Jake's proposal? I don't think so."

"No no. I meant there's another way to look at Bettie's bossiness."

"And that is?"

"Bettie's a lonely woman. Her husband's gone too, you know. She has no children. She's pretty much stuck in her social position—boxed in by it. I think she's jealous of you."

"That's ridiculous. Why doesn't she take her own advice and get married?"

"Maybe no one has asked her."

Lucy found that even more ludicrous. "There are a dozen men around here who would marry her for the store alone," she said.

Poca thought that over. "You're right," she said. "So it must be the store itself that's keeping her from marrying. Now that it's hers, she won't give it up. I'll bet she makes every decision."

"So what does she need Jake for?"

"Actually, Jake's gone."

"Gone?"

"Left day before yesterday, I heard. Bettie's taken her nephew, Will Neal, as her new partner."

"And that just leaves me with the same question. What does she need him for?"

"To maintain her status as widowed matriarch." Poca struck a pose, holding her hands beseechingly in front of her bosom. "I'm just a woman," she said, mimicking Bettie's voice. "I can't run the store, but I can keep it as a memorial to my dear husband." She smote her brow in fine dramatic fashion. "It is my duty to be an example for other widows."

Lucy laughed. "You should be on the stage," she said, but it started her thinking. Bettie had been a magnanimous friend as long as she thought Lucy was dependent on her for welfare and social position. She had seen Lucy as someone she could mold into her own image, someone to take over the reins of matriarchy when the time came. But Lucy had disappointed her. If she carried out her plan to run her own business openly (not behind the scenes as Bettie did), Bettie feared the effect it would have on her influence in the community. After all, Lucy had been her protégé.

Lucy came out of her reverie to hear Poca say, "She has a building for rent, you know."

"Who?"

"Bettie, silly. She's got a For Rent sign on that little section of the old store that used to house cattle feed. Now she's got that big new building, she doesn't need the shed."

"She'd never rent it to me," Lucy said, but already she was envisioning its perfect location.

"You'll never know until you ask."

She shook her head. "Bettie would be there every day, giving me advice I don't want or need."

"You don't have to take it. Are you a woman or a weakling?" Poca said in her flippant way.

Over the next few days, Lucy pondered the possibility of renting from Bettie and finally decided to walk past Faris and Neal, read the sign, and get a close-up look at the building. She hoped she would not run into Bettie.

The shed had a wide window across the front—something she would need for display—and it looked as well-built as James's old storage room.

As she stood on the wooden walkway in front of it, Will Neal came out of the main store and asked if he could help her. Lucy knew him slightly because he had helped out in the store from time to time when Henry was there. He seemed polite and respectful.

"I-I was just noticing that this section of the building is for rent," she said. "Do you know how much Bettie's asking for it?"

"As a matter of fact, I do," he said. "I'm Will Neal, Bettie's new partner, and she leaves all such things to me."

It had not occurred to Lucy that she might be able to rent the building without speaking face-to-face with Bettie.

"I'm Lucy J. Williams," she said, holding out her hand. "My late husband was John Faris's partner."

"I remember you," Neal said, returning her handshake. "I heard about the fire at James Dees's place. You're looking to relocate?"

"Yes," Lucy said. "I need to find something else as soon as I can."

"I'd be glad to rent you the shed," he said. "I can get some of the workmen to clean it out."

This was too easy. "How much?" Lucy asked.

"Let's say seventy dollars a year, and you buy the coal."

A steep price. Lucy asked him the same question she had asked James. "Would I have to pay it all at once?"

"I would need fifteen dollars down and then five a month for the rest of the year. Could you do that?"

He didn't seem like the kind of man who'd barter.

"What about Bettie?" Lucy asked.

Will drew himself up. "As I said, she leaves all such decisions to me," he said.

Lucy still didn't believe him, but she wanted the store, and she was glad not to have to ask Bettie for it. There would be a reckoning, of course, but Lucy was happy to put it off as long as possible.

"I'd need immediate possession," she said.

"Yes, indeed," said Will. "I'll get you the key." He went into the store and came back with a large key on a cord. Lucy had her money ready, and they made the exchange. Once again, she walked home with the knowledge that she had a place to sell her goods.

Chapter Ten

True to his word, Mr. Neal had his workmen clean the shed. By the last week of November, all that was left for Lucy to do was scrub the walls and windows and arrange the shelves to her liking. She had little to put on them, of course, but she had ideas.

The hats ordered by the mountain women had been completed and mailed off. Now the payments had begun to arrive—enough to allow her to purchase a supply of coal to heat both her home and the store, with a little leftover. She would make more hats from the materials she had on hand and pray that she could find buyers for them. If she couldn't, she would not have money to live on, much less buy more stock.

Jarvis was still small enough to sleep comfortably in the carriage, and as long as Lillian had her doll, she was content. Lucy took them along that first morning, and once she had them settled, she filled a pail with water, slivered lye soap into it, and began to wash the wide front window. She had barely started when Bettie appeared outside the window and stared in at her. Lucy knew she would get no more work done until Bettie had said her piece, so she got down off the chair she'd been standing on and motioned her inside.

"Good morning, Bettie."

Bettie nodded.

Lucy pushed the chair toward her. "Won't you sit down?"

She shook her head but said nothing. Lucy waited, dreading the tirade to come. Then to her surprise, Bettie started to cry.

"Oh, Lucy," she said. "I'm so sorry."

Lucy couldn't help the gasp that escaped her lips. An apology was the last thing she had expected.

"S-sorry?" she stammered.

Bettie sank down in the chair and put her face in her hands. "You know what a fool I am—always having to have my own way, trying to run things. I didn't think this would happen."

"You didn't think what would happen?" Lucy's head was spinning.

"I thought I was doing what was best for you when I consented to let Jake make that silly proposal. I thought it would bring you back to me."

"Well, you were wrong," Lucy said, her hackles rising.

"We were so close! I thought of you as my daughter," Bettie sobbed.

"Would you have turned the whole town against your daughter?"

"I saw you heading in a dangerous direction, and I thought it was my duty to-to change that, whatever it took."

"That is the most arrogant statement I've ever heard. You don't—you can't—own me, Bettie."

The older woman kept sobbing.

Lucy didn't want to feel sorry for her, but she did. After a moment, she touched her shoulder. "Hush, Bettie, you'll make yourself sick."

Bettie fumbled in her handbag for a handkerchief and wiped her eyes. "To think that you would go to James and then to Will when you needed help and not to me," she said, her voice shaking.

Lucy was not going to make this easy for her. "You're the one who said you'd washed your hands of me," she said.

Bettie started to sob again. Lillian, who had been clinging to Lucy's skirt through all of this, said, "Don't cry, Aunt Bettie. It only makes things worse."

She was echoing Lucy's words to her, but Bettie seemed to take them to heart.

"You know, Lillian, I believe you're right," she said, straightening up. "What is needed here is action, not tears." She stood and rubbed the handkerchief over her face again. "I'm going home to get my apron, then I'll be back to help you wash that window, Lucy."

With that, she strode out the door. Lucy sat down in the chair with a thump. She knew that something momentous had just happened, but as yet, she couldn't tell if it boded well or ill for her future.

Lucy had dreaded facing Bettie, and so she welcomed the sense of relief that came from having survived the first confrontation with her. Would her apology translate into a meeker, less contentious attitude? Lucy doubted it, but she decided to assume that it would and to treat Bettie accordingly. When Bettie came back a few minutes later, prepared to wade in and take over, Lucy was emboldened to insist on her own methods of cleaning despite suggestions to the contrary. All in all, Bettie took it well. She worked alongside Lucy until it was time to go home and get dinner, and though her lips tightened a few times when her advice went unheeded, she did not make a scene about it.

By the end of that week, the store was ready for occupancy. Lucy's meager stock was lined up on the shelves, and the few hats that she had on hand were displayed in the front window. A hand-lettered sign read, Lucy J. Williams, Millinery and Notions.

But again, her plans were thwarted. Before she could put out her Open for Business sign, news came that Kate was sick with typhoid and needed her. She packed a bag, closed up the house and store, and went to take care of her sister.

She left Lillian with Aunt Margaret and Martha, but she had no choice except to take Jarvis with her. He was healthy and growing well, and she felt she could keep him from contact with the disease while she was there. Her biggest fear was that she would become infected herself.

As when Zack had been ill, his sister, Dora, took Kate's children home with her. Kate missed them terribly. Lucy gathered up the pictures of them that Kate had sitting around and took them into her sickroom.

"Oh, Lucy, I'm so glad you're here," Kate said, trying to smile. "I know it's a hardship for you—trying to get your business started and all—but I don't think I could stand to have anyone else take care of me."

The pain in her voice broke Lucy's heart. She knew that Kate might never see her children again. Not that she didn't have hope, at first. When Kate would have a day or two without the fever and the coughing, Lucy would be encouraged, but then it always came back worse than before. The doctor came regularly and did everything he knew to do, but it was not enough. A week before Christmas, Kate said, "I'm not going to get well, Lucy."

Lucy protested, but Kate went on, "There's some settling up I need to do. I've told Dora to sell the farm and put the money away to educate the boys when the time comes. They'll go to live with her, but I wanted—I wondered, could you take Lucy Dora?" She looked at Lucy as if she thought she might refuse, but how could she? Kate's daughter was dear to her for her own sake, but Lucy was especially anxious to accept the responsibility for her niece so that her sister's mind could be at ease.

"Oh, Kate, you know I will," she said through her tears. "Don't worry about any of the children. Just try to get better."

Kate shook her head.

Lucy sent word to Zack's sister, Dora, and the next day, she came and brought the children. They were not allowed to touch their mother, but at least they got to see her one last time. Kate's condition had so deteriorated by then that it was doubtful she even realized the children were there. Lucy could hardly bear the sadness.

When Kate had been laid to rest beside Zack, Lucy helped Lucy Dora pack up her belongings. The child tried to be brave, but at age seven, she could not help but cry for her mother and for the brothers she would miss so much. Her aunt Dora promised that she would bring the boys to town for a visit soon. Dora and Lucy felt a special bond with the little girl because she was named for the two of them.

The weight of the grief in her heart threatened to destroy Lucy as she drove back to town. What would happen next? Where would she get the energy to take care of her children, help Lucy Dora deal with her loss, and make the store provide enough for them to live on? And then it dawned on her that it was Christmas Eve, and though she did not think Lillian would know what day it was, she wondered what Lucy Dora would expect from the day.

She drove the buggy straight to Aunt Margaret's house. Word of Kate's death had come to town, so she and Martha did not seem surprised when Lucy arrived with Lucy Dora. Martha insisted they come in and have something to eat. Lillian clung to her mother as if she feared Lucy would disappear. Lucy Dora sat at the table, barely nibbling at her food, though Martha tried unsuccessfully to draw her out.

"She's tired, Martha," Lucy said. "We must all go home and rest."

"Lucy, I need to tell you something," Martha said, putting her hand on Lucy's shoulder.

"What?" She dreaded to hear.

"Someone broke into your house while you were gone."

Lucy jumped to her feet, upsetting the coffee she had been drinking. "Who?" she shouted. "Who would do that?"

Martha made soothing noises as she wiped up the coffee. "Now now," she said. "Nothing's missing that we can tell, and only one window was broken out. It could have been much worse."

"But who did it? When?"

"Shhh." Martha eyed the children who had stopped eating and moved closer together at Lucy's outburst. "No one knows who did it, but it was the night before last when Mr. Scoville saw a light moving about in the house. He knew you were gone, of course, so he went over and found the window in the

THE LIFE AND TIMES OF AN EARLY FEMINIST

back door broken, but the intruder must have gone out the front way while Mr. Scoville was in the back."

She handed Lucy the latest edition of the *Mountain Echo* and Lucy read,

Quite an excitement was created here last Saturday night, by the announcement that robbers were in the house of Mrs. Lucy Williams, who was absent visiting her sick sister, Mrs. Kate Faris, ten miles in the country. Lights were seen moving about in the house by Sheriff Scoville's family, next door neighbors to Mrs. Williams. The alarm was immediately given . . . four neighbors visited the house, but could not find any trace of robbers, except that one of the locks to one of the windows of the lower rooms was broken and one of the windows in the upper rooms was unlocked and both inside lower doors, leading into the hall were open, being rather conclusive proof that someone had been in the house, as Mrs. Williams' near relative says that Mrs. Williams locked every window, and closed all the doors before leaving.

Lucy sank back down in her chair. "So what are they saying?" she asked, knowing that the local gossipers would have a theory and that Martha would know what it was.

Martha shrugged. "Some think it was just a tramp who knew you were gone and meant to steal from you until Sheriff Scoville scared him off."

"And others say it was to send me a message about opening the store?"

"Oh, Lucy, I don't know! Why does it matter?"

Why, indeed? Lucy began to gather up Lillian's things. "I'll have to get new locks tomorrow," she said. "And new glass for the window."

"Oh, I took care of that," said Martha. "The window, I mean. I didn't want any varmints taking up residence in your house."

Lucy knew she meant squirrels and birds and such, but she was more concerned with the human kind of varmint. When they got home, she emptied the buggy and put Prince out to pasture with a good helping of oats. She built a fire in the kitchen stove and left the children there while she started fires in the two main fireplaces that warmed the rest of the house. As far as she could tell, nothing was out of place, but she had an eerie feeling. She got Henry's old pistol out of the place where she had hidden it and loaded it. Then she went from room to room—upstairs and down—just to make sure no one was there. Satisfied that they were alone, she went back to the kitchen and began to prepare the children for bed.

Lucy Dora only shrugged when asked if she'd like to have her own room or sleep with Lillian. Lucy's heart ached for her loneliness.

"How about you sleep in with Lillian tonight?" she said. "It'll be warmer, and you can take a few days to get acquainted with the house and decide which room you'd like to have for your own."

Her niece nodded and went to bed without another word. Lillian, who had been getting the undivided attention of Margaret and Martha while her mother was away, resisted going to bed and climbed into Lucy's lap.

There was a question in her eyes. "Lucy Dora?" she whispered, pointing to where her cousin lay asleep.

"Yes. Your cousin," Lucy said. "You remember."

Lillian shook her head.

"She's going to live with us." Lucy didn't try to explain to Lillian why that was necessary.

"She can't have my bed," said Lillian.

Lucy took her daughter's face between her hands and looked into her eyes. "We are all going to share everything we have with Lucy Dora," she said. "She is part of our family now."

Lillian sighed and leaned against her. "All right, Mama," she said.

Later, Lucy remembered Christmas again. She must think of some gift—some treat—to give the children. She went out to the kitchen to see what she had in the way of baking supplies. The water bucket was empty, so she picked it up and went out to the well to fill it. On the porch were two small boxes and a larger package that she was sure had not been there when they came home.

Lucy dragged them inside to the light and saw a note scrawled on one of the small boxes:

> Lucy, I knocked but I guess you and the children had already gone to bed. I forgot to give these to you earlier. They're just trinkets for the children for Christmas—I found something that will do for Lucy Dora, too, I hope. The big box came in yesterday's mail. Martha.

Lucy said a prayer of thankfulness that the children would have a gift to open on Christmas Day. With the tarts she would make and some popcorn balls, the girls would not feel left out. To Jarvis, it would make no difference.

When she looked at the other box, she saw that it was the merchandise she had ordered for the store just before she had gone to Kate's. It contained thread and thimbles, ribbons, sashes, and a half-dozen hat frames. Lucy felt immediately cheered and wished that she could take the supplies to the store right then, but of course, it would have to wait until morning. Never mind that it would be Christmas! Her store would open the next day even if she scandalized the whole town all over again. She had waited long enough.

Chapter Eleven

Lucy had no customers that first day, but she did get attention. Families making Christmas Day calls from house to house strolled down Main Street and stopped short when they saw the Open sign on her door. She stood in the shadows at the back of the room and watched the range of shock, disbelief, and anger revealed on the faces of those who peered through the window at her display of hats. The women lingered, though, until their outraged husbands dragged them away.

Barely a week passed until their family—especially Lucy Dora—suffered another blow. On New Year's Day, her youngest brother, James, died from the same dreadful disease that had claimed her parents. Her aunt Dora was inconsolable.

"I promised Kate I'd keep the children safe and look what's happened," she said to Lucy at the funeral while tears streamed down her face. "How can I explain this to the others?"

Lucy tried to comfort her. "This is not your fault, Dora. Typhoid is an uncontrollable disease. No one knows what to do about it."

Lucy liked Dora and admired her intelligence and strength. Besides Kate's boys, she also cared for her disabled brother, Clay. She did not have an easy life. Not long after little James's death, Dora sold the farm of her late parents on Raccoon and bought a home in London. Then because she had to make a living, she went to work for Vincent Boreing in his store. Though they became good friends, Dora and Lucy were as unalike as two women could be. Dora had an excellent head for business, and Lucy never doubted that she was one of the reasons Boreing's commercial ventures became so successful, but Dora stayed in the background. Her tall thin figure hovered like a ghost in the depths of the store, ready with a column of figures, a list of merchandise, or to help a customer find some item or other, but offering no opinion as her own.

She was ill at ease with those who came in to trade and seemed embarrassed by the necessity of having to make her own way in the world. Lucy wished that her friend were more assertive, but she had to admit that Dora knew what she was doing. Ten years after she moved to London, she was Vincent Boreing's partner in both his store and his mail-route businesses, though hardly anyone knew that.

Sales at Lucy's store were slow in those early days, but she tried not to get discouraged. Her course was set, and she must stick to it. She was counting on her visibility. Women doing their errands around town would have to pass her window display every day, and eventually, their curiosity would get the best of them. Some would, no doubt, use the feminine wiles they'd been reared on to wheedle their husbands into letting them buy one of her hats. She longed to tell them that such ploys were degrading, not only to them but to other women as well, but she was learning to bide her time. She could not change the thinking of a whole community overnight.

Perhaps she would never change it. It could be that her beliefs and practices would result in permanent disgrace. She thought about it constantly during those first dark days. Was it worth risking the children's social acceptance and the opportunities that acceptance could provide to prove her point that a woman must be able to make her own decisions? What had fostered such ideas in her head in the first place? The truth was, she had been brought up in much the same way as the women around her, taught that it was a young woman's duty to fulfill her purpose in life by marrying and producing children. No one explained the sexual aspect, the subservience expected of a wife, or how marriage effectively closed the door on any future except the one chosen for the woman by her husband.

Kate had followed that pattern, and though she had seemed happy enough with Zack and her children, Lucy grieved that there had been so little opportunity for her sister to choose her own path.

"I might have fallen into the same trap if Henry had not decided to establish himself in business before he married," she said to Poca one day. "Those years of waiting for him to be ready gave me time to view the marriages of my female friends and to form opinions about a woman's place in these relationships."

Poca shrugged. "Maybe," she said. "And maybe you're just naturally opinionated."

Lucy couldn't argue with that. "It's possible that I should never have married at all, but I loved Henry and wanted to be with him. I would have married him even if I'd known he would die within three years. We were soul mates." She did not say so to Poca, but she understood that love like that was her only criterion for remarriage, and she did not expect to ever find it again.

Not that her opinion was considered important in the matter. Over the next few months, she had five proposals of marriage, all of which she refused as politely as possible. The men were all widowers who needed a housekeeper and mother for their young children. Lucy sympathized with their plight, but she had no intention of being the solution to it. One man was passing through London and came in the store to buy a sunbonnet for his little girl. While he made his selection, the child wandered to the back of the store and began to talk to Lillian and Lucy Dora, who sat on the floor dressing their dolls.

"My mother owns this store," Lillian said, pointing to me.

"I ain't got no mother," the little girl answered. "But that's my pa over there."

"I don't have a daddy," Lillian replied in a matter-of-fact voice.

"Me neither," said Lucy.

The man was listening, and he turned and looked Lucy up and down. "If you don't got no man," he said, "I'm a' askin' you to marry me right now."

Lucy looked at the little girl, whose clothes were shabby and dirty, her hair tangled. For the child's sake, she forced herself to speak civilly, "Sir, I do not wish to get married, and I have children of my own to care for."

He opened his mouth, but she turned her back on him, refusing to hear what argument he would use to prop up his absurd suggestion. After a moment, he called to the child, and they left without paying for the sunbonnet.

Lucy's first customers, of course, were Aunt Margaret and Martha and Poca and as many of their friends as they could inveigle into coming with them. By the end of January, she had sold a total of ten hats and a few spools of thread. She was almost out of coal again, and much of the winter still lay before her. All day, she tried to think of ways to earn more money. For a short time, she sold staples like flour, salt, and sugar from the porch of her small building, and once or twice, she bartered a hat for food for her children. The first months of 1885 were long and cold and desperate for her little family.

Then it came to her that she could rent out the upstairs space in her house to make ends meet. She brought it up one afternoon when Martha, Poca, and Bettie were in the store.

"Preposterous," said Bettie. "And common."

"It's mostly transients who rent rooms," said Martha. "And they're all men. Even you can't be thinking of living under the same roof with a bunch of strange men."

"Then I'll only rent to women."

"If you only rent to women somebody'll start a rumor that you're running a brothel." Poca said.

Lucy threw up her hands. "So what do you suggest?"

"Forget the whole idea," said Bettie.

"How about a young married couple who could help out with cooking and yard work?" said Martha.

"They'd want to do that in exchange for rent. I need the money."

As usual, Poca cut to the core of the problem. "You need money and you've got three empty bedrooms. Put an ad in the newspaper and see what happens."

And that is what Lucy did.

There were two newspapers in London at that time: the *Mountain Echo* and the *Examiner*. Lucy didn't know the editors of either paper, except by reputation, but it occurred to her that getting to know them would not be a bad idea. As soon as she was financially able, she would need to advertise her business on a regular basis, and she would want the goodwill of those in a position to help her.

Since funds were limited, she studied both papers to see which had the largest circulation and the most advertising before deciding where to take her business. Her heart was with the *Examiner* because of the kind words printed there about Henry after his death, but that paper had few ads and even fewer subscribers. The *Mountain Echo*, on the other hand, claimed that it went out to all the communities in Laurel County as well as to a number of subscribers in the adjoining region. Its pages were full of local advertising from a mere line or two by people with small shops to half-page ads by large stores like Faris and Neal. On that basis, Lucy chose the *Mountain Echo*. She wrote out a small ad and took it to the newspaper's office: "Rooms for rent in Lucy J. Williams's commodious home. Reasonable rates."

That day, she stopped wearing mourning clothes. A widow in a black dress might be treated kindly by the man in charge of the newspaper, but Lucy felt sure she would not be taken seriously in business matters. She put on a dark skirt with a high-collared white lace blouse, completing the outfit with a modest hat and white gloves.

At the front desk of the *Mountain Echo*, she was greeted by the editor, A. R. Dyche, a stern-looking man of indefinite age who seemed less than happy to have his workday interrupted. He seemed surprised when Lucy told him that she wished to run an ad but picked up a pencil from the counter and asked her what she wanted to say. Lucy handed him the ad she had written, and he looked it over.

"That'll be twenty-five cents," he said.

She had thought it would be more. "I'd also like to run a business ad," she said.

He picked up his pencil again. "For what business?"

"For my business. Williams Millinery and Notions."

"Oh yes," he said, and she sensed a coolness in his manner. "I heard about your store."

"Good," said Lucy. "Please tell your wife to come in and see me the next time she needs a hat."

He did not reply, just stood with his pencil poised, until she told him what she wanted to say, "Hats for sale at Williams Millinery and Notions on Main Street, L. J. Williams, proprietor."

Lucy knew that using only her initials on the business ad was misleading, that those who didn't know her might assume that she was a man when they read it, which was the point, of course. She felt that once she got the residents of London and the surrounding county into the store—even if under a misconception—they would have to see that she did good work and that her business was viable. She half expected Mr. Dyche to change the spelling of her name on the second ad, but both ads appeared in the next issue of the *Mountain Echo* just as she had written them.

The rental ad got swift results. Lucy could have let all three rooms the first day, but she had promised herself to be careful of her choices, so she turned down inquiries from two single men who worked for the railroad even though they seemed polite and prosperous. Bettie asked her to rent one of the rooms to her schoolteacher niece, but Lucy refused.

"Your niece doesn't need a room, Bettie," she said. "She has a perfectly good one at your house."

"But, Lucy, she's so respectable. Just the kind of person you need to assure your good name in the community."

"I'm sure she has better things to do than spy on me," Lucy said.

"Spy?" Bettie sputtered. "What on earth are you talking about? I'm just trying to do you a favor."

Lucy sighed. "Thank you. If I need anything, I'll let you know."

Bettie went away pouting, of course, but Lucy knew she'd be back. She was an oddity to Bettie, and the other woman could not resist trying to turn Lucy into someone she could better understand. Lucy found it exasperating.

It took a week, but she did find acceptable renters. One was a young woman from the Lily community named Eva Norton, who had taken a job at the Lovelace Hotel. Eva was neat and clean, and she held her head up as if she had the best job there was though she worked long hours and was usually too tired in the evenings to make conversation. Lucy told Poca that Eva had style though she wasn't sure herself just what she meant by that. Most of the women she knew had a sort of anxious look about them, as if they thought they might be in trouble for some reason. It galled Lucy. How could a woman ever obtain a measure of equality if she willingly made herself a victim?

Tom and Felicia Hammock were her second renters. Tom worked on a railroad section crew. Felicia looked fragile, but she was not. Lucy would come home from the store to find that Felicia had pulled the weeds from the flowerbeds and the vegetable garden or had swept the porches.

"Felicia, I don't expect you to do that," Lucy told her.

"I've got to have some way to pass the time when Tom's at work," Felicia replied.

Lucy was pleased to have found such good people to live in her house, not to mention the blessing of the extra money they brought in.

For the first time, she knew that she could make it. Little by little, she had reclaimed her life—had reconstructed her life—from the debris of loss and pain. She had only a small income, true, but she had plans. And she was beginning to find the confidence needed to bring those plans to fruition. Each time she sold an item at the store, each time she received a rent payment, she divided the money in half. With half she managed her living expenses. The other half she divided again, putting one portion away for the future and the other into new stock for the store. Some months, the store and the savings got only a few cents apiece, but Lucy made the most of every penny.

Chapter Twelve

Lucy Dora was beginning to feel more at home with them by now though she still seemed to be waiting for some miracle to occur that would bring her family together again. Lucy tried to be as patient and loving as she could, to see that her niece had enough food and a warm bed, and to leave the rest to God.

One day, Martha, in her blunt way, reminded Lucy that it was time to enroll Lucy Dora in school. She hesitated to put the child through another drastic change so soon after the tragedy of her parents' and her brother's deaths, but she knew that Martha was right. Girls like Lucy Dora, disadvantaged as they were by poverty and loss, needed an education more than most. She was determined that both Lucy Dora and Lillian would have as much schooling as she could give them. If they chose to marry, fine, but why should marriage preclude a woman's knowing as much as she could about the world, about herself? The subject of education for women was so dear to Lucy's heart, in fact, that she couldn't help but preach on it to the women with whom she came in contact. Most of them were appalled at her stance, and she was appalled at their complacency.

She had taken it upon herself to study the history of education in Laurel County—what little she could find—and one Sunday afternoon in June of that summer of 1885, she took the children for a walk up Main Street to Laurel Seminary. As they walked around the building, Lucy pointed out the classroom where her brothers had been students long ago. Lillian chattered away, as if she knew all about school, but Lucy Dora said little. When they had circled the building and come back to the wide yard with its tall trees, Lucy spread a blanket on the grass and drew her niece down beside her. While Lillian chased butterflies and Jarvis slept in his carriage, she told Lucy Dora the history of the seminary.

"For many years, there was no school in London," she said. "Some parents taught their children to read and write, but many parents didn't know how to do those things themselves, so a lot of children grew up without an education. Besides that, in places where there were schools, mostly boys attended, book learning not being thought necessary for girls.

"Way back, long before your parents were born, the government made a way for counties to establish schools for all children, both boys and girls, by granting land around the state that could be sold to raise money for school buildings. The leaders of Laurel County—who were all men, of course—didn't take advantage of this for more than twenty years, when they finally began to build Laurel Seminary. It opened in 1858. It was a great boost for the community to have a place close to home where children could get an education.

"It hardly got started, though, before the war came along. You're too young to remember that too, but I remember. Anyway, during the war, Laurel Seminary was used as a hospital for the soldiers, and this yard we're sitting in was their campground. After the war, the school started up again. In May, before he died in September, your uncle Henry signed as surety for the trustees of the school. Who knows, if he'd lived, he might have been a trustee himself."

Lucy Dora drowsed against her aunt, lulled by her voice but not interested in what she was saying. Gently, Lucy shook her. "So what do you think of going to school?" she asked.

"It's too big," said Lucy Dora. "I'll get lost."

"No, you won't." Lucy gave her a hug. "This isn't your school. Not this year, anyway." She had tried all summer to save the money for Lucy's tuition to the seminary, but it was not to be. For this year, at least, Lucy Dora would have to go to the common school, a one-room, one-teacher institution not far from Lucy's house. The common school was for poor children and taught only the most basic curriculum. There were no art or music classes like those at Laurel Seminary.

"Your school is much smaller than this one, and you will easily be able to find your way around. A smart girl like you." She put as much encouragement in her voice as she could and was rewarded by a smile from her niece.

The new term was to begin on the first of July. Farmers would have their crops in the ground by then and could spare their children for a few months. Before that time, Lucy made it her business to talk to several mothers with school-age children and get their opinions on the quality of teaching at the common school.

"They mostly treat the youngest ones all right," one mother told her. "But the bigger youngens get a lot of whippings."

Lucy felt faint at the idea of Lucy Dora observing this form of discipline, let alone being made to undergo it. She decided that she would need to be involved in everything that went on at the school in the days ahead.

Despite Lucy's fears, Lucy Dora settled into the routine without problems. Lillian, on the other hand, was inconsolable at the loss of her cousin's company.

"Why can't I go to school too?" she wailed.

"Because you're too young," Lucy said, trying to be patient. "You can go when you're older."

Not for the first time, she wished for a place of learning for bright children like her three-year-old daughter, but when she said as much to Felicia, the younger woman was shocked.

"Why, she's just a baby," she said. "It's bad enough she has to go at all."

"You don't think girls should have an education?"

Felicia looked away. "I know you set great store by it, Lucy," she said. "But outside of knowing how to sign her name and figure a little, I can't see the good of all that learning for a girl."

Lucy knew she was parroting her father and her husband because she had never been taught to think for herself, and she wanted to shake her. But 90 percent of the women she knew were no more enlightened about the need for education in 1885 than those self-righteous men who ran the county until 1858 had been when they allowed the means of raising money for a school to go unimplemented all those years. She decided it was best not to mention her dislike of corporal punishment though she certainly intended to speak out against it if it should become a problem for Lucy Dora.

By the fall of 1885, Lucy and the children had settled into a pattern that worked well. She rose early to do her housework, laundry, and gardening. She then woke the children, fed them all breakfast, and went to the store, taking the little ones along. She tried to open at 8:00 a.m. and was rarely later than that. Early morning was not a good time for customers, so it was then that she sewed on her hats and arranged her stock. She added items to her shelves as she had money to do so. Once the women in London realized that buying from her was not a cardinal sin (and once their husbands decided that Lucy had been punished enough for being uppity), they were willing to pay for the better quality of goods that Lucy offered. Hats could be bought for less money at Cheap John Pearl's on the corner of Sublimity and Main, but they wore out much sooner than the hats Lucy made, and they had no style.

She began to stock bolts of cloth and dress patterns too. In this, she had a lot of competition from Faris and Neal, W. H. Jackson's, and John Pearl's, but here again, she found that most women preferred quality if they could afford it. This desire to expose her customers to the better things in life caused her to stock and sell *Voyage of Life*, a book of engravings by the famous artist, Thomas Cole, accompanied by uplifting moral and cultural essays. She advertised the book in the *Mountain Echo*:

> Mrs. Lucy J. Williams is agent for that famous work, *Voyage of Life*, and it is selling by the dozen daily. It is one of the best books that anyone can place in his library, containing over 400 pages, beautiful engravings, excellently and handsomely bound, "brim full" of the choicest reading matter, and can be had at the remarkably low price of from $1.75 to $2.25 per copy. Be sure and call at her store, examine proof sheets of it, and give her your name.

The response to this book was good, and for a while, Lucy felt that she had made a lasting contribution to the cultural enrichment of the area. Then she discovered that, while London's housewives liked the idea of having the beautiful book in their homes, it was used mostly for decoration and rarely read.

Each day, at 5:00 p.m., Lucy gathered up the children and went home to cook supper, clean the kitchen, and spend some time with Lillian, Jarvis, and Lucy Dora before they went to bed. She had little time to reflect on what she had accomplished or to map out a future direction, but these things were always in her head, roiling about, and they seemed to float into place of their own free will and spring out of her mind full-blown.

At the beginning of October, cousin William appeared on his way to the mountains. As much as she wanted to go with him, to take her hats to those spirited women she had met the year before, Lucy felt that she could not leave the store just when business had begun to be profitable. Instead, she put price tags on the hats she had on hand, boxed them up, and sent them off with William.

"Law, Lucy, I'm no hat salesman," William said, laughing.

"They'll sell themselves," she told him. "And if they don't, I'll know better next year."

So he took them. And when he came back a month later, he'd sold all but three. Meanwhile, Lucy worked long hours to replenish her stock.

One evening, as she bent over her sewing in the dim light of an oil lamp, a feeling of well-being came over her that made her catch her breath. Here she was, snug and safe in her own home with her healthy children asleep nearby, with work that would support them (as long as they were frugal) and even promised a future. She had put Henry to rest deep in her heart, and now she only looked ahead to what she—on her own—could make of her life.

She felt such a sense of freedom. Not that she thought all her troubles were over. She was smart enough to know that there were many struggles ahead and that she would face them alone. Kate's death had left her bereft of family for all practical purposes. She had good friends in Martha and Poca, but she vowed never to presume on that friendship. Only she could make a good life for her children, and if it took developing a thick skin when her methods were disapproved by the London community, she would still rejoice in the freedom she had gained.

It was clear that she would soon need a bigger store. She mulled it over, thinking of this and that place she might be able to rent, but doing nothing about it. Then one day, she saw a For Sale sign on a wooden building next to the Masonic Hall. It was twice as large as her present space, and its location would make her business stand out—not look as if it were somehow connected to Faris and Neal.

The building was just across the street from the Ewell's home, so Lucy asked Poca who owned it.

"I think it belongs to the Masons," Poca said, and Lucy knew she didn't mean a family named Mason but the secret society for men only that flourished in London.

"Who would I see about it?" she asked.

Poca thought for a moment. "I'd say Vincent Boreing would be your best bet. He's got a finger in most every pie in town."

Because he was Zack's brother-in-law, Boreing had officiated at Lucy's wedding and also at Henry's funeral, so Lucy knew him to speak to, but that was as far as it went. He was a full-time merchant and businessman—and a part-time minister—but he was best known as one of several men in Laurel County awarded bids from the federal government for the right to carry the mail to remote areas all over the United States. There was big money in Star Route contracting, and rumors flew that the contractors cheated the government out of millions, but no suspicion had attached itself to Vincent Boreing. Lucy had never heard anyone say a word against him.

She went to see him, taking Lucy Dora with her. After all, he was her niece's uncle, and Lucy thought it could not hurt to let him see that she was being well cared for. He was an impressive figure, sitting behind his wide desk in the office over his store. Lucy's heart pounded as he shook her hand and spoke a few words to Lucy Dora. She saw compassion for the child in his eyes.

When they were seated, Lucy came right to the point, asking Boreing if he knew whom she should contact about buying the building on Main Street that the Masons had for sale.

The look he gave her was part concern and part admiration. "I didn't know you were looking to buy a place," he said.

"I don't know if I am or not," she said, wishing her voice sounded stronger. "But in just a year, I've outgrown my present space, and I'd like to put my rent money toward something I could improve on over time."

Boreing sat back and looked at a spot over her head. "As it happens," he said, "I'm acting as agent for that building."

Lucy was embarrassed. "I didn't know," she said. "I was told you might know who owns it. And what price they're asking."

"As to price," Boreing said, "I'd say you could buy it for a thousand."

He might as well have said ten thousand. Lucy rose, taking Lucy Dora's hand, and thanked him for his time.

"So you're not interested?" He rose too and came around the desk.

Lucy looked him in the eye. "It's not that I'm not interested," she said, "but I have three children to care for, and I cannot mortgage their future by putting every cent I have into that building."

He nodded. "You've done well," he said. "With the little ones and with the store."

His words pleased her, but she could not tell if they were sincere. She thanked him again and turned to go.

"Don't give up," he said.

Lucy shook her head. When had she ever given up?

She considered what to do next as she walked along and, lost in thought, almost ran into Henry's Uncle James on the street in front of the courthouse. They both apologized, and Lucy started on when James called after her, "Lucy, I'll make you a good deal on that piano your daughter likes so much."

She hadn't realized that James had noticed how Lillian ran to the piano and picked out her little tunes every time they were in his store.

She smiled at him. "I'm afraid there's no deal good enough to make it possible for me to buy that piano, James, but I appreciate the thought."

"Now wait a minute," he said. "I'm talking next to nothing for a quality instrument."

"Why would you do that?"

"I'm rearranging things, and that piano takes up a lot of space."

She knew that he was trying to do her a favor because the piano was actually smaller than most uprights and of a sleek design that fit easily into James's furniture display.

She shook her head and said, "Thank you, James, but I can't afford the piano right now at any price."

He nodded. "I just thought I'd mention it," he said, and both of them moved on.

It came to Lucy that in the space of one morning she'd had an option on the two things she most wanted—the Masons' building and the piano—and there was no way she could purchase either. She squared her shoulders and marched back to her store.

Salesmen had begun to call on her at regular intervals, trying to get her to carry everything from ready-made dresses to housewares in her store. She was intrigued, but she had neither money nor space to increase her stock beyond a few unusual items that she believed would bring a quick sale. The success of *Voyage of Life* had not been lasting, so she soon gave up carrying that type of merchandise and concentrated on hats and fabrics, which was, after all, her area of expertise.

Every waking moment was taken up with the house, the store, and with monitoring what went on at the Common School for Lucy Dora's benefit. Lucy found that beyond learning the ABCs and counting to one hundred, little education took place there. She had taught Lucy Dora those things before she started going to school. Each day, she hoped that her niece would come home excited about something she had learned, but that did not happen.

She paid the school a visit. Miss Randall, the teacher, showed her to a seat at the back of the room and went on with her work. Lucy could not help but feel sorry for her as she tried to keep order among fifty children of assorted ages in one small room. Such an environment could not lend itself to learning.

One class after another went to sit on the bench in front of the teacher's desk to make recitation. There was much pushing and shoving by the older students and many whacks with a long ruler by the teacher. Lucy watched Lucy Dora to see how these actions affected her, and she saw that each time the ruler came down on someone's hand or head or shoulder, the child flinched and gripped the top of her desk. When it came time for her class to go to the bench and recite, Lucy Dora's voice was barely audible, and Lucy was afraid that she would receive a blow from the ruler. She did not, but neither was she praised for knowing the answer. Lucy went back to the store more worried than when she had come. Surely, there was a better way to educate London's children.

At the store, Vincent Boreing was waiting. Lucy offered him a chair in the tiny office she had made for herself in one corner of the room.

"I wanted to talk to you," he said when they were seated.

Lucy could not imagine why, so she waited, saying nothing.

"I wondered if you would be interested in locating buyers for some buildings and land that I own around the county," he said after a moment. "I travel a lot, so it's difficult for me to give these properties my full attention."

"I'm a very busy person myself," Lucy said.

"Yes, I know, and it's been my experience that busy people always get the most done."

"What exactly did you think I could do?"

"My proposition is that you act as selling agent for these properties, and for each one you sell, I'll give you a commission for your work. Sell three or four properties and you've got the money for a down payment on the Masons' building."

She was stunned. "What makes you think that I could do this? I've had no experience at selling anything except my hats."

"Selling is selling," he said, smiling at her.

"Why?" she had to ask.

"Because I need someone to keep an eye out for my property..."

She opened her mouth, but he held up his hand to stop her from speaking.

"And because I admire your determination," he finished.

Lucy did not know what to say. Was this just another favor being offered her by a man? Would she be expected to give favors in return? But even as she tried to find an ulterior motive for his offer, she heard herself telling Boreing that she would like to give it a try. It wasn't a gift. She would have to work for it. What did she have to lose?

Boreing drew up a contract saying that Lucy would advertise the properties for sale, deal with those who inquired about them, and get the paperwork in order for his signature. She would get 5 percent of any payment he received.

Lucy took on this new responsibility with fear and trembling. If she failed, the fragile respect she was beginning to win in the community would be eroded and her business would suffer. On the other hand, if she succeeded, she would be able to buy her own building and her business would grow. She took a deep breath and dived in.

The first thing she did was post flyers in the windows of the store, advertising the various properties that Boreing had put into her care. Since her customers were mostly women and women didn't buy property (at least, most of them didn't), she gave each woman who came in a flyer and asked her to pass it on to the man in her household. Then she tacked up some of the flyers in the post office and on the door of the courthouse.

She found that men love to buy land. "It makes them feel rich, I suppose," she said to Poca. "Proprietary."

"But will they buy land from a woman?" Poca asked.

"It's not my property they'll be buying," Lucy replied. "But I do worry that they'll suspect me of doing it for free. I want them to know that it's a business transaction, not something I'm doing to curry favor with Mr. Boreing."

But she had no control over what they thought, and she tried to let their remarks about a woman's "place" just slide right off, to think only of her commission. And as she was able to sell more of the acreages Boreing had entrusted to her, she cared less and less about what the buyers thought of her. By the end of 1885—only one year after she had opened the doors to Williams Millinery and Notions—she purchased the Masons' building and moved her store into larger quarters where she could expand.

And then, though Poca and Martha and Bettie laughed at her, she insured the building for $8,000.

Chapter Thirteen

Lucy continued to spend most Sunday afternoons with Poca though she no longer attended First Christian Church. Poca's family was entrenched at First Christian, but Lucy did not feel comfortable there. She realized that her motive for attending church in the first place was not pure, so it was no wonder that she often felt she was there under false pretenses. If the children had not loved Sunday school so much, she might have dropped out altogether despite the negative impact this would have had on her business.

One day, as she walked to work past the Methodist Church that stood on the corner of Long and Sublimity, she stopped to read a notice in the window indicating that Miss Sue Bennett would speak at the Sunday morning service. Since one of the reasons she found church less than fulfilling was that women seemed to take no active part in the worship services, she was intrigued. Maybe she would go and hear this woman who was purported to be a leader in the women's missionary work of the Methodist Church. Lucy had had a strong belief in God since childhood, but no church she had attended had ever given her the peace and satisfaction it promised. In her experience, women were considered good only for cooking Sunday dinner for the pastor or for teaching the youngest children in Sunday school. Rarely had she known a woman to speak before a mixed congregation or to participate in the decision-making processes of the church. When the day of Miss Bennett's appearance came, Lucy took the children and walked up the street to hear her speak. After the service, she shook Miss Bennett's hand and decided to become a Methodist.

At first she worried that doctrinal disagreements between the Christian and Methodist churches would separate her from Poca and Martha, but neither of them seemed to give her defection a thought. She felt blessed to know them.

One Sunday afternoon in the spring of 1886, Lucy sat with Poca on her porch, drinking tea and watching the children as they played in the backyard.

"I'm going to run for superintendent of public schools," Lucy said.

"What!" said Poca.

"I'm tired of the poor quality of education Lucy Dora's getting. I'm tired of all the politics in the school, so I'm going to run for superintendent."

"You are the craziest person I've ever known," Poca said, shaking her head.

"Maybe. But something has to be done, and I can't just sit by and not try to change things."

"Lucy, women can't run for public office. Remember how Emma Smith took her husband's place as clerk of the circuit court after he died? She was thrown out."

"But she served four years before someone realized there was a law against it," Lucy pointed out. "I've researched this, and for the time being, there is no law that says I cannot run for superintendent."

"How?"

"What do you mean how?"

"How did you research it?"

"I wrote to the state office of education and asked for the rules. I was told that there is no law against a woman running for the office of school superintendent."

"But women can't even vote!"

"And isn't that the silliest thing you ever heard of? Women can teach in the school, they can bear the children that attend the school, they can take part in every activity the school has where there's work to be done, but they can't vote on who they want to run the schools!"

"So how could a woman actually be superintendent?"

"I don't know. I'm sure some man, somewhere, has made a mistake, but since there is no current law that says I can't run, I'm running."

"Well, I wish I could say that I'd vote for you."

"Just because you can't vote doesn't mean you can't have influence."

Poca put her head in her hands. "Oh no, I see where you're going with this. You want me to drum up support for you with the men I know."

Lucy smiled.

Poca said, "What makes you think they'd listen to me?"

"But, Poca, you're so persuasive. You have such a way with men." She ducked the fan that Poca threw at her.

"I don't think I like you as a Methodist," Poca said.

They laughed together.

Lucy's race for superintendent of public schools began with her putting a small ad in the *Mountain Echo* to announce her candidacy. She wrote it out and gave it to Mr. Dyche:

> To the Voters of Laurel County:
>
> The Hon. J. D. Pickett, Superintendent of Public Instruction, informs me that a woman is eligible to hold the office of County Superintendent of Common Schools. I, having examined the law defining the duties of County Superintendent, find that I am qualified to discharge these duties. I declare myself the Peoples Candidate for the office of County Superintendent of Common Schools of Laurel County and earnestly request the support of the people regardless of politics as I am not a political candidate.
>
> Respectfully, Mrs. Lucy J. Williams

Mr. Dyche's face showed nothing as he took her money and wrote out a receipt, but Lucy was sure he disapproved. She couldn't think of a single man of her acquaintance who would approve unless it was cousin William. No doubt her candidacy would be dismissed and ignored by men. She was surprised, then, to find a comment from A. R. Dyche on the front page of the same edition in which her ad appeared.

> In an appropriate place in this issue will be found the announcement of Mrs. Lucy J. Williams as a candidate for County Superintendent of Schools. Mrs. Williams is the widow of Mr. H. J. Williams who was prior to his death in 1884, the junior partner in the firm of Faris & Williams. Mrs. Williams is intellectually well qualified for the position to which she aspires, and we hope that her candidacy will receive that consideration at the hands of the voters of Laurel County, which it so richly deserves. She announces herself as the "people's candidate," although in sympathy and in heritage she is a Democrat.

His words were faint praise. Saying that Lucy was Henry's widow would, no doubt, bring back to mind, for many people, her unwomanly venture into business before Henry was cold in his grave, and his remark about her richly deserved consideration was probably meant to be sarcastic. And then he had to point out that she was a Democrat when almost everyone in Laurel County was a Republican. But he had said that she was "intellectually well qualified." She liked that though she had no idea what effect it would have on her campaign.

One morning, Dyche dropped into the store. When Lucy asked how she could help him, he admitted that he'd just wanted to take a look at her establishment for himself. And in that week's paper, he wrote, "We stepped into Mrs. Lucy Williams' store a few minutes last Wednesday and were utterly surprised at the magnificent stock of millinery goods she had just received and the immense trade she was having in consequence of her low price."

Had Dyche decided to scrutinize her more closely now that she was a candidate? Had he just awakened to the fact that a woman was actually running for public office and felt compelled, as editor of the newspaper, to make sure she wasn't hiding anything? Or were his visit and his kind words simply an effort to be friendly? Lucy recognized her tendency to suspect the motives of those who were kind to her as reflective of the shell she had built around herself since Henry's death, but if she threw off that armor, could she handle the exposure? Her political venture would help her determine that, if nothing else.

A few days later, she had another visit from Vincent Boreing. "I heard you're running for school superintendent," he said without preamble.

Lucy nodded, wondering what was coming.

"I thought . . . That is, I'd like to make a contribution to your campaign fund," he said.

She couldn't help but laugh. "I have no campaign fund, Mr. Boreing," she said. "All I plan on spending is what I've already spent on a small ad in the newspaper."

"You want to win, don't you?"

"Of course."

He leaned against the counter and looked at her. "Then you need financial support."

Lucy was no politician, but she knew enough to know that when financial support was offered to a candidate, it usually meant that the supporter wanted something. What did she have that Vincent Boreing wanted?

She shook her head. "I have no intentions of owing anyone when this is over," she said. "If I win, I'll do my best to make a good superintendent. If I lose, I'm no worse off than I was before."

"I wasn't suggesting a loan."

She looked him in the eye. "Then what are you suggesting?"

He seemed startled. "Please don't take offense," he said. "It's just that I admire your courage, and I'd like to help."

"Thank you," she said, trying to be gracious. "But I wouldn't feel right taking money from anyone. You've already helped enough, as it is, by letting me manage those properties."

"You've done a good job with that," he said. "I believe you can be a good school superintendent too."

"I appreciate your confidence."

"Then why won't you let me help you?"

"Why do I need help? As long as the word is out that I'm running, what more is there to say?"

"You need to make up some posters, arrange a rally or two, be out there where people can see you."

"I'm here in plain sight every day."

"That won't be enough, believe me," said Boreing. He turned to go, shaking his head at Lucy's lack of political understanding.

"I hope you'll vote for me," she called after him.

He looked back with a nod and a smile.

In June, Lucy's father wrote to say that her mother was very ill, and before she could arrange for the long trip to Nebraska, she received word of her death. Though she had become used to the absence of her mother, she grieved for the loss of this parent who had meant so much to her. Her once-large family was all but gone, and she was more than ever aware of the necessity to prepare her own children for the time when they too would be alone.

As she had done after the stress of Zack's death and the trip to the mountains with William, however, she became ill. Spells of the heart, the doctor called these episodes, though they were in truth more a dizziness of the head that left her incapacitated. Martha nursed her as before, and she was soon on her feet again and surprised to read of her swift recuperation in the *Mountain Echo*: "Mrs. Lucy J. Williams who was quite ill at the time of our last issue, has quite or entirely recovered," said Dyche.

Lucy had gone to Frankfort at the time she filed for the office of school superintendent and had fulfilled what she believed were all the necessary requirements, so it was with dismay that she received word from the state superintendent of schools that her papers were incomplete and she would need to be recertified. She felt confident in her ability to pass the test, but she couldn't help wondering if this second examination had to do with the fact that she was a woman.

"You've got to get over this persecution thing," said Poca, but she agreed to watch the store for her while Lucy went to be retested.

She left the children with Martha and took the train to the capital city. Once there, she was pleased to see several other candidates—all men—who were there to retake the test, just as she was. She threw off her fears and gave the test her fullest attention and, much to her relief, was assured that she had passed and would soon receive her certification in the mail.

The *Mountain Echo* reported on it,

> Mrs. Lucy J. Williams returned last Thursday evening from Frankfort, whither she went to be re-examined for a certificate of qualification for county Superintendent with the assurance that her certificate would be forwarded in due time.

Not that it mattered. Although she cut into the other candidate's vote considerably ("Reducing the Republican majority from 400 to 132," said Dyche), she did not win the election. And even though she hadn't taken a cent of anyone else's money for her campaign, Dyche hinted that she had. After writing that she was "a lady against whose private character and Christian life no one can truthfully say aught," he went on to write that she had been backed by "men of ability and means," which was the same as saying that she had neither means nor ability in and of herself. Vincent Boreing could have nipped that in the bud, but he chose not to. Her refusal to take his money had obviously wounded his pride.

Lucy had no time for pride or even for anger. Her children still depended on her for food and shelter, and her business would not run itself. But losing did not mean that Lucy gave up her desire to see Laurel County's children better educated. If she could not be superintendent, she would just have to make her mark on the system in some other way.

Lucy subscribed to the Louisville and Frankfort newspapers and read them eagerly. She did not want to lose sight of the fact that there was a wider world out there, that events and inventions she could scarcely believe would become commonplace in the lives of her children. If she could help it, they would not close their minds and live in fear the way so many of her acquaintances did; they would look to the future with excitement and relish the possibilities it held.

One day, when Bettie was in the store, Lucy asked her if she had seen the item in the Louisville paper about a man in Germany, a Mr. Benz, who had patented what he called an automobile—a motorized vehicle that ran without the aid of horses or mules and much faster.

"I don't read those foreign papers," Bettie said. "They're full of lies."

"But think of it, Bettie," Lucy said. "Think of the time it would save."

"If I want to go fast, I'll take the train," was Bettie's answer.

Lucy laughed. "There was a time when no one believed in trains either, Bettie," she said, but Bettie pretended not to hear.

Reading the newspaper made Lucy angry sometimes, like when she read of the killing of black people in Carrollton, Mississippi, or the battles for equal rights by the Chinese immigrants in Seattle, Washington, but she grew tired of trying to convince those around her that the changes taking place in the world were natural and beneficial. She just kept reading and storing up the things she learned.

Chapter Fourteen

In her new store—her very own building—Lucy had room to expand. And thanks to her ability to dispose of Vincent Boreing's property quickly and to his satisfaction, she had money to increase her stock and buy two display cases.

The first floor of the building had three rooms, one of them double the size of the other two together. Lucy put shelves around three walls of this big room and filled them with stock. Along the other wall, near the front door, she enclosed space for a small office with a desk to hold her till and her account books. This cubicle had a wide glassless window where she could speak with customers and have a view of the store at all times. On the outside wall of the office cubicle, she hung a large mirror so that women could see if the hats they tried on suited them. The two long windows that looked out on Main Street held the new display cases filled with her prettiest creations.

In the larger of the other two rooms, she put a secondhand stove, a round table, four straight chairs, and her sewing machine; the third room she used for storage. The second story of the building consisted of one large room with a closet. As soon as it was cleaned and freshly painted, Lucy planned to rent it.

That decision was part of her ongoing experiment in alternate ways of generating additional income. Since London was always crowded during the days that Circuit Court was in session, it occurred to her that she could sell soup and crackers to those who had not brought food with them from home. There were other places to eat, of course, like the dining rooms of the several hotels about town, but these were frequented mostly by lawyers and judges. The common people who came into town for court could not afford to eat at those places and were looking to find nourishing food at a small price.

Whenever court was in session, Lucy kept a pot of vegetable soup or pinto beans bubbling on the stove. On those days, she put a sign in her window advertising a first-class lunch for five cents. To go with it, she offered a slice of the excellent cheese she bought from Mrs. Emmelman, a resident of the Swiss Colony that had recently been established in the western part of the county. For an extra penny, the customer could buy a slice of cake. During the two or three weeks court was in session, Lucy made an extra fifteen to twenty dollars that way.

The Swiss people and their migration intrigued her. They had established their colony about the time she had married Henry. They were said to be industrious and thrifty people, and Mrs. Emmelman was one of the best examples of these qualities. She came regularly to town with her wonderful homemade cheese, and Lucy always bought a block of it.

Mrs. Emmelman was a tiny wizened woman with the merriest eyes Lucy had ever seen. She seemed to vibrate with goodwill and energy. It was from her that Lucy learned the story of the Swiss colony—Bernstadt, it was called—the last of its kind to be established in America.

In her broken English, Mrs. Emmelman told of how the Swiss families had bought land in Laurel County based on the recommendation of two of their countrymen and how disappointed they had been to find on their arrival that the land was a virtual wilderness. The time they had intended to use to plant crops and start businesses had to be given up to clearing the land. Many families moved on to other previously established colonies, but most swallowed their disappointment and fell to work to make a home in this strange place.

The Swiss had naturally expected to make grapes their main crop, and the Kentucky Bureau of Immigration had given every indication that this could be done. In this, they were to be greatly disappointed, for despite planting the cuttings they brought with them from Switzerland and those obtained through the Kentucky Bureau of Immigration, the dream of vineyards for commercial wine making was destroyed by the American temperance movement of the 1880s. For a short time, the Kentucky legislature agreed to suspend the new law against the making and selling of spirits for any Swissman living within the colony of Bernstadt. They were free to make wine for their personal use, but not to sell it.

"That law did not last long," Mrs. Emmelman told Lucy with a shrug. "But long enough." Her eyes twinkled when she said it. It was common knowledge in London that excellent wine for any occasion could be purchased at Bernstadt.

Mrs. Emmelman, a widow, had come to America as part of her son's household. She was the oldest of the Bernstadt immigrants and, as such, enjoyed a high degree of respect, which she accepted as her due. Lucy loved to watch the range of expression that marched across her face as she told her story. Often, she talked of the Old Country and of how she did not expect to return there, but her cheery disposition never changed. In her neatly pressed dress and apron, she drove her cart to town, sold her cheese, and went back to Bernstadt to make more.

Animosity against Lucy's business ventures seemed to have, at last, receded. London women regularly bought yard goods and thread and other sewing notions from her, and her hats were now in demand. At church one Sunday morning, she counted a dozen of her creations gracing the heads of women in attendance. Lucy supposed that the town's two other churches boasted roughly the same number.

The best part, for Lucy, was seeing women who had once shunned her because of her independent lifestyle begin to make their own small statements of self-sufficiency. It had been a while since a woman considering some item in her store had said, "I'll have to ask my husband."

Another idea brewing in her mind was to hire Eva Norton as a full-time clerk. She hadn't mentioned it to her because she wasn't sure she could pay her enough to make it worth her while. Maids didn't make much, true, but they did sometimes get tips from the prominent people who stayed at the hotel. Maybe Eva wouldn't want to give that up.

Lucy set an amount in her mind and asked Eva about it. Her response was surprising.

"Lucy, do you mean it?"

"Of course."

"There's nothing I'd like better. I'm so tired of emptying slop jars and washing sheets."

"But I can't pay . . ."

"I'll manage. I don't have much expense." It was obvious that she really wanted to do it.

"What if I let you live here rent free and paid you what the hotel does without the tips?" Lucy asked. "Would that do?"

"Oh, Lucy, it's perfect."

Eva was a natural, and it wasn't long until Lucy felt free to leave her in charge of the store when she needed to shop for stock in Louisville or Cincinnati.

She was still selling an occasional tract of land for Vincent Boreing to supplement her income, but it seemed to her that he had been distant since the election. Besides that, his mail business and his rising prominence in politics took most of his time. And she'd heard from Dora Farris that Vincent's wife, Dora's sister, was ill.

Lucy had liked selling his properties, though, and she wrestled with the idea of going into the real estate business for herself. Then two incidents occurred that drove all else from her mind. At the end of August 1886, an epidemic of flux swept the area, leaving several people dead. As it had been with typhoid, no one was sure if the condition could be spread from person to person or, if so, just how that was done. Both the common school and Laurel Seminary closed because of the illness. Everyone was on edge. The worst of it was said to be in the eastern and southern regions of the county, but there were plenty of cases in London as well. Remembering past epidemics, Lucy kept a close eye on the children.

Then just as things had begun to settle down, there was an earthquake. Lucy had gotten the children to bed and was preparing to go herself when she felt the house shiver like an animal in the cold. Several items toppled off the shelves. She heard raised voices and ran outside to find her neighbors in the street, speculating on the cause of the disturbance. Everyone had an opinion. One man insisted that a river flowing underground could explode in that way. Another said it was compressed air being released, but what Lucy heard most often were fearful cries that the end of the world had come. When there were no further rumbles, the crowd dispersed, and in the next day's paper, Lucy read that Charleston, South Carolina, had been virtually destroyed by an earthquake felt throughout the United States. That was an exaggeration, of course, but the residents of London, Kentucky, could certainly vouch for its having shaken the ground a long way from Charleston.

Altogether, it was an uneasy time. Sermons on getting right with God were very effective the next Sunday.

Chapter Fifteen

What the earthquake did for Lucy was to focus her attention on the need to further supplement her income in order to save money to send her children to college where they could learn about such things as the earth's geology.

She put a sign in the window of the store saying that she would act as agent to sell houses or lands on a 10 percent commission. That was twice what Vincent Boreing had given her, but she reasoned that she could always come down if necessary. Between October and December, she listed two houses and sold them both. Half of her commissions went into savings, a fourth into the business, and a fourth into her personal account.

With Eva to help in the store, she had time to spend on making additional real estate contacts. No license to conduct such a business was required. If someone wanted help to sell a piece of property, all they had to do was list it with Lucy and agree to the commission. Sometimes, the owner would sell it himself and not bother to tell her, and she would lose her 10 percent. After that happened a few times, Lucy made up a contract that said she must be given a certain length of time (say three months) during which she had exclusive rights to sell the property and draw her commission. Some men signed this and then went ahead and sold the land themselves. Some men refused to sign; a few agreed to her terms. It was discouraging, but she stuck with it. It was only right that she get something for doing both the legwork and the paperwork. She rode Prince back and forth across the whole of Laurel County that fall, looking for land to list or showing property she already had under contract.

Charles Duber, a tailor who had moved to London from Louisville, rented the top floor of her building. He was a quiet little man who did good work and soon had many customers. Lucy did not expect to keep him, for it was clear that before long he too would need more space than she could give him.

James's piano continued to fascinate Lillian. One day, when they were in his store and Lillian had rushed to the instrument and began to play her little songs, James said, "You sure you don't want to buy that piano, Lucy?"

"How much are you asking, James?"

"Well, let me think. It's an older model, you know. How about a hundred?"

She thought of her hard-earned savings and of depleting it by that amount. If she bought the piano, she would have to find the money for lessons too. But not until Lillian was older. Maybe she could swing it.

"Okay," she said to James, "I'll take it."

"I'll have it tuned for you and deliver it myself, say, Saturday afternoon."

All that night, she wrestled with her foolishness, but when she thought of the surprise and delight she would see on Lillian's face when the piano came, she felt better. Though Lillian was only four years old—not even in school—Lucy believed that she had musical talent, and she did not want to see it go to waste. Her daughter's excitement when the piano was delivered wiped away her doubts about the purchase. Lillian had music in her blood.

It was too early to get a sense of what direction Jarvis's life might take, of course. At age two, he had no playmates except Lillian and Lucy Dora, and they considered him much too young to join their games. He liked best to play alone, making his own toys from sticks and stones and the boxes Lucy discarded at the store. He had an active mind, and Lucy knew he would find his place when the time came, but she worried about what the absence of a father could mean to a little boy. Did she owe it to Jarvis to marry so that he would have a male influence in his life? She went over in her mind all the eligible men she knew in London and the surrounding area, and she could not think of one that she would be willing to marry, not even for Jarvis's sake, so she put the idea to rest and decided to trust herself to know what was best for her children.

In December, Campbell Moore came to visit and was amazed at how far Lucy had come since that sad fall of 1884 when he'd made that first little sign to advertise her business. She introduced him to her boarders, showed him her building, and explained how she had gotten into real estate.

"I can hardly believe it, Lucy, but I'm not surprised," he said. "I always knew you had gumption."

This praise from her father was good for Lucy's morale.

And while he was there, they spent hours talking about Mama. Campbell told Lucy how ill she had been and how she'd longed to see her daughter again. He told in great detail of the funeral and burial. Lucy let him speak of those things as much and as often as he liked, and she felt some of her own grief dispelled by the telling. On New Year's Eve, she put him on the train for Tennessee where he was to spend the winter with her brother Evan.

That night, she sat up late and welcomed the arrival of 1887. She knew from experience that security could be a fleeting thing, but she could not help but think that the next two years would surely be easier than the two just past.

Chapter Sixteen

From the time of the typhoid epidemic that had taken Henry's life, Lucy had made it her business to speak out against what she considered dangerous sanitary conditions that existed within the town's borders. It was not just that the streets were muddy and cluttered but that some private citizens allowed debris and filth to accumulate around their homes and made no effort to clean it up. Lucy missed no opportunity to bring this to the attention of the town fathers, and in her zeal, she offended many people who felt that how they kept their property was none of her business. Lucy knew they had a point, for she herself felt strongly that government should not interfere in the lives of private citizens. Community improvement, on the other hand, seemed, to her, to be everyone's business.

Finally, a Board of Health consisting of all local doctors was formed to take action. A. R. Dyche at the *Mountain Echo*—who, like Lucy, supported a cleanup—used his newspaper to tell his readers what was being done and what they might expect in the future. Lucy cheered when she read,

> The Local Board of Health have decided that to prevent sickness, more attention should be paid to the sanitary condition of London. All property owners may, in the early Spring, expect to receive notice from the Board of Trustees, to clean up their back yards, alleys, adjoining etc., burn all garbage and remove all accumulated filth.

Dyche could have used a good copy editor, but his message was right on target. In the next week's paper, he wrote (tongue in cheek) that "the town board will soon have to put out a proposition for bids for the establishment of ferries. What for? My friend, just tackle the mud and see."

And in the same humorous vein, he wrote, "To any person who contemplates committing suicide we say; Don't go to Rockcastle river; don't spoil the water in a well or cistern, just flop right out in the middle of one of London's streets."

The muddy streets were especially difficult for women who had either to hike up their skirts when they walked and be thought unladylike or let the hems be ruined as they dragged in the mud. Lucy often had to cut off several inches of muddy hem and replace it with a ruffle or flounce of the same or contrasting color in order to get sufficient wear out of a dress. Most of the time, she wore boots and held up her skirts and let people think what they would.

Dyche advised property owners to be careful about where they located privies and wells so that "water from the former will have no chance to drain into the latter."

He went on to say that,

> People should be very careful about depositing the refuse from sick persons, so that it will have no chance to come in contact with water running into their wells or cisterns. The germs of disease might be communicated to other persons in this way. Even if the water may be drained into brooks, it may be communicated to persons by drinking milk coming from cows that have quenched their thirst in the waters of the brook.

Though his narrow-mindedness on certain subjects sometimes irritated Lucy, she totally agreed with Dyche's efforts in regard to sanitation. It was clear that he and other of the town's leaders, like Vincent Boreing, had the good of the community at heart. Lucy admired that and wanted to help in any way she could. Women were never appointed to governmental boards, of course, but at every opportunity, she spoke out about sanitation and other issues, like education, that were dear to her heart. Bettie complained that Lucy embarrassed her, but Poca cheered her on.

With the death of Vincent Boreing's wife in 1888, he became one of the town's most eligible widowers, and though he was forty-nine years old, many young women set their caps for him. Lucy knew from experience that a quick remarriage after the death of a spouse was not only expected but also applauded. She and Bettie had broken that rule—Bettie because she would not relinquish her wealth and Lucy because she refused to marry without love. She liked Vincent and hoped that he would find someone who could make him happy. There were times when she even thought that she might be that person. Just when she began to think that Vincent was considering courting her, he once again grew cool. Lucy was disappointed, but not heartbroken. Pleasant as the friendship had been, she knew that she did not love Vincent and he did not love her. It was no secret that he was headed to the legislature, and in order to further his political agenda, he needed a woman with background and influence. Though Lucy continued to speak to him when she saw him at church or other public places, he no longer seemed to take a personal interest in her welfare. In 1889, he married Sarah Randall, whose father had been a well-known lawyer and judge in the London area.

Lucy worried that her business affairs would cause her to neglect her children, so each Saturday afternoon, she left the store in Eva's care and took time out to be with Lillian, Jarvis, and Lucy Dora. On winter days, they would read and talk or bake cookies, and when the weather was nice, they would take a picnic lunch and walk to the Falls, a popular and scenic spot not far from town. Dora's move into town had been a wonderful thing for Lucy Dora, who could now spend much of her time with her brothers. The more often she did this, the more she bloomed, so although all of them—especially Lillian—missed her when she stayed at her aunt Dora's, they knew she was doing what was best. Dora had carefully invested the money she received from the sale of Zack's farm and meant to share it with Lucy Dora as well as her brothers. This left Lucy free to concentrate on providing for her own children's future.

Once a month, Lucy took the children to visit Henry's parents. Lillian and Jarvis did not enjoy these visits because, as Till and Sally aged, their interest in the children took second place to their various ailments. Lucy understood that such concerns had little appeal to youngsters, but she was not willing to relinquish such an important family bond just to make Lillian and Jarvis more comfortable.

The children liked best to simply stay home on Saturday afternoon to go about their play, knowing that Lucy was in the kitchen or entertaining Poca on the back porch. They loved Poca dearly because she was always as much child as adult.

One Saturday afternoon in late May of 1889, she and Poca sat in rockers on the porch as the children came and went. Poca seemed restless as Lucy told of her plans to attend the State Convention of the Woman's Missionary Aid Society in the town of Carlisle, Kentucky, in the middle of June.

"It will no doubt be boring," Lucy said. "But I was elected a delegate, so I feel I must go."

Instead of teasing Lucy about taking her duties too seriously, Poca said, "Hmm. I think I have plans for that weekend too."

"What plans?" asked Lucy.

Poca kept rocking. "I may go to Knoxville," she said.

"Do you have relatives there?"

"Hmm."

"But Poca . . ."

"Listen, Lucy, you know that white hat you've got in your display case?"

"The one with the little veil?"

"Yes, that's the one. Will you put it aside for me? I want to take it with me if I go."

"Of course," Lucy said. "I saw you trying it on the other day. It's very becoming."

Poca smiled. "I thought so too," she said.

Lucy could not have been more surprised, on her return from Carlisle, to read in the *Mountain Echo*:

> Mr. Mac Fitzgerald and Miss Poca Ewell, accompanied by Col. W. C. Kelly, left on the south bound express last Monday morning bound for Knoxville, where they were married that same morning at 11 o'clock. They remained in Knoxville until Tuesday night when they returned home. The Knoxville Daily Tribune had this to say about the wedding: "The early train from Louisville yesterday morning brought to our city Mr. Mac Fitzgerald and Miss Poca Ewell of London, Ky. They were accompanied by W. C. Kelly, who has been for the past two years a special examiner at London. After they had taken rooms and had breakfast Mr. Kelly informed the clerk of the Hattie House that Mr. Fitzgerald and Miss Ewell were to be married at 11 o'clock. For that purpose the clerk granted the use of the private parlor. At 11 o'clock sharp Mr. Kelly appeared with marriage license and the Rev. Mr. Jones, of the First Baptist Church. The only persons present were the officiating minister, the Rev. McGowan, George Sevier, Frank Blair and W. C. Kelly. The ceremony was short, beautiful and rich in allusions to the divine institution of marriage. Mr. Fitzgerald is a prominent young man and the leading druggist of London, and Miss Ewell is the beautiful and accomplished daughter of Hon. R. L. Ewell a prominent politician of the same place, and late a candidate for Congress against Gov. McCreary."

Lucy was both hurt and angry. She had thought she knew Poca. Why had she not been told about her upcoming marriage? It seemed impulsive, even for Poca. Lucy stewed for a day or two before admitting that such impetuousness was really quite in keeping with her friend's personality. She went looking for Poca and found her at her father's home.

Poca laughed when she saw Lucy.

"Oh, Lucy, don't take it so hard! Did you think I'd stay single all my life?"

Lucy ignored her frivolous manner. "Of course not," she said. "But I did think you'd tell me before you took the big step."

Poca gave her a hug. "It was very spur of the moment. No one knew."

"So you just bought that hat on a whim?"

"Hmm. I was hoping it would come in handy."

"I wish you all the best," Lucy said, trying hard to sound sincere.

"No, you don't," Poca replied, laughing again. "You think I've made a gigantic mistake and you're mad at me."

"Oh, Poca . . ."

"Hush, Lucy. You'll always be my best friend. Married or otherwise."

Lucy smiled through her tears. "I just wanted to keep you otherwise for a while longer," she said.

"You think my being married will change things?"

"How could it not?"

"In some ways, maybe," she said. "But not in any way that matters."

Lucy looked at her and knew she spoke the truth. The friendship she and Poca had forged was not one that could be so easily broken.

"May I give you a reception?" Lucy asked.

Poca smiled and hugged her again. "Why not?" she said. "Let's give everyone a look at the runaway bride."

Just before school started that fall, Lucy took Lillian and Jarvis to Nebraska to visit their grandfather Moore. Her two living brothers and her younger sister came from their homes in California and Kansas, and they had a reunion. It did Lucy a world of good. The children enjoyed the train trip and seeing scenery different from what they were used to, she and her siblings said a proper good-bye to their mother, and Campbell had what was left of his children around him once again.

Then almost as soon as they returned home, Till died from a stroke. She and the children had gone for their Saturday afternoon visit. Lillian and Jarvis were telling their grandparents all about the Nebraska trip when Lucy noticed that Till was staring into space and seemed unable to move. She and Sally got him to bed and sent a neighbor for the doctor, but nothing could be done. Till lingered until Tuesday and died without speaking.

Soon, the little house was overflowing with his children and grandchildren. Two of Henry's sisters, Lucinda and Malinda, were far away and could not come, but his other sisters, Sarah and Jane, and his brothers, John and Bill, were close by. Then there were his half siblings, Nancy, Charles, Sidney, and Ed.

The weather was nice, so the crowd spread out into the yard. Lucy did her best to help John's wife, Virginia, and Bill's wife, Kitty, keep food on the table and the house in order. When she heard whispered discussions of who would get what of Till's property, she said nothing. One look at the dozens of descendants made it plain that an equal division of Till's assets would not give any descendant enough to buy a good meal. Besides, it all belonged to Sally for her lifetime.

The next day, Till was buried at McNeil Cemetery. Lucy and the children went back to London, leaving Nancy to comfort Sally. Lucy grieved for the man who had been her staunch friend from childhood long before he was her father-in-law.

Before leaving for Nebraska, Lucy had arranged to add two rooms to the back of her house and to have the whole house repainted, inside and out. She was without boarders temporarily (except for Eva), Tom and Felicia having bought a small house in the country, so it seemed like a good time to make improvements.

She had also contracted with Leuenberger and Bendel, two Swissmen who did excellent carpentry work, to remodel her store building. Her corner lot was narrow, but deep. It ran east from Main all the way to Hill Street, so there was easily room for an addition. On the advice of the contractors, she decided to add a large room at the back of her present building and to build an additional structure at the back of the lot to be used as a rental. She was pleased with the contractors' work and told them to feel free to use her as a reference. She was amused to find an ad in the newspaper of December 12, 1890 that read,

> Leuenberger & Bendel, Carpenters and Builders:
> As we have a long experience in Carpentering, we desire to call the attention of all who desire to erect any building to call on us. We guarantee satisfaction. For reference call on Mrs. L. J. Williams, London, Ky. 203 Main St.

Naturally, when anyone asked about the work of Leuenberger and Bendel, she gave them a good recommendation.

She had no trouble renting the new building on the rear of her lot. Andy Johnson, a realtor from Pineville, Kentucky, and W. S. Jackson, another of Lucy's cousins, opened a real estate office there. Right away, she told them that she sold real estate too, but they said that would not be a problem; and the longer she knew them, the more she learned from them.

The first thing Johnson and Jackson did was to advertise that they would give away lots to persons who would agree to build on them at once. These lots were part of a large tract of land Jackson owned just west of the railroad and to the left of Sublimity Street. When Lucy asked how that could possibly be good business, she was told that the number of free lots were limited and the houses built on them were meant to initiate what would be called the New London Addition. "They'll be like seed from which a community of other houses will grow," Jackson said.

London tried hard to be forward-looking—a cultural center for the region. Speakers on various subjects were regularly booked to appear at some public building, and musicals and plays were often performed at the opera house. Lucy attended the lectures of Ka Ka Koo-Ka, a Cheyenne Indian, who spoke to large crowds at the courthouse two days in a row. He was also known as Star, Son of Shining Star, because his father was a second chief of the Cheyennes. He was quite civilized, wearing an expensive suit and speaking perfect English. His subject was the Indian Question. There had been no danger from Indians east of the Mississippi River for decades, but people still liked to discuss it, and the majority of Laurel Countians agreed that Ka Ka Koo-Ka had the right idea when he maintained that the only way to settle the Indian question satisfactorily was for all Indians to be educated, civilized, and Christianized. Lucy asked him if making Christians of all Indians would mean that they gave up their own cultural customs, and he said, to much applause, "That is what is needed." It made Lucy wonder what the long struggle of the Indian had been about if they were now called on to reject their heritage.

This and many other questions about what was right and what was wrong kept her mind active but often made her wish for a better education or, at least, simpler sensibilities.

Another time, Laura Clay, president of the newly founded Kentucky Equal Rights Association and daughter of the famous Cassius M. Clay, spoke in London on the Relation of Society to Woman.

"For as long as women are dependent upon men for bread, their whole moral nature is warped," she said to loud jeers from the small group who had come to hear her. They jeered even more when she spoke of a woman's right to vote or be awarded property in the event of divorce. Lucy searched the familiar faces around her and saw no inkling of respect for Miss Clay's effort to improve their lives. It was as if she spoke a language they could not understand. Her speech opened new vistas for Lucy, but she went away wondering if real equality for women could ever happen where such attitudes were the norm.

Chapter Seventeen

By the fall of 1890, Lillian, Jarvis, and Lucy Dora were all enrolled at Laurel Seminary. Instruction there was adequate, but Dora was looking into boarding schools where Lucy Dora could further her education now that she was thirteen.

Lillian was eight in October of that year, and Jarvis seven. Lucy had found a piano teacher for Lillian, and more and more, she felt that music could become a vocation—even a career—for her daughter. She listened to the mothers of other students complain that their youngsters had to be forced to practice, but she had no such problem with Lillian. The child was never happier than when she was at the piano.

Lucy's days were filled with seeing to her business ventures and working throughout the county to forward the cause of education. Her businesses flourished, but her efforts to raise educational standards were a failure. The question she asked was, Why should our young men and women have to go away to get the kind of education they need to make a good life for themselves? The answer she got most often was that girls could learn all they needed to know at Laurel Seminary and that there were good colleges for boys in either Lexington or Louisville. Her suggestion that a local institute of higher learning where both girls and boys could go would be best was ignored.

Mr. Duber had moved out of the top story into his own building, and Lucy now used this space for storage. She needed all the downstairs rooms, including the new one, to display her ever-increasing stock. Fewer and fewer of her hats were made from scratch now, for she had found a supplier who furnished a basic shell to which she and her staff could add ribbons, feathers, and artificial flowers according to a customer's wishes.

Since Lucy had opened up the possibilities, several other women in London had gone into business. Most didn't last long, but there was some viable competition. Bettie had designated a corner of her spacious new building to hats and other small items of interest to women and presided over it herself. Lucy had to laugh, remembering Bettie's outrage when she had opened her first store, but she took her seriously. Of all the women in business, Bettie was the only one who could afford to keep going even if she took a loss. Still, Lucy was the only store offering a custom-made option, and it served her well. Women liked to wear a hat that was one of a kind.

She now carried every type of accessory, from handkerchiefs to handbags, and she had a special line of satin fabric for lining coffins. This was kept in a corner away from the other stock so that when a bereaved woman came in, she could have privacy as she made her selection. Vincent Boreing sold ready-made caskets at his furniture store, but few people bought them. The tradition of men and women from the community gathering to build and line a coffin after a death comforted the family.

Besides Eva, Lucy had two other women working in the store, and all of them were kept busy trimming and sewing. She believed each of her employees to be ambitious and trustworthy, so she was surprised to come to work one morning in September to find that Mattie Blauvelt, who had worked for her for about six months, had not come in. Eva, Dora Parsley (her other clerk), and Lucy worried that Mattie had fallen ill, and they discussed going to her home to see if she was all right. While they were deciding who should go, Mattie walked in, arm in arm with Joe Farmer, and announced that the two of them had been to Jellico to get married.

"I'm sorry, Lucy," Mattie said, "but I won't be coming back to work anymore. Joe doesn't think I should."

Lucy had been preparing to congratulate Mattie and offer her a choice of merchandise as a wedding gift, but she suddenly felt too angry with her. "I would like you to stay until I find a replacement," she said.

Joe spoke up, "I'm afraid she can't do that. She no longer needs to work because I'll care for her from now on. We've taken rooms at the Riley Hotel."

"I don't understand why you have to quit working here just because you got married," Lucy said to Mattie, ignoring Joe. She felt sure that Mattie was the kind of person who would be bored doing nothing in a suite at the Riley Hotel all day long.

Mattie looked at her husband, but Joe put his arm around her shoulders and drew her away, beaming as if he'd just discovered the secrets of the universe. He made Lucy think of a dog, staking out its territory. She managed to smile and wave as Mattie went out the door, but it wasn't easy.

Lucy watched the big-city newspapers to see which styles of hats and accessories were popular and then ordered the ones she thought most suitable for her clientele. She never sold the same design twice, and the reputation of her store as a place where one could buy quality products grew.

Bettie said she was taking on more than she could handle. "You're trying to compete with the city stores, but you don't have the space or the capital," she said.

Bettie had mellowed some with the years, but her tendency to criticize rather than praise continued to be a sore spot in Lucy's relationship with her. She nearly had a stroke when Lucy placed an ad in the *Mountain Echo* that said, "Muslim underwear in great quantities at L. J. Williams."

Bettie also thought it crass that Lucy insisted on cash when she had a big sale. She came into the store, waving the newspaper. "What is this?" she cried, reading.

> I am needing the money, and for this reason I have cut the prices on many of my goods far below the usual price and will positively sell any grade of goods in my line for less than you can buy them elsewhere. But you must understand that in order to get the advantage of my cut prices you must pay cash. I do not credit anyone. L. J. Williams

"Have some pride, Lucy." Bettie was near tears. "You make it sound like you and the children are starving."

When Lucy didn't reply, she said, "You aren't, are you?"

Lucy knew that Bettie was hoping she would tell her how much money she had saved up, but Lucy wouldn't do it. She had earnings and savings enough to give her confidence in her ability to pay for the items she put up for sale in her store, and besides, it was none of Bettie's business whether she did or not. Nor did she let Bettie in on her plans to go even bigger in the future. As soon as she could afford it, she meant to build a brick store with adequate space for expansion and an apartment for herself and the children above it. Then she could rent out her whole house.

"We will never starve as long as I can get up and go to work every day," she said.

Bettie tried a different tactic. "You never have any fun, Lucy," she said.

"What do you mean by fun?"

"Well, you don't belong to clubs or play cards, and you never entertain."

"That's not true. I spent the weekend at Rockcastle Springs a while back, and I had a pound party at my house just last week."

"I'm talking about a social event, not a food gathering for white trash."

Lucy's expression told Bettie that she was in danger of going too far. With a sniff and a shake of her head, she picked up her pocketbook and left.

Chapter Eighteen

Most of the buildings in London were frame and of shoddy construction. In their zeal to become a regional center of commerce, the town's leaders encouraged quantity over quality and ignored the problems this could cause. J. T. Williams—no relation to Henry—had lost his store to fire in 1889, and a second fire had wiped out the Lovelace Hotel in October of 1891, but even though the city trustees had asked the townspeople for permission to buy a combination chemical and hand pump fire engine, their request was turned down. This did not stop the trustees from approving more and more building. They seemed to want every inch of frontage along Main Street filled even if the nature of one business conflicted with the other businesses around it. Near Lucy's building was a blacksmith shop where, all day long, the loud clang of iron on iron, the whirr of tools being sharpened on the grindstone, and the hiss of the bellows could be heard. Not to mention the considerable detritus left everywhere by the horses, which caused the walking public no end of trouble. Lucy placed throw rugs both outside and inside her front door and that helped a little, though it meant a lot of extra laundry.

Short on funds and impatient with the time it was taking to save enough money for a more spacious building, Lucy rented her house to a young lawyer and his wife and moved her own family into the small apartment above the store where Mr. Duber had run his business. It was crowded and hot, and she immediately repented her decision. There was no room for Lillian's piano in the apartment, so it had to go in the sewing room of the store. This meant that Lillian could practice only after the store closed.

The children had nowhere to play after school except the street. They didn't seem to mind, for there were always other children there, but at the end of the day, they came in dirty and full of neighborhood gossip that Lucy felt they were too young to hear. For the first time, she saw that her zeal to increase her income had caused her to make a bad decision. The apartment was just too small and crowded for them.

She compounded her mistake and scandalized both Bettie and Poca by taking a suite of rooms at Mrs. Brown's boarding house across the street from Laurel Seminary.

"Lucy, I despair of you," Bettie said. "What will people think?"

"Whatever they like," Lucy replied, trying not to show her own wavering faith in what she had done.

"You won't have a moment's privacy," said Poca. "And how is Lillian going to practice?"

That problem had just begun to dawn on Lucy, but it was too late to change her mind. She knew it was foolish to be renting when she had a perfectly good house, but she did not feel she could ask her tenants to leave when they had only just moved in. She left the piano at the store so that Lillian's practicing wouldn't disturb the other boarders. In an effort to equalize expenses, she rented the apartment over the store to J. A. Riley, a produce salesman who traveled a lot, and his rent partially paid her rent with Mrs. Brown.

Other than the crowded living conditions she had forced on her family, life was good that fall of 1892. Lucy felt secure in her business. In less than ten years, she had proven that she could support her children in a man's world, and though she knew she was considered a bit strange, she had at last garnered respect from the community as a whole.

Some of the women with whom she had forged friendships did their best to find her a husband on the assumption that she would be happier married, but she ignored them. She missed the intimacy of marriage, and she was not so naive as to think that such intimacy could not take place outside of a legal arrangement, but she chose not to go that route. Loneliness seemed a small price to pay for living life on her own terms.

On January 12, 1893, just after midnight, gunshots and dinner bells announced that fire had broken out in town. Lucy quickly woke the children and dressed them in warm clothing in case there was a need to evacuate. The fire was south of Fourth Street, however, and she saw with relief that her store was in no immediate danger. She told the children to stay inside, and then she went to see how she could help her neighbors.

When she came back at dawn, they were all awake. Jarvis talked excitedly about how he had watched the flames shoot into the air, but Lillian said little. Lucy drew her close. "And what about you?" she asked. "What did you think of the fire?"

Lillian shivered. "I was scared."

"Well, it's over now," Lucy said, giving them all a hug.

But for Lillian, it was not. She had frequent nightmares about the fire and would wake screaming.

"My piano, Mama, my piano. It's burning, it's burning!"

Lucy held her until she was quiet. "It was just a dream, lovey," she told her.

"No no," Lillian protested. "There's going to be another fire, and it will burn my piano," she sobbed. Lucy could not convince her that it wasn't real.

In the days that followed, Lillian devised a dozen ways to save her piano from the flames that she was sure were coming. "We could bury it, Mama," she said.

"Lillian," Lucy remonstrated with her. "We can't put a piano in the ground. The dirt would ruin it."

Lillian thought it over. "Then let's put it in the root cellar behind the store," she said.

"But the door is too low," Lucy said, amused at her daughter's creativity.

"No," Lillian said. "Me and Jarvis and Lucy Dora play in there sometimes. Lucy Dora can walk through the door standing up, and she's taller than the piano."

"And how would you practice?"

"After the fire," she said. "I'll practice again as soon as the fire is over."

"Lillian, we can't put the piano out in the weather just because you had a bad dream."

"Please, Mama. The root cellar is warm, and we can wrap the piano in a quilt."

Lucy could see that she would not be calmed until something was done. That night, after the other stores had closed and the streets were empty, she sent Lucy Dora to get Poca.

"Don't tell her what we're doing," she said. "Just ask her to come to the store with you."

"What now?" Poca said when she arrived and saw Lucy leaning two old boards against the back of the wheeled cart that she kept in the store for moving stock.

"This is supposed to be a ramp," Lucy said. "Help me roll the piano up the boards, and I'll tell you about it."

Poca moved to her aid at once, and when they had pushed the piano up onto the cart, stabilizing it as best they could with a sturdy rope, she said, "Now tell me why we did that."

So Lucy told her about Lillian's dreams. With her natural tendency to identify with the children and their problems, Poca did not laugh but gave Lillian a hug and said, "Well, let's get going. Where are we taking it?"

With Lillian holding the lantern and Jarvis trailing behind, the two women, with some help from Lucy Dora, managed to get the cart out the side door and across the rough terrain to the root cellar.

They were all relieved when the door proved high enough to accommodate the piano, cart and all, just as Lillian had said it would.

As they stood observing their feat by the light of the lantern, Poca whispered to Lucy, "How long are you going to leave it here?"

Lucy shrugged. Who knew how long it would take to convince Lillian that the piano would once again be safe inside the store? She sighed as she covered the piano tightly with a piece of canvas and an old quilt and bolted the heavy metal door behind them.

"Not a word about this to anyone," she told the children when they were back inside.

"Can't I tell Billy Smith?" Jarvis asked.

"Not a word," she said, and her voice was sharp.

Lillian and Jarvis looked about to cry.

"It's a secret, Jarvis," Lucy Dora came to the rescue. "A secret just for our family. No one must know but the four of us and Poca, of course."

Jarvis, who loved secrets, was easily won over, but Lillian was dejected. "I don't see why I can't tell somebody," she said.

"Maybe later," Lucy said. "But for now, just do as you're told."

To ease Lillian's mind, Lucy promised that they would move back into their house as soon as she could find another place for her current renters. "Now let's get back to Mrs. Brown's," she said.

When the children had trooped outside, Poca gave Lucy a look and said, "You are the strangest women I've ever met."

"Well, I've been called worse, I'm sure," Lucy said, and Poca went home laughing.

The following night, January 30, 1893, a fire started in the attic of J. D. Smith's storehouse next door to Lucy's store, and before morning, a block and a half of London's downtown, on both sides of Main Street, had burned to the ground.

When she saw the labor of so many years in ashes at her feet, Lucy's pain was almost more than she could bear. She felt panic and despair and guilt. Was she being punished for her single-minded devotion to making money?

But thanks to Lillian's dreams, the piano was safe.

Lucy Jackson Moore Williams
1857-1925

Henry Jarvis Williams, Sr.
1854-1884

Lucy's house in London, Kentucky

Photos courtesy of Tricia Nellessen Fowler, great-great-granddaughter of Lucy and Henry Jarvis Williams

Lillian as a young child

Lucy in her mourning dress

Lillian models a hat

Lillian as a girl

Photos courtesy of Tricia Nellessen Fowler

Lucy with Jarvis and Lillian

Reproduction of sketch in the *Mountain Echo* supplement,
"Glimpses of London" ca.1895

Henry Jarvis Williams Jr.
as a young man

Photo courtesy of Tricia Nellessen Fowler

The building Lucy erected after the 1893 fire. In more recent years, it housed the Hob Nob Café in London on its lower level and lawyers' offices above. It stood until about 2005.

Photo courtesy of Shirley Acton Smith whose parents, Obert and Marie Acton, ran the Hob Nob Café from 1940-1955

Lucy (with shovel) breaks ground for Sue Bennett Memorial School (later Sue Bennett College). Though Belle Bennett and Dr. J. J. Dickey were in the crowd that day, they are not identifiable here. Second Laurel County Courthouse in the distance on right.

Lillian at a special event

Lillian and Jack

Photos courtesy of Tricia Nellessen Fowler

Jarvis Jr. and his nephew, Jack

Lucy and two of her sales clerks

McTeer Homestead in Deming, New Mexico, ca. 1908

Photos courtesy of Tricia Nellessen Fowler

Lucy (at right) on horseback in the New Mexico desert.
Man is unidentified

Always Clean
Comfortable

Phone 73

Reasonable Rates
Close in

When in Avalon stop at

The Williams Cottages

217 Sumner Avenue

Parties of from 6 to 15 a specialty

Cooking Privileges

Call for Mrs. Williams

REAL ESTATE AND INSURANCE

Reproduction of Lucy's business card, ca. 1922
Photos courtesy of Tricia Nellessen Fowler

Jarvis in his military uniform

Lucy as she grew older

Style of dress and Lucy's age indicate that this photo was taken while she lived on Catalina Island. The windows of the house in the photo look like the windows in the Sumner Avenue house, which was still standing in 2007.

Photos courtesy of Tricia Nellessen Fowler

Lucy's gravestone at
Forest Lawn in Los Angeles, California

Lucy's memorial stone at
A. R. Dyche Memorial Park in
London, Kentucky

Henry's original gravestone, which was moved from the Randall Cemetery in London to what was first the Jackson-Parker burial grounds, then became Pine Grove Cemetery, and is now A. R. Dyche Memorial Park, London, Kentucky

Photos by author

Chapter Nineteen

As Lucy stood looking at the devastation, Poca came and put her arm around her. She and other kind neighbors had rescued about $500 worth of the store's stock, but it was soiled and wet. Hardly worth giving away, let alone selling.

"I'm so sorry, Lucy," Poca said.

Lucy could not speak. Not since Henry's death had she felt such desolation of spirit. How could she start over once again? Why all the struggle if it was to end this way?

"You need to go and see the children," Poca said.

As they approached Mrs. Brown's rooming house, Lillian came to meet them. Her little face was streaked with tears. "Oh, Mama, what did I tell you?" she said, running into Lucy's arms. "What will we do?"

"Look up, my child," Lucy said. "Look up." She did not know what else to say. She knew she should be grateful that she still had her family and her faith. No one had been killed or seriously injured in the fire. And surely, this would make the city fathers aware of the need for better construction and a fire engine if London was to survive.

Mrs. Brown was kindness itself. "Here, Mrs. Williams," she said. "Sit down and I'll bring you a cup of tea."

"I just came to see about the children," Lucy said. "I must go back to the store . . ."

"The children need you just now," said Mrs. Brown. "They've been very worried, but they'll be fine. You must rest before you tackle any cleanup."

She was right, of course. Lucy took the children to their rooms and gathered them around her. She told them what the fire had done and what they were facing as a family. They looked at her with trusting eyes, sure that she would make everything all right.

"I have insurance," she said, though she knew they didn't understand the significance of that. "Eight thousand dollars worth. I'll build a new store, a store made of brick, a fireproof store."

Their faces lit up. Mama had said it, so they had no doubt that it would happen. Lucy felt a surge of energy despite the weariness of her body. She was better off than many of her neighbors. And the reason for that was because she had been prudent when others—men believed to be wise in the ways of business—had not.

Uncle James, for instance. He and Aunt Phoebe had lost everything—even their home.

"I never thought to need insurance, Lucy," James had said as they stood watching the fire consume their buildings. "Just seemed like a waste of money."

They watched the sparks fly into the air and land on the roof of Mrs. Wren's house across the street. "I wish I hadn't talked you into buying that piano," he said after a moment. "I reckon you lost it along with everything else."

Lucy smiled at him. "No," she said. "Thanks to Lillian's bad dreams, the piano is safe inside the root cellar behind the store."

"Well, if that don't beat all," said James, shaking his head. "I must tell Phoebe. It'll cheer her up."

They were all sad for a long time after the fire. Grateful as she was for God's blessings on her and her family and upon the other townspeople, Lucy felt the loss of her business keenly. All the sweat and tears, all the time and energy that had gone into reaching her goal of supporting her children without help seemed wasted. In a sense, she was back where she had started after Henry's death in 1884. That wasn't strictly true, of course, because now she had money in the bank and insurance, but still there was that feeling of being lost without a guide. She had managed to keep that feeling at bay for years, but now she was afraid she couldn't muster the courage to go on.

"Lucy, this isn't a bit like you," Poca said, and Lucy heard the echo of her father's voice years before when she had believed everything taken from her.

"I don't know what's come over me," she said. "I feel like I'm drowning."

"You and half the other people in London," Poca said. "Are you going to let the men around here see you give up, or are you going to best them like you always do?"

Poca had a way of looking at things from a different perspective. The next day, Lucy went looking for space to set up shop until her new store could be built. Mr. Weaver, the postmaster, offered to let her use a portion of the building that housed the post office. There wasn't much room, so she ordered only a stock of notions and hat frames. She filed her insurance claim and hired Leuenberger and Bendel to help her draw up plans for a new building.

It was now mid-February and the weather was bad. Lucy fretted because there were days on end when the contractors could not work. Business was slow too, and she began to wonder if there would be enough money to live on and pay for the new building as well. S. A. Lovelace, one of London's druggists and a prominent member of the Baptist congregation, came into the store one day to buy some ribbon for his wife. He was all excited about plans for a church building the Baptist were going to erect on the corner of Long and Seventh streets. They had purchased a lot and a half adjoining Lucy's property, and on the half lot, they intended to build a home for their pastor, Rev. R. A. Mahan, so he could bring his family to London.

"Do you need any extra land?" Lucy asked him, thinking of the unused portion of her lot that abutted the lot they were buying.

"Not at the moment," he said. But later that day, he came into the store again with his pastor. Lucy had not met Rev. Mahan, but she was impressed with his bearing and intelligence.

"I've been living in quarters over J. L. Yaden's building, which, as you know, was damaged in the first fire a few weeks ago," Mahan said, shaking her hand. "It's possible I may need additional land when I build my house, and I wondered if you would be willing to sell me the uppermost portion of your lot."

"You have come to me at a time when I am in need of money," Lucy told him. "I will be happy to sell you the lot if we can come to terms."

His eyes twinkled. "I've heard that you are an astute businesswoman," he said.

Lucy smiled back. "I'm just a woman trying to raise her children, Reverend."

"The Bible says in Proverbs 31:10 that the price of a virtuous woman is far above rubies," said Rev. Mahan in the flowery way of his profession. "I have long admired your zeal and honesty. I assure you that I'm willing to meet any reasonable terms."

Later that week, she deposited the money for the upper quarter of her lot into the bank and breathed a sigh of relief that, once again, she had a little something put by for emergencies.

As the Baptist Church and Rev. Mahan's house began to take shape, so did Lucy's new building. By the middle of March, despite the bad weather, it was well underway. A. R. Dyche wrote in the March 17 issue of the *Mountain Echo*: "Mrs. L. J. Williams has the foundation of her new brick store house completed. The building is 24 x 70 feet and will be one of the most substantial and handsome buildings when completed that there is in Southeastern Kentucky."

In another place, he mentioned that the builders would soon be ready for the brickwork and praised Lucy for her effort to erect the kind of building that would last. Her energy and confidence returned by leaps and bounds. She could hardly make herself stay at her rented shop for wishing to be at the building site all the time—to watch this dream come to pass. Since the fire, however, she had had to cut staff, which meant that she had to stay in the store herself most of the time. This necessity also kept her from going to see her father, who was very ill. He and her youngest sister had recently moved from the homestead in Nebraska to a small farm in Kansas. Lucy decided not to go to them though she was torn between the need to know that they were taken care of and the pressing responsibility of making a living for her children.

On March 31, Dyche wrote, "Mrs. Williams has the walls of the second story of her commodious new brick storehouse well nigh completed." That was a bit of an exaggeration, but the building was coming along well, thanks to the help of many kind friends and neighbors.

In building the store from scratch, she had been able to design it to suit her needs. The front display windows were wide and high, allowing for better lighting than she had had before. The layout was much the same as the old store in that there was the large front room with its displays of stock, its mirrors and comfortable chairs, and the corner arrangement for her office. And she had installed a cash register on top of the new wooden desk in which she kept her account books.

The upstairs apartment, where she and the children would live—at least for a few more months—was spacious with double windows that opened for air in the heat of summer but were sealed well to keep in warmth in the winter. The back rooms of the store were larger than the old ones had been and were used, as before, for sewing and for storage of stock. She even had space left over, but she had plans to fill it.

Lucy set May 1 as the day she would move into the new store and ordered large amounts of all kinds of stock, but small delays here and there caused her not to open until May 5. That day dawned clear and sunny, and she could barely contain her happiness. She had called Eva and two other clerks back to work, and they had spent all the week before cleaning and polishing and arranging everything just so. Of course, Lucy advertised the reopening in the newspaper.

That morning, they dressed in their best clothes and threw open the doors to the new store promptly at eight o'clock. People were waiting in line, and all day there was a steady stream of customers. Such a feeling of blessing and fulfillment swept over Lucy that she thought she might begin to shout the way some of the women at the Methodist Church did when they got happy, but she restrained herself.

In the May 12 issue of the *Mountain Echo*, Dyche wrote,

> The women of our town seem to be the only class blessed with a spirit of public enterprise and energy judging by experience. Mrs. Williams and Mrs. Thompson were the only two ladies depending upon their own energy and resources for a livelihood who lost property by the recent fire, where there were three or four times that number of men who lost, yet they are the only ones who are making active preparations to rebuild anything like fireproof buildings.

Then he went on say,

> The opening of Mrs. L. J. Williams' new brick store last Saturday was a most remarkable success. Early Saturday morning witnessed the hoisting of the American colors, the stars and stripes, over one of the handsomest business houses in Southeastern Kentucky. About nine o'clock a.m. the London Cornett Band in their beautiful uniforms were called together by the blast of their leader's horn and rendered many delicious pieces of music for the occasion. The commodious store room was well filled from floor to ceiling with beautiful summer patterns of dress goods, hats, laces, ribbons, etc., and Mrs. Williams and several clerks were kept reasonably busy all the day waiting on the trade. The occasion was indeed worthy of commendation and Mrs. Williams deserves much credit for her indomitable energy. Beginning life a widow with two very small children depending upon her for support with but very few dollars she succeeded in the course of five or six years in building a commodious business house, filling it with $5,000 to $6,000 worth of goods and building up a trade extending over several counties and the envy of all competitors, only to be licked up in half an hour on Jan. 30, 1893, by the furious flames, leaving her only the ground on which her building stood and about $500 worth of soiled and damaged goods. Although she had but little earthly possessions left she possessed a world of energy and at once she resolved to

retrieve her lost fortunes and today witnesses her occupying one of
the handsomest brick buildings in the State, and a handsome stock
of all kind of millinery, dress goods, shoes, notions, etc.

As usual, Dyche's spelling and punctuation could have used some
improvement, and Lucy laughed when she read that she had begun life as a
widow, but on the whole, she was well pleased with the story. Poca and the
women who clerked in the store all came around to tell her how unusual it was
for a woman to get such high praise from Dyche. They wanted to know how
she managed it.

"I have no idea," she said, but in her heart, she thought it was because of
that first small ad she had taken out when no one (certainly not Dyche) had
expected her to succeed. She believed that, in his pompous way, he felt he was
responsible for getting her started. For whatever reason, she was glad to have
his support. She floated through that first week on a cloud of euphoria.

Then overwhelmed by the heightened expectations thrust upon her by a
demanding public and the residue of long months of tension, she hit a wall of
despondency so complete that she was ready to sell the store and move away.
She even went so far as to post an ad in the paper to that effect: "A handsome
new brick store on Main Street, good business location, for sale. Call on Mrs.
L. J. Williams. My purpose is to locate in some Northern town to educate my
children."

That evening, she was surprised to find a delegation of her closest friends
on her doorstep.

"What is the meaning of this?" Poca yelled, waving the newspaper at her.

"I-I've decided to move, to take the children where the schools are
better . . ."

Poca shook her head. "You can't be serious," she said.

Lucy looked around at the others: Aunt Margaret and Martha, James and
Phoebe, Dora, even Bettie. Each face mirrored Poca's astonishment. She did
not know what to say.

After a moment, James spoke up, "Lucy, you were an inspiration to me
after the fire with your determination to build back as soon as possible and
your refusal to pity yourself. This is not the time to sell out."

"We need you here," said Martha. "Please don't go."

The others nodded in agreement.

Lucy looked at each of them in turn: Aunt Margaret, feebler than ever
(by the end of that summer she would be gone); Martha, sturdy and resilient;
James and Phoebe, greatly aged since the fire; Dora, quiet and refined; Bettie,

her erstwhile nemesis; and Poca, her true friend. It was a moment like none before. She felt the warmth of their love and support, and she realized the extent of her foolishness. How could she let despair seep in when she had, at last, reached the apex of the mountain she had begun to climb all those years ago? Now was the time to relish the journey, to enjoy the scenery, to settle in.

"I will take the ad out tomorrow," she said to her friends, and they cheered.

"Sometimes you are just so . . ." Poca began.

"I know. I'm just so crazy."

"You said it."

Chapter Twenty

The next years were the most profitable Lucy's business had seen. She ran ads in the Manchester, Barbourville, and Mt. Vernon newspapers; and she regularly had customers from all those areas, plus from as far away as Berea and Richmond. She now had four women working for her, and she valued each of them for their special skills. In the years that Eva had been with her, she had learned the management of the store so well that Lucy felt no qualms about leaving her in charge when she went away on buying trips or personal business. Dora Parsley was a skillful trimmer, much in demand, and Blanche Sweeney's kind smile and genteel manner endeared her to even the most disagreeable customer. Mattie Blauvelt Farmer, as Lucy had supposed, soon tired of sitting in her room day after day while her husband was out and begged to be allowed to work at the store again on a part-time basis. Lucy was glad to have her and did not ask how she had gotten Joe to give his consent.

During this period, her real estate business picked up as well. Andy Johnson and W. S. Jackson had taught her a lot about what makes property valuable, and she was careful not to contract for land that she did not believe she could sell. The profits on her real estate transactions made up the bulk of the money she was able to put away for the children's education.

After a few months of occupying the apartment over the store, she notified her tenants that they would have to vacate her house so she and the children could move back in. What a relief it was to be home, in the house Henry had built for her so long ago. Busy as life had become, evenings and Sundays in their own home became treasures for both Lucy and the children.

She continued to work for a better educational system in Laurel County, but in that, she was not encouraged. Laurel Seminary, the pride of London in its day, had been plagued by poor management and erratic funding and, for the past several years, had been used as a common school. Efforts by some of the town's leaders—including A. R. Dyche—to establish a nine-month graded school in London on the seminary grounds was put on the ballot in the fall of 1895. Dyche wrote,

> The proposition to establish a graded school in London nine months out of the year was defeated last Saturday by a vote of 84 to 96. To our minds this was the most severe blow ever administered to our town, and the people of the county generally, and when those who opposed it have time to consider the matter and view it in all its phases, we are constrained to believe they will recognize and acknowledge it. We say that it was a severe blow to the people of the county from the fact that if the proposition had carried, it would have assured the people of the county a first class high school, at least nine months in the year, to which they could send their children for one third less tuition than they can now procure here or elsewhere . . ."

With a graded school still in the future, Lucy needed to find other options for her children. They were growing up, and she was pleased with them. Dora arranged for Lucy Dora to attend boarding school in Tennessee, where she would study to be a teacher, so Lucy sent Lillian and Jarvis to a private school in Hazard, Kentucky. Both were unhappy there, so Lucy allowed them to come home at the end of the term. That next year, she kept Jarvis at home in the common school, but she sent Lillian to Asbury, a Methodist school in Wilmore, Kentucky.

She had decided to send Jarvis there for the next term, but something happened that caused her to change her mind. Lucy had become friends with Belle Bennett, head of the Women's Parsonage and Home Society of the Methodist Episcopal Church, South (the official name of the church she attended, which everyone just called the Methodist Church) on the state level. She admired Belle because she looked at things from a woman's viewpoint and because she was in a position to make a difference. Lucy had not forgotten that Sue Bennett, Belle's sister, had been the first woman she had ever heard speak from the pulpit of a church.

Belle was a tireless worker in a thankless job. Her main focus was on establishing schools of higher learning in the mountainous areas of the state, a cause Lucy also embraced. For every person who professed an interest in seeing this come about, ten more were against it. Lucy had dealt with that attitude for years, but Belle was used to success in her endeavors, and she was dismayed by the apathy among those from whom she sought support.

It was through Belle that Lucy met Dr. J. J. Dickey, a minister and newspaperman whose interest in locating a school in the mountains coincided with hers. Dr. Dickey was interesting, but strange. As a minister, he was narrow in his beliefs, but he had a newspaperman's thirst for knowledge and a strong will, and he had set his heart on seeing a school built that would benefit mountain youngsters. When Lucy met him, he was living in Manchester and trying to interest the people in Clay County in supporting a school. It was not going well, and at Belle's urging, he had come to London to take the pulse of that community on the subject.

Not in years had anything excited Lucy as did this campaign to bring better education to the children of London. She was not appointed to the committee, but she got accurate reports of everything that went on from Belle. Dr. Dickey took up residence in London around the first of 1896 and began buying land and making preparations for the school while Belle frequently traveled from her home in Richmond to meet with him.

Dr. Dickey's choice of land for the school was on Sublimity Street, on a prominence that would allow it to sit high and overlook the town. He asked Lucy about it, and she told him the land he wanted was owned by Mr. Callaway. He and the committee began immediate negotiations. The committee—all men, of course—consisted of E. H. Hackney, W. L. Brown, and C. R. Brock. Belle attended meetings when she could, but she trusted Dr. Dickey to make decisions about the land and buildings.

The Women's Parsonage and Home Society proposed to endow the school with $20,000 if the community would raise a matching amount. At first, interest was keen and subscriptions came in easily, but then dissention about who gave what and who would get the most glory from it began to arise. One major subscriber refused to give his money because of a rift he had with another member of the committee, and Dr. Dickey had to use his best diplomatic skills to keep both men on board for the project. At times, he grew quite dejected, but he pushed ahead.

Lucy met him on the street one day and asked how the plans were progressing. He answered as if he were in the pulpit, pulling himself up straight and clasping his hands together over his waist.

"The enterprise has so far been attended with difficulties and delays, Mrs. Williams," he said. "But that is common to such undertakings. I'm sure you understand."

She replied that she did, indeed, and they went their separate ways.

The next week, the newspaper reported that the bids for construction had been made and a builder chosen. The contract was awarded to Clark and Howard of Lexington for $12,000. Groundbreaking was set for May 11 with completion expected by November 1. It was to be called Sue Bennett Memorial School, to honor Belle's sister who had, by then, passed away.

Lucy read this while sitting at her desk in the store. As she considered what this school would mean to the future of London's children, Dr. Dickey and Belle came in. She greeted them with enthusiastic congratulations on their success.

Belle came around the counter and gave her a hug. "Thank you, Lucy," she said. "Now we have a favor to ask of you."

"Of course," Lucy said. "Anything."

"We would like you to throw out the first shovel of dirt at the groundbreaking ceremonies."

Lucy could not believe it. As she tried to stammer her acceptance, Dr. Dickey said, "You represent the education movement in London better than anyone else. You have worked for it over the years."

"But I have accomplished so little," she said. "No one listened to me."

"But they did," said Belle, "as you can see."

Lucy got tears in her eyes. "I can think of no honor greater than breaking ground for this school," she said. "Thank you so much."

And so it was that on the afternoon of May 11, 1896, she stood among a large number of patrons and curiosity seekers, and with a steel shovel borrowed by Dr. Dickey from J. F. Brown's hardware store, she dug up a large clod of earth and tossed it into the air amid the applause of the crowd. It was one of the most satisfying moments of her life.

Late into the night, she relived it: The people—Dr. Dickey estimated that there were two hundred—the way the weather had threatened but did not interfere, the songs, the speeches, Mr. Ogg, the local photographer taking pictures of it all, and that glorious moment when she had shoveled away the first ground for the school she had dreamed of for so long.

Belle and Dr. Dickey had planned an even bigger ceremony to take place on June 23 when the cornerstone would be laid. This took place with much fanfare. The cornerstone contained various papers and memorabilia and was to be opened on the one hundredth anniversary of the school. *What a great day that will be,* Lucy thought. If only she could live to see it!

She felt such pride in the people of London that day. Most impressive were the words of Methodist Bishop Hendrix, who said in his speech that "this mountain school will be a great plant where boys and girls are to be fashioned into men and women whose influence will be felt to the uttermost parts of the earth." And though, on that day, she could not envision how the actual buildings would look, she nevertheless felt she was seeing the future of London as she stood on that hill above the town.

Chapter Twenty-One

Lucy's store—now called the Emporium—was beginning to have a lot of competition. In the wake of her campaign to raise their level of independence, other women had opened shops offering much the same merchandise and services that she did. These businesses did not cut into her profits appreciably, but any sign of a downturn in sales aroused old anxieties in her mind.

She made trips to Louisville and Chicago in search of new and unique items to sell in the store in an effort to assure that her goods were superior to those of her competitors. She found travel stimulating and resolved to do more of it in days to come.

For some reason, her friendship with Belle seemed to put a strain on her friendship with Poca. Or maybe it was just that in her busy life as one of London's foremost matrons, Poca had other things on her mind. Mac had given up his career as a druggist and now had an important job with First National Bank.

He built a fine house and the family moved into it early in 1897. Poca threw a big party to show it off, and Lucy was invited.

"It's just lovely, Poca," Lucy said as Poca showed her around.

"It's not as big as Bettie's," Poca sighed.

"So what?"

"Oh, it's just that Mac admires Bettie's house so much. He never passes it without commenting on its style and graciousness."

It was true that the Faris house dominated the landscape from its eminence on the corner of Broad and Second streets. It was what Lucy called an enduring house, destined to remain an icon for generations to come.

She patted Poca's hand. "Don't worry," she said. "Your house is beautiful. And not as quiet and lonely as Bettie's."

"Well, hers won't be quiet much longer."

"What do you mean?"

"I hear she's taken in her brother's children. Four girls, I think."

Once the idea of Bettie as a mother would have been beyond Lucy's imagination. Now she only said, "Bettie has a good heart."

It was at Poca's housewarming party that Lucy was first introduced to E. K. Wilson. A lawyer, Wilson had been in London for several years, but strangely, she had never actually met him. Wilson was handsome and suave with his gracious manners and educated accent, and all the young women at the party vied for his attention. The fact that he was a graduate of prestigious Centre College in Danville was not lost on the mothers of these young women, either. He represented intelligence and ambition and that fit perfectly into their plans for their daughters' future.

Lucy and Dora sat on the sofa and watched as several mothers invented ways to draw Mr. Wilson aside and introduce him to their eligible offspring.

"I'm glad Lucy Dora and Lillian aren't here," Dora said.

Lucy nodded. There was something about young Mr. Wilson that sent a shiver up her spine.

"I wish I could be sure that I've done my best for Lucy Dora," Dora said with a sigh.

When Lucy turned to answer her, she noticed, for the first time, the pallor of her friend's face and the listlessness in her eyes. It gave her a jolt.

"Dora, are you ill?" She asked.

"No," Dora said quickly, but she did not look Lucy in the eye.

"Dora, what is it?" Lucy demanded.

"I'm just tired, Lucy. We've been terribly busy at the store lately, and Vincent's gone so much."

Lucy patted her hand. "You mustn't worry about Lucy Dora, you know," she said. "She is well able to take care of herself."

"It's so different now than it was when I was a girl," Dora said. "I don't know how to advise her."

"She has your example to go by," said Lucy. "How can she go wrong?"

They watched as another mother cornered E. K. Wilson. "I'm not much of an example of how to attract a man," Dora said with a smile.

Lucy laughed. "If Lucy Dora wants to do that, she'll figure it out," she said. "It may be that she's happy just the way she is."

"I have been happy, Lucy," Dora said. "I could have married, but . . ."

"Dora, you don't owe anyone an explanation," said Lucy. "Least of all, me."

This time, the smile reached Dora's eyes. "No, I don't believe I do," she said. "You are a woman with clear vision, if ever I knew one."

"Thank you for the compliment," Lucy said.

Dora died in June of that year, and Lucy grieved for her and for Kate's children to whom Dora had been an excellent mother. Her funeral was well-attended, and Dyche's obituary in the *Mountain Echo* was one of the longest Lucy had ever known him to write.

> Miss Dora Faris, daughter of the late James M. and Marium Faris, died at her home in London, June 26th, 1897. Miss Dora was a model business woman, quiet and unassuming, scrupulously conscientious in all things, prompt and accurate in all business transactions, withal one of the purest and best women within our knowledge. After the death of her father she lived for several years in the family of her brother-in-law, Judge Vincent Boreing, for whom she worked, first as a clerk, later as a partner, under whose teaching she developed splendid business talent, and at the time of her death she had acquired considerable property and bid fair to be a rich woman. She had for some time past had charge of and conducted the office work of the mail contract business of Parker, Jones & Steele, also W. H. Steele & Co., and was at the time of her death a member of the mail contract firm of Jones & Faris. She was also a member of the firm of Boreing, Faris & Brown, undertakers and dealers in furniture. She owned a beautiful home in London, where she lived with her niece, Miss Lucy D. Faris, to whom she willed the home and a large portion of her other property. She was much devoted to Miss Lucy and her little brothers, whom she had taken to educate, all being the children of her brother, Z. T. Faris, who departed this life when they were infants, their mother following two months later. She also provides for her brother Clay Faris liberally in her will, and remembered the Methodist Episcopal Church of which she has been a consistent and valuable member for many years.
>
> Notwithstanding her success in business her health had always been delicate, and while she was strictly a business woman, she entertained none of the ideas of the new woman, and seemed to have no sympathy with the women's organizations that have

for their object the procuring of more rights and wider scope of privileges for women, but she was a splendid illustration of what a woman with business capacity can accomplish under existing social and political conditions.

She died in the 39th year of her age, of inflammation of the stomach and bowels. Her sickness was long and her suffering great, which was borne with Christian fortitude. Judge Boreing was summoned home from Washington on account of her sickness, and his daughters, who loved her as a mother, were constantly at her side, and her niece, Miss Lucy, was as faithful, loving and devoted to her as Ruth to Naomi. Dr. McMurtry, of Louisville, visited her as did Dr. Ramsey, of Danville, and no effort was spared by the local doctors, Pennington and Coldwell, to save her. Two professional nurses from the hospitals in the cities waited on her. It seems that every possible effort was made to raise her up, but the skill of physicians and the attention of nurses and the prayers of the church were unavailing, and at 12:30 o'clock Saturday morning she passed peacefully to the unseen world to join her father and mother, sisters and brothers, leaving behind only John B. and Clay Faris, her brothers.

The funeral service was conducted by Bro. Hughart, the pastor at the M. E. church at 9 a.m. Sunday, from which one of the most splendid funeral processions that ever went out of the town followed her remains to the family burying ground, 7 miles in the country where a large assembly of the friends and acquaintances of her childhood had assembled to witness the burial of one whom they loved and appreciated on account of her strength of character, purity of life and integrity on all matters.

Miss Dora's death has created a vacancy in our town that no one seems prepared to fill. It is said she appointed Judge Boreing the executor of her will. The Judge had been her teacher from childhood and always had the most implicit confidence in her ability and business integrity, and therefore entrusted to her the most important details of business transactions, and feels deeply the loss he has sustained in her death, and the same may be truthfully said of all others who entrusted business matters to her management. A modest and unpretentious great woman has been transplanted from the visible to the invisible Kingdom of God, leaving many friends and no enemies behind.

Lucy cried as she read Dyche's words because he had captured Dora's life so beautifully. Never mind that he had managed to preach his usual anti-women's-rights sermon when he said,

> While she was strictly a business woman, she entertained none of the ideas of the new woman, and seemed to have no sympathy with the women's organizations that have for their object the procuring of more rights and wider scope of privileges for women, but she was a splendid illustration of what a woman with business capacity can accomplish under existing social and political conditions.

Maybe Dora hadn't articulated her belief that women were equal to men, but she had practiced it. Because of Dora, men like Boreing, Parker, Steele, and Jones were able to absent themselves from their businesses for long periods of time without the slightest fear that those businesses would fail while they were away.

By the time Sue Bennett Memorial School was established, Lucy's children were nearly past the level of education it offered. She kept them there for two years, though, during which time Lillian was able to study music with Florence Campbell, who was head of the music department, and take private lessons with Lucy's friend, Blanche Sweeney. These two women had a great influence on Lillian, and it was through them that Lucy became aware of Ward Seminary in Nashville, Tennessee, and its exemplary music program. At once, she began the process of enrolling Lillian as a student there.

Lucy worried that Jarvis had no niche such as Lillian did with her music. He was a good student, but his interest varied from one day to the next. All his life, he had been a follower rather than a leader. She told herself that this would change as he studied, as he found that field for which he was best suited.

A year before she died, Dora had put Kate's two sons on a waiting list to attend a boarding school in Mt. Hermon, Massachusetts. When Lucy questioned her about why she would send them so far away, Dora had gone on at length about the school and its high academic standing. She suggested that Jarvis might like to go there too, and when Lucy mentioned it to him, he was willing—if not as enthusiastic as she would have liked. Had she sheltered her son too much? Maybe it was time for him to strike out on his own. After all, he would have his cousins for company, and they had always gotten along well. With that in mind, Lucy applied for Jarvis to go to Mt. Hermon and prayed that he would be accepted.

During her years in London, Lucy had watched the town change from a tiny village with mud lanes and a lawless bent to a growing town whose leaders did their best to improve the conditions of streets and buildings and put a damper on crime. This worked well a large part of the time, but of course, there were lapses. In January of 1898, thieves broke out the rear window of her store and stole hundreds of dollars worth of goods, along with the $17 in petty cash that she kept in her desk. While she was insured for the loss, Lucy was angry and unsettled, and it did not help that only a night or two later she awoke to the raucous sounds of gunshot as riders on horseback raced up and down Main and Broad streets, shooting out windows and yelling at the top of their lungs. In the next week's paper, Dyche wrote that "the good people of the town are determined to put a stop to this, as well as all other violations of the law."

The Board of Trustees of the town took up money for a reward to be given to anyone whose identification of the prowlers led to their conviction. Lucy contributed when they came to her, but she had little hope that this would help. She installed bars on the rear and side windows of her store and shutters across the plate glass in the front.

That same month, she was called to Tennessee to nurse her brother, Evan, and his wife during a typhoid epidemic there. Her sister-in-law died, but her brother finally improved enough for her to return home. She had never lost her dread of typhoid, and though cases of the disease were few and scattered in London, she lived in fear for her children. And just when she felt the danger had passed, there was an outbreak of smallpox. There was a vaccination for this plague, of course, and the town fathers arranged to have it offered to everyone. Lucy and her children were first in line though many of her friends and acquaintances believed the horror stories that were circulating about the effect of the vaccine and were afraid to get it. Dyche reported,

> The Board of Trustees of London have passed an ordinance requiring all inhabitants of London over 21 years of age who have not been successfully vaccinated, to be vaccinated, or re-vaccinated, as the case may be, by March 25, 1898. The ordinance also directs all parents, guardians and employers of minors to have them vaccinated by the above date, and provides that a fine of not less than one nor more than ten dollars shall be inflicted on those who violate the provisions of the ordinance. Infants under one year of age and persons whose health will not permit of vaccination with safety are excepted from the operation of the ordinance.

As usual, Lucy was torn between her strong belief that government should not be able to dictate personal preference and what was clearly a need to protect the populace from the spread of disease. Without seeming to mandate their response, she nevertheless tried to encourage her friends and employees to have the vaccination.

She longed for spring, and when it came, she threw herself into a flurry of cleaning, painting, and repairing. She discovered that there was nothing like a fresh coat of paint to raise one's spirits. Evan and his son came from Tennessee and stayed for three weeks. He worked alongside Lucy, and by the time he left, he had begun to lose some of the gauntness left from his bout with typhoid and the haunting pain of his loss.

The telephone had made its appearance in London, and electricity was talked about. Anxious as she was to see these conveniences come, she could not guess how they would revolutionize life as she knew it. Imagine not having to go in person to the *Mountain echo* to post advertisements of items for sale at the Emporium or for acreages offered through her real estate business. She could simply lift the receiver, ask the operator for Dyche's number, and, from her desk, tell him what she wanted the ad to say. She could call the bank if she had a question about her account; she could even call the market and tell them what groceries she wished to have delivered to her home and when. And electricity, when it came, would be equally amazing, she felt sure. It was said that one could read or sew into the night without straining one's eyes. Even Bettie embraced this magic though she predicted that the wires would get hot and burn people's houses down around them as they slept.

Bettie had become dear to Lucy with the passing of time. Her life had not been easy in the years since John's death, and Lucy acknowledged that, despite her punitive attitude and her bossy ways, Bettie's goodness was not in doubt. She had raised her brother's children after his death, and this had an enriching and humbling effect on her. She no longer railed against Lucy's views on women's rights though she had not changed her opinion of them. Lucy began to feel like the daughter Bettie had once said she'd like her to be.

The sinking of the battleship *Maine* in February brought on war with Spain, and though London did not have its own company, several of its male citizens signed up with neighboring companies and went to fight in Cuba. In April, E. K. Wilson was actively recruiting men. He announced that he had enough for a Laurel County company, but it never materialized. Around the first of May, an announcement in the *Mountain Echo* read,

CALL FOR CALVERY (sic): I am receiving applications for enlistments in Theodore Roosevelt's Special Corps, better known as "Rough Riders." Applicants must be between eighteen and forty five years of age, and in addition to regular physical qualifications must be expert riders. In the event of Col. Roosevelt's failure to get his full quota of 1500 cowboys, this company will be mustered in at Lexington and transported immediately to San Antonio, Texas. ROGER D. WILLIAMS, LEXINGTON, KY.

That put an end to recruitment in London because all the young men wanted to ride with Roosevelt, and they rushed to Lexington to enlist. The war was of short duration, and by the time the Treaty of Paris was signed in December 1898, the soldiers from London had all been to the war and returned home.

Lucy and her children closed out the year of 1898 by attending a musical entertainment at Sue Bennett Memorial School in which Lillian had the leading role. It was her last performance there for she had been accepted at Ward Seminary and would be leaving for Nashville at the beginning of the new year.

Chapter Twenty-Two

At the beginning of 1899, scandal rocked the London community. Mary Cloyd, a cook at the Catching Hotel, died an agonizing death as the result of an infection from a forced abortion. Lucy knew Mary slightly because she had come into the store once or twice to buy small items like thread or straight pins. She was a simple country girl, shy and pretty. The Catching Hotel was the largest and most impressive hotel in London and catered to the influential leaders of the town. Many young women from the rural areas of Laurel County, like Mary, found employment there.

With growing shock, Lucy read the story behind Mary's death:

> A sensation that had been smoldering and brewing in London the past four weeks burst forth with all its hideousness and desolating fury upon the peaceful inhabitants of our usually quiet little mountain city last Saturday and Sunday. It was the exposure of one of the most hideous, black and damnable crimes that ever disgraced our favorite town or blacked the record of our court. It was the story of the bewitching conduct of a wily, cultured, daring and handsome young barrister; the betrayal, seduction, ruin and agonizing death of a sweet, innocent, confiding, pretty, though unlettered young lady and servant girl at the Catching Hotel.
>
> The young man implicated and charged with the crime is none less than Mr. E. K. Wilson, who, though he has been a citizen of our county only about nine years, has been honored more than once by the good people of this county, at one time chosen by the suffrage of the people to preside over the interests of the county as its legal adviser and representative as County Attorney, and came within a few votes of being called to preside over the county as its chief officer, County Judge.

The young lady who met with such a sad misfortune and tragic death was Miss Mary E. Cloyd, daughter of Mr. Thomas Cloyd, who resides near McWhorter, this county, twelve miles north of London, but who has been serving in the capacity of a cook at the Catching Hotel for the past two and a half years. According to the proof adduced at the examining trial, the facts and circumstances are about as follows:

About two years ago Mr. Wilson began paying his respects to Miss Cloyd in the capacity of a sweetheart and continued to do so regularly about once a week, sometimes not so often, and sometimes oftener, calling on her in the parlor of the hotel where Mr. Wilson was a boarder and where the girl was a domestic. Mr. Wilson, all the while, using every means known to the wiles of man to accomplish his purpose to have carnal knowledge of her and her ruin. Finally, yielding to his persuasive genius and under the solemn promise of marriage, she yielded to his lusty desires and her ruin and death followed. Mr. Wilson's confession, the girl's dying declaration, substantiated by a volume of other evidences, is insurmountable proof that the girl was a pure girl up to the time of his knowledge of her, that he had given her medicine and that with his own hands, after she had refused to use it, he had used the instrument which caused her death. This interview closed, this meeting ended by Mr. Wilson saying that before he would be forced to marry the girl he would kill himself. With this Mr. Wilson left the room, the town, the county and was never again seen in our county until last Sunday morning when he was arrested by the authorities of Madison County at Richmond and brought back here under the charge of murder. The dying declaration of the girl, made in the presence of Mrs. McLear, and Drs. Ramsey and Pennington, was in substance as follows: That she was 25 years of age, that no other man save Mr. Wilson knew her carnally, that he accomplished her ruin under the most solemn promise of marriage, that Mr. Wilson was the father of her unborn child, that he had given her twelve pills with directions how to use them, one three times a day, that she took seven of them, that two days later on about Dec. 27, Mr. Wilson told her that the pills might bring her all right, but that she did not want to run any risk, that he wanted to use an instrument, that he inserted it into the uterus by the use of a wire, cut it off, leaving a portion of it in the uterus, and by this produced abortion,

caused her illness and destroyed her life. Dr. Pennington, assisted
by Dr. Ramsey, attended the girl during her entire sickness and
everything known to medical science was done to save her life.

Dyche went on to list the names of the attorneys for both sides, and Lucy
was surprised to see that Poca's father was one of those defending Wilson.
Of course, she understood that the accused is entitled to a good defense
and that he is innocent until proven guilty, but she could not reconcile the
straight-laced, religiously conservative Mr. Ewell that she knew with the
defender of a man charged with the crimes of abortion and murder.

Ewell and his associates, D. K. Rawlings and A. L. Reid, entered a motion
for bail, but it was denied by Judge Stanberry, and Wilson was remanded and
taken to the Richmond jail for safekeeping. This was a wise decision, for in the
beginning, sentiment against Wilson ran high throughout the county.

Dyche published his "trial notes" wherein he wrote of the crowd's
breathless attention to the testimony of Dr. Foster, who testified that Wilson
had come to him earlier asking him if cotton-root or ergot, taken orally, would
produce an abortion or if a catheter inserted into the uterus would bring that
result. When told that those methods could work, Wilson asked the doctor
to write a prescription for the drugs, but Foster refused. Next, Wilson asked
the doctor to perform the abortion himself, and when the answer was no, he
asked for the loan of a catheter. This request Dr. Foster also refused. To aid
in destroying the life of an unborn child was strictly against the law, and Dr.
Foster's unwillingness to defy the legal and moral temper of the time, even to
save Mary, was supported by everyone.

Lucy kept her own counsel, but she couldn't shake the niggling thought
that something more could have been done to save Mary's life. Since Dr.
Foster could not, in good conscience, perform the abortion, why didn't he
take steps to remove Mary from danger by reporting his suspicions of Wilson
to the sheriff? He must have known from Wilson's questions that the young
lawyer meant to take matters into his own hands if the doctor would not help
him. The situation opened up a whole new area of concern for the rights of
women in Lucy's mind.

Mr. and Mrs. McLear, managers of the Catching Hotel, were called to
testify and stated that after the girl's condition became known to them and
when death was imminent, they pled with Mr. Wilson to marry her to protect
her reputation, but he would not even when Mary begged him from her
deathbed to do so and save her from further disgrace.

Lucy thought it strange that this should have been a concern for Mary. She must have known that she was dying and that marriage could save neither her life nor her reputation at that point. She supposed the McLears, fearing a reflection on their status as proprietors of the town's best hotel, felt that marriage could gloss over the fact that one of their employees had become pregnant out of wedlock while under their roof.

As the case evolved and Wilson's obviously wealthy and socially prominent family began to arrive and circulate among London's elite, a shift in opinion occurred. Many refused to accept that Mr. Wilson, with his polished good looks and charming manner, could have been responsible for such a dastardly crime and began to circulate a petition to that effect to be used in his defense.

To his credit, Dyche continued to focus on the crime, ignoring the swing in attitude of many of the townspeople. He wrote,

> How shocking it is for one who once enjoyed the confidence, support and admiration of the people, one with such an education, refinement and ability, one who possessed such an honorable and venerable father and mother, such pure, lovely and cultured sisters as Mr. Wilson has, to fall so low by the violation of his own acts as to be brought face to face with the penitentiary for life, if not the gallows.

That is not to say that there was a loss of sympathy for Mary and her family. In London and around the county, there was outrage at the senselessness and cruelty of her death. A large contingent of mourners had accompanied her body to McWhorter for burial and her brother, J. C. Cloyd, a student at Sue Bennett Memorial School and a veteran of the war with Spain, was shown every possible respect during his sister's final struggle. He published a note in the *Mountain Echo* expressing his thanks to "the good people of London for the kindness and hospitality shown my sister during her sickness and death, a favor to me, which, if an opportunity is ever afforded, I shall be only too glad to reciprocate."

Though Dyche had called it a trial, the proceedings of which he wrote were merely a hearing and did not determine E. K. Wilson's fate. Lawyers for both sides made motions and countermotions, and the case was waived to another session of the court, where it resulted in a hung jury. In the paper, Dyche condemned the judge for throwing out the dying girl's declaration while allowing an unknown woman brought in by the defense to testify that Ms. Cloyd had told her that Wilson was not the father of her baby. Dyche's prediction of life imprisonment or death for Wilson became more and more unlikely.

After many machinations and appeals by his lawyers and despite the circulation of numerous petitions to the governor for pardon, signed by his friends, Wilson was finally sentenced in Rockcastle County to five years in the state penitentiary.

What struck Lucy about the case was the number of people she encountered who believed that because Mary Cloyd was "a loose woman" who had "brought her trouble about by her own immoral behavior," E. K. Wilson could not be blamed for taking her life. She thought of the bashful girl she had waited on in her store. Surely, that young woman had not left the safety of her home and family with the intention of ruining her life. She had no history of promiscuity. Like so many others before her, Mary fell for the line of a charming, unscrupulous man, to her detriment, and her drama was played out in a sanctimonious community whose moral scale tipped heavily in favor of men on any sexual question.

Wilson was successful and wealthy and handsome. He came from a fine old family. For the socialites of London to believe that one with such gifts could be guilty of murder was to believe that their own children could act in the same way. It was unthinkable.

Chapter Twenty-Three

The cold was intense during the first part of 1899. It was fortunate that no one of importance died during the cold spell, for the ground was so frozen that burials could not take place in the new Jackson-Parker Cemetery at the south edge of town. Dyche remarked in the *Mountain Echo* that it was about time the city had its own burying ground and that Articles of Incorporation were being prepared to make it official. He lauded Ed Parker, who had donated six acres adjoining the family plot near his home, and W. H. Jackson, who gave three more acres adjacent to Mr. Parker's, and encouraged everyone to purchase a plot before they were all gone.

Lucy did not rush out to buy one because she expected to be interred beside Henry on Randall Hill when her time came. If the new cemetery had been available to her when Henry died, she would probably have chosen it for its beauty and roominess. The Randall Hill cemetery was now crowded and overgrown, and rarely was someone buried there.

Kate's sons, Amon and Evan, received their letter of acceptance from Mt. Hermon, effective in September of 1899. Lucy received a letter from the school, urging her to wait another year before sending Jarvis since he was only fifteen. She was disappointed, but Jarvis evidenced no distress at all. He continued to read his books and play ball in the streets with the neighborhood children. If he missed his cousins who had lived in Lucy Dora's house only a block away, he made no mention of it.

A rainy spring followed the long cold winter, and the summer was extremely hot. A pall had hovered over the town since the Wilson trial. It seemed that at every gathering, one faction or the other would insist on voicing an opinion, and those who wanted to remain neutral were often drawn into the discussions despite themselves. Lucy found it wearing and avoided as many social events as she could.

With the fall, however, the excitement of the installation of a new telephone exchange and the upcoming gubernatorial race lifted the dark cloud over the town, and life fell back into its normal pattern. The weather went from sticky summer heat to balmy fall breezes overnight, and one could almost hear the collective sigh of relief from London's citizens.

Unlike the cooler weather, the race for Kentucky governor was hot, and London was the site of two political gatherings featuring the oratory of men from both sides. Like most everyone else, Lucy attended both events.

The Democrats presented the nominee for state attorney general, Robert J. Breckenridge, a man of great eloquence, who spoke in favor of the Democratic candidate for governor, William Goebel. Lucy was moved by Breckenridge's speech, and though she knew nothing about Goebel, she leaned in his direction. What did it matter since she could not vote? Dyche had labeled her a Democrat when she ran for superintendent of public schools because her father had supported that party, and Lucy saw no reason to dispute him. Even though she often disagreed with him, she admired A. R. Dyche because he was not afraid to stand up for his beliefs and because of his strong efforts to improve the quality of life in London. He was a good man, but intractable when it came to politics.

A week after the Democratic meeting, the Republicans rallied in London. Their keynote speaker was the current attorney general and candidate for governor, W. S. Taylor. The Republicans had much the bigger and more enthusiastic following, as well as a larger slate of speakers. Edward Parker and Vincent Boreing represented London's local leaders along with Breckenridge's opponent for attorney general, Clifton J. Pratt, and the Republican candidate for secretary of state, Caleb Powers. Dyche waxed poetic about Powers, calling him "the pride of the mountains."

Powers, a lawyer from Knox County, spoke with great persuasion, but his words did not reach into Lucy's heart. Most of the crowd was enthralled, however. She noticed the same worshipful looks on the faces of the young women around her that she had observed when they were introduced to E. K. Wilson on the night of Poca's housewarming party.

The cooler temperatures gave Lucy a new surge of energy despite the fact that Eva Norton, who had worked for her since 1886, had announced her plans to retire, and Lucy had no idea who would take her place. She was not surprised that Eva was leaving because she knew that she planned to be married as soon as her fiancé finished law school and returned to London to practice, but she felt keenly the loss to her business. Unless she could find another clerk with Eva's qualifications, she would have to confine herself to the store for longer periods of time, which would cause her to neglect her real estate work and curtail her travel. She racked her brain for a suitable replacement, and then Poca came to her rescue.

She had not seen Poca for a while. Besides being tied down with young children, Poca had kept a low profile since her father's involvement in the Wilson trial, for fear of saying something to offend that might reflect on Mac and his job at the bank. Marriage had changed her though Lucy couldn't say quite how. She just knew that her friend was not the same, and she wished for the old Poca who never cared what she said or who might not like it.

One day, when Lucy was having lunch at a small café near her store, Poca came in. Lucy beckoned her to come share her table, and they laughed and talked as they had in earlier days. Lucy told her that Eva was leaving and about her search for a replacement.

"May I suggest someone?" Poca asked.

"Of course," Lucy said.

"My cousin Lucy Brown is in town and looking for work. She's a good seamstress and a fast learner."

"Send her around, by all means," Lucy said, deciding that she would hire her even if she found her skills deficient because she wanted to do something for Poca. As it turned out, Lucy Brown was just what she was looking for. Lucy sent her to Cincinnati for two weeks training to bring her up-to-date about styles and materials, and when she came back, she slid easily into the store's routine.

On the Saturday evening after Miss Brown's first full week at the store, Lucy stopped by Poca's house on her way home. "I just wanted to say thank you for sending Lucy to me," she said.

Poca seemed not to know who she was talking about. "Lucy who?" she said. Her eyes were red-rimmed and her hair had fallen out of its neat chignon.

"I'm sorry," Lucy said hastily. "I've come at a bad time. We'll talk again soon." She backed away toward the door.

Poca made a motion with her hand. "No, stay. Please," she said. "I guess I've just got too many children and too many Lucys."

When Lucy didn't answer, Poca laughed and waved her arm again. "I think I know too many people named Lucy," she said. "You know. There's you and Lucy Dora and Lucy Brown . . ." Her voice trailed off.

"Here, Poca," Lucy said, taking her arm and guiding her to the sofa.

Poca sank down, drawing her knees up under her chin in a childish way. "I'm a foolish woman, Lucy," she said. "And a bad mother." Her voice was tragic.

"Stop this nonsense and tell me what's the matter." Lucy wanted to shake her.

Poca leaned back and covered her face with her hands. "Oh, Lucy," she said. "Mac has left me."

"Poca! I'm so sorry."

Poca sat up straight. "I'm not," she said. She looked at Lucy to see if she was shocked, but Lucy returned her stare without blinking.

"What?" said Poca. "No 'what did you do'?"

"Even if I wanted to say that—and I don't—you know I wouldn't. Besides, I don't believe it."

"Don't believe what?"

"I don't believe Mac has left you. Anyone can see how much he loves you, and he's devoted to the children."

"Well, okay, I made that part up, but sometimes I wish he would. I'm tired of being a housewife and a mother. I never get to go anywhere or do anything, and Mac is always traveling to Lexington and Louisville, and well . . . even Lucy Brown got to go to Cincinnati."

Lucy managed to contain her laughter. "Poca, you're having the same attack of self-pity that I had after the fire."

A grin threatened to escape Poca's lips. "Oh, I know it," she said. "But I just hate it when Mac is away and there's no one to talk to but a six-year-old. I start to feel like all I'm good for is to bed and breed . . ."

"Poca . . ."

Suddenly, Poca laughed, and the color came back into her face. "You're the only person on earth that I can talk to this way, Lucy," she said. "God, how I've missed you."

"And I you," Lucy said. "So what are you waiting for? Get the children together and come home with me. We'll sit up all night and gossip about everyone in town."

"Really?" Poca's voice was breathless.

"Absolutely."

"I won't be a minute."

Chapter Twenty-Four

W. S. Taylor was elected governor and inaugurated on December 12, 1899, but the excitement of London's political leaders was short-lived. Almost immediately, Goebel's forces contested the election on the basis of a law he had pushed through the legislature when he was a senator. The law said that the state must appoint three men from each county to canvass all elections to make sure the vote was correct. These committees were supposed to be equal, but since each consisted of three members, generally two Democrats and one Republican, no one expected an honest recount. If Taylor was ousted, then the whole Republican slate was in danger.

The Republicans insisted that the law was unconstitutional and that, besides, their margin was sufficient to establish the winner, but the Democrats refused to concede the election. The debacle consumed the whole month of January 1900, and still nothing was decided. Caleb Powers organized thousands of mountain Republicans who rode special trains to Frankfort, declaring themselves ready to fight this injustice. Then on the morning of January 30, as Goebel walked toward the capitol building, he was shot in the stomach and taken to the Capitol Hotel in dire condition. The shot was said to have come from the office of secretary of state elect, Caleb Powers.

Taylor, the inaugurated governor, declared a state of insurrection and announced that the legislature would leave Frankfort and move to London until the furor was over. Republicans complied, but Democrats refused to move. With the legislature divided between Frankfort and London, and meeting separately, nothing constructive was accomplished.

Local politicians made much of the senators and representatives who came to London during this period. Edward Parker, the county chairman, made arrangements to house and feed them and provided them with fetes and entertainment.

In Frankfort, the Democrats, meeting at the Capitol Hotel, announced that the canvassing committee had declared Goebel the winner and administered the oath of office to him just before his death on February 3. Goebel's young lieutenant governor, J. C. W. Beckham, was sworn in as governor, paving the way for a legal battle that ended up in the Court of Appeals before being resolved in favor of the Democrats.

Lucy found the political infighting distasteful, to say the least, but it was clear to her that just by being alive at this particular time, she had become part of an event that would reach far into the future. Because of that, she decided to attend Goebel's funeral in Frankfort, telling only Lucy Brown where she was going. She knew that the crowds would be large and that with emotions on both sides at a fever pitch, she could be in danger, but she was determined to experience history firsthand.

Goebel's family—two brothers and a sister—had chosen to take his body first to his hometown of Covington, where it lay in state overnight at the Odd Fellows Hall there. Then it was to be returned to Frankfort for a formal funeral service and burial in the Frankfort Cemetery. Lucy knew the schedule because the Louisville newspaper to which she subscribed printed dates and times of the public rites, along with features about Goebel's life and highly biased editorials on the political implications of the assassination.

She recognized no one among those waiting for the train though she was sure that others from London would go. No doubt A. R. Dyche would cover it for the *Mountain Echo*.

The train was crowded and noisy, and of course, the assassination was the main topic of conversation. It was impossible to rest, so Lucy took out the newspaper she had brought from home and tried to read. One headline caught her eye: Goebel's Body Will Not Ride the L & N, it read. The article told how, because of Goebel's hatred for the Louisville & Nashville Railroad's executives, whom he believed to be corrupt and intent on influencing Kentucky politics, the body had been taken over a circuitous route to Covington and back to Frankfort on the Frankfort & Cincinnati Railroad, greatly lengthening the trip. "Even in death Goebel's purity of heart shines through," said the writer.

A letter to the editor took the opposite view, saying that Goebel had slandered the L & N executives and was himself the epitome of corruption. Lucy thought of how a newspaper could shape the opinions of its readers. Surely, she had been predisposed to believe Robert J. Breckenridge when she read about his oratorical skills prior to his speech at the London rally. It had made her sympathetic to Goebel's campaign, but over the course of the month and a half since the election, she had come to think of the fallen candidate as a politician willing to do anything to further his own interests. And she felt the same way about the Republican candidate. After an honest analysis of the rhetoric from both sides, she concluded that there was no moral difference between the two. However, Goebel was dead, and death would deify him in the eyes of the people. For as long as his name was spoken, he would be thought of as a martyr for the cause of truth and right.

In Frankfort, the crowd was so massive that it was nearly impossible for Lucy to make her way from the train station to the Capitol Hotel, site of Goebel's bier. In addition to the swarming hordes of people, there was a large contingent of both civil and military police officers who moved among the crowd with guns in evidence. She had a moment of panic and wished she had not come. The smallest of incidents could start a riot in which innocent people would be killed. But she had come to see history being lived out, and she would not leave.

At the hotel, the wait to pass by the coffin was hours long, trailing down the steps of the impressive building and up the street as far as the eye could see. A steady rain added to the misery, and Lucy was thankful that she had formed the habit of carrying an umbrella with her wherever she went.

By the time she walked past the casket, she was so tired she could barely stand. Afterward, she stumbled out into the street and took refuge from the rain at a nearby church where visitors who had no place to stay were being housed. There she was able to buy food, dry her clothes, and get a few hours' sleep on one of the benches.

The next morning dawned clear and cold, but soon the rain began again. Thousands of onlookers lined the Main Street in front of buildings draped with black crepe while other thousands watched from windows and balconies along the route. The street wound and twisted up the hill from the center of town, past the arsenal, and beyond.

The funeral procession proceeded past the crowds and up the hill to the cemetery. Once they had seen the casket pass, many people fled the rain and did not follow the cortege up the hill, but Lucy had not come so far to stop at that point. She trudged on until she arrived at the grave site—or as close to it as she could get. Just as she reached the summit, there was an announcement that burial would not take place that day because of the water that stood in the grave. Instead, Mr. Goebel's body would lie in the cemetery's chapel, and the various prayers and eulogies would take place there as well. This meant that very few of the common people who had made such an effort to attend Goebel's funeral would be able to hear the speakers. Lucy was not concerned about that because she knew that the text of each eulogy would be in the next day's newspaper, but she was sorry not to get a glimpse of a dignitary or two. The cemetery overlooked the little town of Frankfort with the wide ribbon of the Kentucky River winding through it. She took in that view before turning back down the hill and making her way to the railroad station.

No one knew that day that the burial site would be changed on request of the family to a spot near the edge of the bluff above the river or that interment would not actually take place until the day the legislature adjourned on March 13. During this period, Goebel's friends stood guard in the chapel.

Lucy got back to London late in the afternoon and went straight home to rest. It was not until the next morning that she began to be greeted by customers and people she met on the street with "I was sorry to hear that you lost twenty dollars while you were in Frankfort." When she asked what they meant, some would not look her in the eye while others said it was just something they'd heard from someone else. Since she had told no one but Lucy Brown where she had gone—and since she certainly had not lost twenty dollars—she was at a loss to know where the rumor had come from or why it should be of interest to anyone. Lucy decided to ignore it, but after two or three men found excuses to come into the store and remark about her "bad luck," she asked Lucy Brown if she knew why this was happening.

"I'm not sure," the other woman said. "But it may be my fault."

"What do you mean?"

"Freda Thomas and her nephew were in the store just after you left, and I'm afraid she said something facetious about your gambling on getting a hotel room in Frankfort . . ."

"Who is Freda Thomas?" Lucy asked.

"She comes in sometimes to buy quilting thread. Her nephew, Ben, is a little off—if you know what I mean . . ."

"But what does that have to do with the rumor that I lost twenty dollars?"

Lucy Brown ducked her head. "Well, I guess Ben's been telling everyone that you went to Frankfort to gamble . . ."

Lucy spoke to her employee sharply, "You were not supposed to mention to anyone where I had gone."

"I know, I know." The clerk wrung her hands. "It just came out before I thought. I'm real sorry."

Lucy was angry with her, but for Poca's sake, she tried not to make too much of it.

But then, when the *Mountain Echo* came out, there it was—"Mrs. L. J. Williams had the misfortune to lose twenty dollars while attending the Goebel funeral..."

She marched over to the newspaper office and asked Dyche where he had gotten his information. He was all apology. "I'm sorry to say that I don't know," he said. "The paper was all set to go to press when I returned from Frankfort and I did not check it. I should have."

"What's done is done," Lucy sighed. "But I'd like to post a notice of my own." She handed him what she had written. "Mrs. L. J. Williams informs us that the statement that she lost $20 while attending Mr. Goebel's funeral at Frankfort was a mistake."

Given the crowds at the funeral, it was a wonder that she hadn't lost her purse and everything she had taken with her, but the idea that she had gone there to gamble—in such a mob, at such a time—was so ridiculous that it was funny. And so she laughed.

Later that month, Caleb Powers and several others were arrested and charged with murder in Goebel's death, and after that, no one could talk of anything else.

The year of 1900 was profitable for Lucy and for the whole of London's business community. No one was sure what made this so, but all were appreciative. Lucy felt secure enough to make her real estate business official by opening an office, separate from the store. Prior to that time, she had looked upon real estate as a sideline, but now she began to see it as her future. The Emporium ran smoothly most of the time in the care of her clerks.

One day, Lucy Brown announced that she was leaving. She had not been comfortable at the store since the incident of the twenty-dollar gambling story. Lucy did not beg her to stay but began, at once, to look for her replacement. She remembered a woman she had met on one of her buying trips to Louisville, and she contacted her to ask if she'd be interested in coming to London to run the Emporium. Catherine Bauer had worked in a similar business in New York City, and Lucy was not hopeful that she would consent to leave, but Catherine surprised her by taking her up on her offer. This time, Lucy was as businesslike as she could be. She had legal papers drawn up to show what Catherine's duties would be, what she would be paid—and in general, what was expected from her. This was the way Catherine had been accustomed to working, and she signed the contract with no questions. Lucy Brown told Poca that she was homesick and did not want to stay in London any longer and left it at that. Poca seemed unconcerned.

"Lucy's a free spirit," she said. "She'll never be happy in one place for very long."

Lucy told Poca about Catherine and her background in sales, and Poca made it her business to see that Catherine met all the leading women in London, introducing her as "my friend from New York." Poca was a bit of a snob. Once Catherine settled in, Lucy began to leave more and more of the work to her and spend most of her time traveling and selling her numerous properties.

In August, Jarvis received his letter of acceptance to Mt. Hermon, and in September, Lucy sent him off to Massachusetts, going with him as far as Cincinnati. As she watched the train move away, she wondered if she was doing the right thing.

She now had her house to herself, and she found it lonely. She arranged with Dr. Dickey to board Sue Bennett Memorial School students who came from other areas but for whom there was no room in campus housing. These young women became like surrogate children to her. Through them, she was able to be involved in events at the school, make friends with the faculty, and get an education of sorts as she listened to their chatter. They were a new breed, expecting to take the world by storm as soon as they were educated, and Lucy reveled in the independent spirit they exhibited. Probably, in the end, most of them would fill the same roles their mothers had, but at least they would have had the experience of thinking for themselves for a while, and that was bound to do them good. She encouraged them to take a stand when they saw women being treated with disrespect. One day, one of them brought her a copy of the *Mountain Echo* with a passage marked.

"Miss Lucy," she said. "What is newsworthy about this?"

Lucy put on her glasses and read the headline: Two Large Women. Underneath was written, "Mrs. Lizzie Owsley, of Goff, Kan., and Mrs. Robert Huff of this county, sister-in-law, while in London a few days ago, were weighed, the former weighing 219 pounds and the latter 200."

Lucy shook her head. "Nothing that I can see," she said, and in her head, she could hear the laughter the statement would bring from men and the smug derision from women who had no such problem as excess pounds. Dyche had not printed it out of malice; he simply did not understand that it belittled women to make an issue of their weight at all, much less to write about it in the newspaper. She was proud that her young boarder had gotten that message.

In the early part of 1901, Lucy heard, through the rumor mill, that Vincent Boreing's young wife had left him and filed for divorce. She was further shocked to read about it in the *Mountain Echo*. Dyche usually did not print negative articles about highly respected members of the community though he sometimes slandered with careless words lesser citizens or those of whom he did not approve. Perhaps because the matter went to court and so was public record, he wrote,

> The case of Mrs. Sarah Randall Boreing against Judge Vincent Boreing was tried during the week before Judge O. H. Waddle, of Somerset, special Judge, and resulted in the plaintiff being granted a divorce but denied alimony. The cost of the suit was assessed against Judge Boreing.

Lucy felt sorry that Vincent, who had done so much good for the community with his money and public spiritedness, should not have found lasting love and companionship with Sarah. She was not surprised, however, to note that a man could withstand the whispers and innuendo of a divorce much more easily than a woman. Vincent held his head high as if nothing had happened, coming and going between London and Washington as usual, but Sarah moved away, and Lucy never knew what happened to her.

In March, Lillian got the opportunity to accompany a group from Ward Seminary to Washington City to witness the inauguration of William McKinley to the presidency. Lucy encouraged her to go, to participate in history, as she had done at the Goebel funeral. This was a much longer journey, of course, and on the way, they were to stop at Luray Caverns and Natural Bridge, among other points of interest. Dyche wrote it up for the *Mountain Echo*, and Lucy clipped it out and saved it to show to Lillian when she came home for the summer. By the time she went back to school in the fall, McKinley had been assassinated.

Both Jarvis and Lillian made plans of their own for that summer of 1901. Lillian spent several weeks at the home of one friend or another, and Jarvis announced that he wanted to go to the country with his cousins, Amon and Evan, and work on the farm. Lucy Dora had kept the land on Raccoon left to her by her aunt Dora, and each summer, she and her brothers went there to live and make a crop.

Lucy was pleased that Jarvis wanted to go because he had a winter pallor that she knew the summer sun and exercise would erase. With both children gone again almost as soon as they came home, she accepted the invitation of her cousin Adelaide Jackson to accompany her on a trip to the West Coast. It was a splendid adventure, and she came home feeling that she had learned a great deal about this enormous country in which she lived.

Dyche stopped her on the street to ask questions about where she had been and what she had seen and then wrote,

> Mrs. L. J. Williams, who has been away for some time, returned home Monday last from an extended tour to the Pacific slope. She expresses great admiration for the country visited. Among the points touched are Pikes Peak, Salt Lake City, Denver, San Francisco, the celebrated Shasta Springs and many other places of celebrity. She was gone five weeks and enjoyed the trip to the fullest extent. We found her looking remarkably well, kind, polite and obliging. She is now at home to her numerous friends and customers at the Emporium, where she will have a kindly greeting for all.

That caused many others to ask about the trip, and Lucy was happy to tell them of the vast acres of land and the breathtaking scenery of the West. She could not stop her mind from thinking about the land and its possibilities, and though she was glad to be home, she promised herself that she would someday go West again.

Chapter Twenty-Five

With the store in the capable hands of Catherine Bauer, Lucy turned her attention to selling the properties she had listed. Business was slow in the early months of 1902, and she thought dreamily of the West and the opportunities she believed were there. She wrote to the government offices of Colorado, New Mexico, and California for information on commerce, particularly the price of land in their respective states. She received few answers, but she refused to get discouraged. Someday, she would investigate the situation for herself.

One spring morning, she walked up to the Randall Cemetery, to Henry's grave, and found that a large branch from the most recent storm had fallen across the stone and cracked it. Several huge trees swayed ominously nearby. That afternoon, she bought four plots in the new cemetery, now called Pine Grove, and arranged to have Henry's body moved there. Though she could have bought a new larger headstone, she had the old one repaired and moved too, for she remembered the sacrifices made to purchase it back in those days when money was so dear. The new site was well kept and overlooked the main road into town, but it was far enough away so that the passing of wagons and horses, with their accompanying dust, would not mar the site.

As usual, Dyche reported on her action by saying, "The remains of Mr. H. J. Williams, which were buried in the Randall cemetery some twenty years ago, were removed to the Piney Grove cemetery during the week." Lucy braced herself for accusations of desecration, but she heard only a few murmurs. *Everyone has grown used to my odd ways,* she thought.

Meanwhile, Lillian was getting ready to graduate from Ward Seminary. Lucy expected her daughter to fall in love as other girls her age were doing, but Lillian seemed to have little interest in men. Her music came first. Before long, she was giving concerts in the Nashville area and even as far away as Charleston and Atlanta. Near the end of her senior year, she wrote to say that she was to be the featured performer at the school's commencement program in June.

Lucy begged Poca to go with her to hear Lillian play and see her graduate. With her children and Mac's busy schedule, it was not easy for Poca to get away, but somehow she arranged it. By the time they reached Nashville, they were hoarse from talking and sore from laughing.

"Good thing I don't travel with you much," Poca said when they finally reached their hotel and could take off their shoes and stretch out on the bed. "I'm exhausted just from listening to you! Where do you get all that energy?"

"It's a gift," Lucy teased her. "The Moore girls have it, but the Ewell girls don't."

"Oh, Lucy, I'm so glad we're friends. I don't have that many. Never did."

Lucy scoffed, but she knew it was true. She and Poca had bonded from their first meeting. Was it because neither of them fit the standard mold for a woman? Goodness knew that since her marriage, Poca had tried, yet she always seemed a shade off the mark.

They dressed in their best clothes and presented their tickets entitling them to seats in the special section reserved for family. Lucy's seat was on the end of the row, and across the aisle from her sat a handsome young man who seemed anxious for the evening's entertainment to start. She smiled at him. "Do you have family graduating?" she asked.

He shook his head and looked back down at his program. Lucy started to tell him that her daughter was the star performer for the evening, but just then, the lights dimmed and the curtain opened and she forgot everything except Lillian as she was introduced and began to play.

Lucy listened, entranced. Could that accomplished young lady on the stage be the little girl who had picked out tunes on the piano in James's store and whose insistence on the danger of another fire had kept that precious instrument safe so that she could continue to develop her musical skills? Her repertoire was classical and brought the audience to its feet in wild applause. Lillian bowed her acceptance of this adulation with grace and dignity. Lucy could not stop the tears as she stood clapping with everyone else. How she wished that Henry could have lived to see this day, to see their daughter graduate from college, and to witness her talent.

From across the aisle, a loud bravo was heard, and Lucy realized that it came from the young man to whom she had spoken before the performance. He was looking at Lillian as if seeing a member of royalty. Was he a secret that her daughter had been keeping from her?

By the time Lillian had gathered up her belongings and introduced her mother and Poca to her friends and teachers, Lucy had forgotten about the young man from the auditorium. When they reached the lobby on their way out, however, she saw him waiting by the door. Lillian walked right past him, and Lucy watched his face fall.

She put her hand on her Lillian's arm. "Darling," she said, "I think there is someone here who wants to meet you."

Lillian turned and Lucy saw her glance at the man, a question in her eyes. The awkwardness of the situation was not lost on her, but she forged ahead.

"I'm Lucy J. Williams," she said to the man. "This is my daughter, Lillian. I couldn't help noticing that you seemed to enjoy her music."

Lillian gave her mother the same look she'd given her when she had been made to shake hands with the school principal on her first day of school. It said, "You are putting me in a terrible position and I will get even." But she was more mature now. She offered the man her hand and said she was happy to meet him.

He just glowed. "The pleasure is all mine, Miss Williams. I'm John M. McTeer, and I came to hear you play tonight because I heard you, quite by accident, in Atlanta a few weeks ago. I cannot tell you how much I enjoyed it."

"Thank you," Lillian murmured, tapping her foot.

"You heard her play in Atlanta?" said Lucy.

"Yes, ma'am. I'm a pharmacist—that is, I used to be and now I sell products to pharmacists—and I was calling on a store next door to the Episcopal Church in Atlanta when I was drawn to the music coming from the sanctuary. There was a poster on the outside of the door, and it told me who Lillian—who your daughter—was and a little bit about her. It mentioned that she was to play tonight, so I made it a point to be here."

Lucy didn't know whether to believe him or not, but his admiration certainly sounded heartfelt. She could see, though, that Lillian and Poca thought she was taking his interest much too seriously. They wanted her to drop the matter and go with them to the Italian restaurant down the street.

"Well, it's been very nice to meet you, Mr. McTeer," Lucy said, taking the hint. "I run a store in London, Kentucky. If you're ever in that vicinity, please stop in and see me."

They were on the street by then, and John walked along beside her for a minute. "You run a drugstore?" he asked, surprise in his voice.

She laughed. "No no. I run a clothing and notions store. I just thought that if you were calling on pharmacists in the area . . ."

"That's out of my territory."

They bid him good-bye at the corner, but Lillian and Poca did not let up with their bantering all through dinner.

"Your mother has made a conquest," Poca said, eyes twinkling.

"Better she than me," said Lillian.

Lucy laughed with them, but she couldn't keep from asking Lillian what she'd thought of John McTeer.

"He's very smooth," Lillian said.

"Smooth? What does that mean?"

"Oh, you know. Sincere. Polite."

"Yes," Lucy said, "that's what I liked about him."

"Why do I get the feeling that you're trying to marry me off?" said Lillian.

That stopped Lucy short. She had spent the whole of Lillian's life telling her that she could become anything she wanted to become, that she was capable within herself to fulfill her own dreams. Had she said, by her example, that men were not important to those dreams? Now looking at her daughter's beauty and talent, she wanted her to choose her own life more than ever, but she was surprised to discover that she also wanted Lillian to know the love of a good man, as she had. She was further shocked to find that she was picturing John McTeer—a stranger she had only just met—as that man. She told herself she was just mesmerized by the grandeur of the evening.

Chapter Twenty-Six

The store continued to thrive, but it no longer interested Lucy as it had when the struggle to keep it going had consumed her every waking thought. With a competent and trustworthy staff of four clerks and a seamstress, the store was easily managed. Lucy spent her time selling the houses and lots she had purchased with her own money or had listed for other people. Men who had once sneered at her efforts to make a living for her family on her own terms now came to her wanting to list their properties. She liked to think she was gracious when she brokered a sale for them though she couldn't help but enjoy the feeling of victory it brought.

They were just beginning to hear of migration to the southwest part of the country where large acreages were available. New Mexico was especially appealing, and some of the other realtors were talking of making a trip to the area to assess the situation. Lucy wanted to go, but she felt tied down to her London businesses. She decided to spend a few days at Rockcastle Springs Resort and think about her situation. There among the trees and waterfalls, she came to the conclusion that she had taken the Emporium as far as she could, and she made up her mind to sell it. On her return to London, she began to look for a buyer.

She had expected it would be easy to find someone interested in purchasing the store since London's economy was healthy at that time, but she was wrong. None of those who made offers were willing to pay the price she had decided she must have. The Emporium was one of the largest and most profitable businesses in the region, and Lucy did not intend to negate twenty years of struggle by giving it away.

She improved the appearance of the building, both inside and out, and increased her stock. Just before Christmas of 1902, she put everything on sale and kept the store open late in order to make the most of it. It was like a carnival had come to town. The new sidewalks that now ran alongside the major streets were crowded with bargain hunters, all of who seemed to be making the Emporium the object of their attention. Neither snow nor rain fell to impede the shoppers, and Lucy and her staff reveled in the long lines and the ring of the cash register. This frenzy did not abate until midafternoon on Christmas Eve when everyone went home to begin their yuletide celebrations. Lucy sent her staff home too and only stayed long enough herself to settle her accounts. She was locking the door at dusk when she saw Poca running toward her. Her face was ashen.

"What is it?" Lucy met her and took her in her arms.

"Logan . . ." Poca said, trying to get her breath. "Logan has shot Elmer Moore," she leaned into Lucy, sobbing.

There must be some mistake. Poca's brother, Logan, was a mere boy of ten.

"Hush now," Lucy said, "and tell me what's happened."

Poca had begun to calm down. "Papa allowed Logan to take the shotgun and go hunting with Elmer. He jumped across a branch and the gun went off . . ." She started to cry again.

"Is Elmer all right?"

"I don't know. They've taken him to Dr. Pennington's. Oh, Lucy, will you go there with me?"

"Of course I will," she said, and they set out.

That Christmas Eve was spent waiting for the verdict on Elmer's condition to come in. Lucy would have left once Mac arrived, but Poca begged her to stay. So while her children attended the Christmas Eve gatherings to which they'd been invited, Lucy stayed where Poca could find her if she needed to.

About midnight, the doctor came out and announced that Elmer would be all right. The sheriff judged the shooting accidental, and Logan, though much shaken, was allowed to go home with his parents. Poca pressed Lucy's hand as they went out but said nothing.

In the next week's paper, Dyche wrote,

> At a late hour last Saturday evening while out hunting, two and a half miles South of London, Logan Ewell accidentally shot and wounded Elmer Moore with a double barrel shot gun. Moore was 12 or 15 feet in front of Ewell when Ewell in jumping across a branch with his gun in hand had the hammer of it to catch in his coat, discharging one barrel of it, the charge taking effect in Moore's hip, but fortunately he had on heavy clothing beside his hunting coat, also had a rabbit in the pocket of his hunting coat

which caught the greater portion of the charge, so that did not go very deep. Until physicians were called it was thought that he was mortally wounded, in fact one report came to town that he was dead . . .

Of course, by the time the paper came out, everyone knew the truth of what had happened, and any talk there had been had died down. Lucy worried that Logan would have long-lasting effects from the incident, and she wanted to shake his father for letting him out with a gun at his age, but she knew it was common practice. Boys must learn to shoot—and the sooner, the better.

A week or so later, Poca came to see Lucy on a Sunday afternoon. "You must have thought I was crazy," she said when they were settled in the kitchen with their tea.

"You *are* crazy," Lucy teased. "But what specific incident did you have in mind?"

"When I came running to you the day Elmer was shot. Instead of looking for Mac."

"I was nearby," Lucy said.

"No. That's not it. Whenever there's a crisis, I think of you first. I need your-your steadiness. No one else I know can deal with upheaval the way you can."

"I've had a lot of practice," Lucy said.

"Promise me you'll always be around when I need you."

Lucy took Poca's face between her hands. "Poca, I will always be your friend, but I cannot promise to always be around."

"Why not?" said Poca, her voice petulant.

"Well, for one thing, I'm thinking of going West. As soon as I can sell the Emporium."

"Sell the Emporium? Why, Lucy, London would not be the same if you and your store were not there on that corner!"

"So things would change. Life's always changing."

"But why?"

"I want to try something new. There's so much more to the world than London."

Poca sighed and closed her eyes. "I know. I used to think I would be the one to see it—that you would always be here running your store—but now I'm the one who's stuck."

"Poca," Lucy chided, "your children will not be at home forever. When they're grown, you and Mac can travel."

"I want to travel alone—or with you," she said.

"You can come visit me as soon as I'm settled."

"Stop talking like that. You're not going anywhere. Who's going to buy your old store, anyway?"

"We'll see," Lucy said.

The conversation disturbed her—not Poca's pretended dependence. Lucy knew that was only a ploy to manipulate her. But she was greatly concerned about her friend's insecurity, her unhappiness. She thought of how Poca had befriended her when no one else would, and she wanted to tell her how grateful she was. But she didn't know how.

Chapter Twenty-Seven

In January of 1903, Lucy accepted an offer from Vincent Boreing and R. M. Jackson to purchase not just the Emporium but her building and lot as well. They agreed to give her sufficient time to collect her accounts and close out her books.

One morning, she went to the store early to work on this. Now that she had agreed to sell, she found that she had become increasingly nostalgic about the building, wondering what changes Boreing and Jackson would make and how she would feel about seeing other people in this place she had constructed from the ashes of the great fire. She hoped that her staff would be allowed to stay, if they wanted to, and that those who had chosen to trade with her over the years would find the new management to their liking.

From the desk in her small office, she looked out on Main Street and was surprised to see a man's face pressed against the glass window. While she was deciding whether to ignore him or open the door and ask his business, he stepped back and she saw that it was John McTeer. She ran to the door and invited him in.

"I'm sorry, Mrs. Williams," he said. "I didn't think you were open."

"I'm not. I just came in to get a head start on the day."

"I can understand that," he said, standing just inside the door as if he might want to run any minute.

"Please, sit down," she said. "It's so good to see you again."

He sat on the edge of the chair she offered him. "Thank you. The southeast region of Kentucky is going to be my territory from now on. I remembered that you said if I was ever here . . ."

"Of course," she said. "I'm glad you looked me up. Do you know where the pharmacies are? Maybe I can introduce you to the proprietors."

"That's very nice of you. The name I have is . . ." He took a slip of paper from his pocket and read. "S. A. Lovelace."

"I know Mr. Lovelace very well," Lucy told him. "His drugstore is just down the street. He's probably not open yet."

"In that case . . ." John said, rising from his chair.

Lucy did not want him to leave. "How about a cup of coffee?" she asked. "I have some made in the back room."

"I'd like that," he said.

And so they sat drinking coffee until it was time for the other stores to open.

"Thank you for the coffee," John said later, turning toward the door.

"You're welcome," Lucy replied. "Anytime you're in town."

He paused and looked back at her. "How is your daughter?"

"She's very well, thank you. She's on a concert tour at the moment, but she'll be back soon."

His smile lit up the room. "I'll be coming through here about once a month," he said. "Perhaps I'll run into her on my next trip."

"Perhaps you will," Lucy said, trying not to laugh. If ever a man was transparent, it was John. She wondered what he'd had to do to get his territory changed.

She wrapped up her affairs at the Emporium and turned the keys over to Boreing and Jackson. They said they approved of how she had run the business and were ready to carry on in the same vein. Jackson was to have the day-to-day running of the store because Boreing was still in the legislature and traveled a great deal.

When they had signed the final papers and Lucy was preparing to leave, Vincent shook her hand and said, "Lucy, I wish you the best. What do you plan to do now?"

She told him she intended to increase the scope of her real estate business.

He nodded. "I do not think you will have any trouble in that regard," he said. "You are a fine businesswoman."

This was high praise from a man who had accomplished so much himself, and Lucy thanked him for his faith in her. He looked weary and frail, but she knew better than to inquire if he was ill. There was something forbidding about Vincent, even when he was at his kindest and most cordial. When he died from pneumonia on September 16 of that year, the whole town mourned and Dyche wrote with all the elegance he could muster.

A NOBLE LIGHT GOES OUT
Judge Vincent Boreing
After a Terrible Struggle With Dread Pneumonia Passes Peacefully
Into the Great Beyond

Congressman Vincent Boreing was born March 24, 1839, in Washington County, Tenn.: removed to Kentucky in 1847 with his father, Murry Boreing, and settled in Laurel County; was educated at Laurel Seminary, London, Ky., and Tusculum College, Greenville, Tenn: volunteered in the Union army, in Co. A, 24th Kentucky Volunteer Infantry, Mar. 1, 1861, as a private soldier on account of meritorious conduct was commissioned First Lieutenant from the ranks by Gov. Bramlett; was severely wounded in the battle of Rasaca, Ga., May 14, 1863; was elected Superintendent of the public schools of this county in 1868 and re-elected in 1870; founded as editor and publisher The *Mountain Echo*, at London in 1875, the first Republican paper published in South eastern Kentucky, and now the oldest Republican paper in continuous publication in Kentucky; was elected County Judge in 1886; president of the Cumberland Valley Land Company in 1887, and president of the First National Bank of London, in 1888; the latter two positions he held at the time of his death. He represented the Kentucky Conference as a lay delegate in the General conference of the Methodist Episcopal Church at Cincinnati, O., in 1880, and at Cleveland, O., in 1896; was Department Commander of the Department of Kentucky Grand Army of the Republic in 1896; was elected to the Fifty-sixth Congress, re-elected to the Fifty-seventh and Fifty-eighth Congress, being elected to the latter position last November. Soon after the war he was married to Miss Martha Faris, daughter of Mr. J. B. Faris, of this county, now deceased, to which union there were nine children born, three of whom died in infancy, the other six still survive him.

Judge Boreing was born of poor and dependent parentage, having to work away from home much of the time at very meager prices for sustenance for himself and his father's family. After carrying home at night on his back the proceeds of his day's wages in meal, corn or bacon. From his youth he was an indomitable and untiring worker, and by dint of his own industry and economy he succeeded in accumulating a comfortable fortune for a man in this section of the state. Being reared by a pious mother he very early in life imbibed the spirit of Christianity, and attached himself to the Methodist Episcopal Church, in which organization he was a strong pillar at the time of his death. This spirit prompted him through life to be faithful to every trust imposed in him. Discharging the duties of every position of honor or trust to which he was called with great credit to himself and marked fidelity to his constituency. In his death the family loses an affectionate and devoted father the community an exemplary and valued citizen; the Church a strong pillar, and the State a most devoted and most influential citizen and official. Congressional District loses a friend and representative who has done as much, if not more, for his constituency than all former Representatives, and his sudden call from time to eternity leaves a vacancy well nigh impossible to fill.

The funeral of the Hon. Vincent Boreing was held from the M. E. Church, South, last Friday, by Rev. G. N. Jolly. It was not first intended to hold it from the M. E. Church, but on account of the sizes of the churches it was transferred. For a half hour before the appointed time the church was crowded and a large number of persons were standing on the outside. The floral display was the prettiest ever seen in London, and was contributed in memory of Judge Boreing by his many friends from over the State. His remains were interred in the Parker Cemetery amid a multitude of friends and relatives. The Honorary Pall Bearers present were Judge W. H. Holt of Porto Rico; J. H. Tinsley, of Barbourville; A. T. Siler, of Williamsburg; D. B. Logan, of Pineville; S. B. Sharp and Postmaster Reynolds of Covington. The active pallbearers were Judge J. S. Cooper of Somerset; D. C. Edwards, Prof. J. C. Lewis, A. R. Dyche., E. A. Chilton and D. F. Brown. Among the prominent persons here to attend Judge Boreing's funeral were, Napier Adams and Judge James Denton, of Pulaski; John Jarvis and D. McDonald, of Knox; Judge J. S. Bingham and R. C. Ford, of Bell; R. D. Hill, S. Stanfill, Luke Moore and Harve Davis of Whitley; B. J. Bethurum, A. G. Lovell, Jno. S. Cooper, J. W. Rider, and Sam Ward of Rockcastle; T. H. Baker, J. A. Craft, Congressman Swagar

Sherley, of Louisville, and Congressman D. Kehoe, or Maysville, and South Trimble, of Frankfort.

Lucy missed Vincent on a personal level because of the connections she'd had with him through the years. Not only had he married her to Henry, but he also had taken the time to instruct and encourage her in her failed run for superintendent of public schools and had given her her start in the real estate business. Remote and austere as he sometimes was, she had great respect for him, and she grieved his loss.

Once again, the pall of trouble and sorrow hung over the town, but it was not long until, politics being what they are, the gloom was displaced by the fierce machinations of those seeking to replace Vincent in the legislature. After a hotly contested battle at the polls and in the courts, D. C. Edwards was chosen to fill Boreing's shoes.

Lucy watched Lillian closely when she told her that John would be coming to London from time to time. As far as she could tell, it made no difference to her daughter at all. In fact, Lillian pretended to think that he was coming to see Lucy, but Lucy did not dignify that idea with a comment. The next time he came to town, she invited him to dinner, and afterward, he pleaded for Lillian to play the piano. She was always being asked to play when she was a guest at the homes of friends, so Lucy had made it a rule never to ask her to do the same for her own guests. She looked at Lillian to see how she would respond and was surprised when she rose and went to the piano, saying, "Certainly, what would you like to hear?" Lucy left them there in the parlor, Lillian playing the old standards while John stood beside her and sang.

From that night, their relationship developed into love, and in November, they became engaged. The *Mountain Echo* duly noted it:

> Mrs. L. J. Williams announces the engagement of her daughter Lillian to Mr. John M. McTeer. The marriage will take place February 4th. Mr. McTeer comes from an old Virginia family and was formerly a druggist of Louisville, but is now one of the most popular traveling salesman of the city.

They were married at Lucy's home. She whispered to the memory of Henry that their daughter was beautiful, that she was talented, that she was going to be happy with John; and she felt his presence there in the house he'd built for her so many years before.

Dyche wrote of the wedding:

> Another brilliant event in London society was the marriage of Miss Lillian Williams to Mr. John McTeer, a prominent drummer of Louisville, at the home of her mother, Mrs. L. J. Williams, Thursday morning at 10 o'clock. They left on the morning train on their honeymoon, and will make their home at Ft. Smith, Ark.

Lucy had wanted them to have an evening wedding, but everything had to be planned around the train schedules. They settled for the 10:00 a.m. ceremony with only relatives and close friends and followed that with a brief reception.

Jarvis and Lucy saw them off at the station, and as they walked home, Jarvis told her that he'd accepted a job as a salesman with a tapestry company, and though he'd be based in Cincinnati, he would be traveling around the Midwest most of the time. She could see that he was eager to begin this new phase of his life.

That night, she made up her mind to focus on the future and relinquish the past. She had done the best she could for her children, and she was pleased with the way they'd turned out. It was time to move on.

She could now devote herself to increasing the number of properties she offered for sale in and around the London area and also listing land in surrounding counties. Her goal was to sell enough to pay for an expedition to New Mexico and see for herself what real estate possibilities lay in that direction. However, in the spring of 1904, Lillian wrote to say that she and John were expecting a baby, and she begged Lucy to come stay with her for a few months. They had not gone to Ft. Smith as they had expected to do—that is, they had gone there to begin with, but then an opportunity had opened up for John in Roanoke, Virginia, where he had family, and they had gone there to live instead. Lucy sensed that Lillian was not at ease with her new in-laws, so she closed her house in London and went to help her daughter. But as soon as her grandson, Jack, was born and Lillian safely recovered, she returned to London to take up where she had left off. And then Jarvis wrote to say that he was to spend a few months in the home office of his company in Cincinnati, and he would like her to come for a visit. She felt she could not do less for him than she had done for his sister, so she went. By the time she got back to London in the fall of 1905, she was weary and her real estate business was woefully lacking in both property and clients.

London seemed different. Part of it was the lack of day-to-day contact with people that she had enjoyed in the store, but she also missed old friends. While she had been away, Bettie had died after a short illness, and as she had for Vincent Boreing, she grieved for her because of their long association—and because she had not been able to say good-bye. And then early in 1906, her father died. It was not unexpected but it was nevertheless heart-wrenching. Lucy could not imagine life without him.

With a sense of starting over once again, she rented space in the Catching Building and threw herself into finding new property listings. A simple contract between owner and agent, giving the location of the property and the terms of sale, was all that was required between buyer and seller. Lucy found real estate easier than running the store because there was no stock to buy and no accounts receivable, but since she worked alone, she had to keep up with the contracts herself, as well as visiting all the sites to make sure they were as she represented them to be.

She ranged far and wide looking for land to list, but it took more than a year for her business to start to thrive again. During that time, she met many old friends and made new ones, and to all of them, she talked of the Southwest and the possibilities there.

"How do you know that land in New Mexico would be a good investment?" Poca asked. "Have you ever been to that area?"

"I've seen it," Lucy said, "when I took that trip to the West Coast. You cannot imagine the vastness of it—the space. People from the east are sure to discover it before long, and I want to buy land there while it's cheap."

Poca shook her head. "Don't you ever think of just settling down in your beautiful home and letting the world go by for a while?"

"As a matter of fact," said Lucy, "I'm thinking of selling my house."

Rare tears sprang to Poca's eyes, but she quickly brushed them away.

"Poca, what is it?"

"Lucy, if you sell that house, you will leave London and never come back."

"Well, I'm not going tomorrow," Lucy told her. "So let's don't worry about it." But she knew Poca was right. Once she relinquished that last tie with Henry, there would be no reason to return.

That fall, she held an auction on nine town lots she owned in East London, and she made $1,950 on them. These were lots she had bought across the years as part of one deal or another and had held on to. Now the town was stretching in that direction and it was rumored that the railroad was soon to be rerouted from its current location on the west side of Long Street, behind her house, to the east side of town, with the crossing on Manchester Street. Her lots were near the proposed crossing, and where they had been worthless before, they were now valuable as commercial sites. The reverse was true of her house. Now that the noise and soot from the trains would be on the other side of town, it was more attractive as a residence. She had no trouble selling it.

She continued to talk of land in the West to her customers, and many of them expressed an interest in buying land there. But before she involved others in her plans, she needed to see the possibilities for herself. Not wishing to use money that she had put away for her children's inheritance on a project that might not work out, she took $500 from the sale of the town lots to stake her, left the rest of her money in the bank, and took the train West.

Chapter Twenty-Eight

Deming, New Mexico

When she stepped off the train in Deming, New Mexico, in 1907, Lucy thought it the most desolate place she had ever seen. The terrain was perfectly flat except for blue-hued mountains in the far distance. The heat was oppressive. Several well-dressed American men were arriving or departing, but she saw no other women at the train station. Besides the Americans, there were a few Indians and some dark-skinned natives of Mexico, the border of which was only about thirty-five miles away. One of these men carried her baggage to the nearby platform. When he did not answer her questions, she realized that he spoke no English. She was startled to think that the basic communication of speech could be a problem in her own country, but then she remembered that New Mexico was still a territory and not a state.

She had come to Deming alone with plans to assess the real estate market, but now she doubted her judgment in the matter. How could she learn what she needed to know in this strange place? She, who so craved adventure, now wished for the safety of the familiar. But she was here, and she must make the best of it. She asked the ticket agent where she might find a place to stay. He looked at her with curiosity, and she thought he would not answer, but finally, he pointed to the street and said, "Rooming house, two blocks down."

There seemed to be no means of transporting her trunk, and since she certainly could not carry it, she pushed it against the wall and went out with just her pocketbook and a small bag. She found Rabb's Rooming House without any trouble. It was built of adobe in the classic style of the Southwest. Lucy walked up three flat steps to a long covered porch held up by round poles. Midway of the porch, an arched door led into the cool, dark interior of the building. While her eyes were adjusting to the dimness, she heard a voice ask if she could help her.

Lucy approached a high counter along the back wall where a woman of about her own age stood, smiling.

"I'd like a room for a few days, perhaps as long as a month," Lucy said.

"Yes, ma'am," answered the other woman. "I can rent you a room for one week, and if you want to stay on, you just let me know before Saturday."

Lucy told her that would be fine, and she asked if she could send someone to the depot for her trunk.

"Certainly," said the other woman and rang a bell that sat on the counter.

An old man came from the back of the building, and the woman instructed him to take the wagon and go to the station to pick up Lucy's trunk.

"It's very heavy," Lucy said, thinking about the man's advanced years, but he had already gone out.

"Are you Mrs. Rabb?" she asked the woman.

"Just call me Nannie. And that was my husband, Thomas. We've run this place for nearly twenty years. Used to be we'd have a boarder every now and again, but lately we stay full up most of the time."

She pushed the registration ledger toward Lucy and said, "Fourteen dollars for the first seven days, and that includes three meals a day."

By the time Lucy had paid and signed the book, the old man was back.

"Room 124," Nannie told him, and the man shuffled off, pushing the little cart that held Lucy's trunk.

Nannie turned back to her. "Here's your key, Mrs. Williams," she said. "Supper's at six o'clock."

Lucy thanked her and followed Thomas down the hall.

The room was nicely appointed with a woven bedspread to match the colorful rugs on the floor. There was also a comfortable chair with a footstool, and as soon as she had put away her things, Lucy stretched out there to think about where she should go to get the information she needed. Strange as her new surroundings were, she was, nevertheless, eager to take on her new business venture.

The next morning, she set out. First, she walked the length of the town, taking note of the kinds of businesses along the street. The layout of Deming was easy to follow, a simple east-west, north-south grid. The streets had names like Gold and Silver and Copper and Iron. There were a lot of saloons, and the men standing outside of them stared at Lucy as she went past. She held her head high and pretended not to notice.

When she grew tired, she sat down on a bench under a pine tree to catch her breath. She still did not know who to talk to about land prices and availability; she wasn't even sure what she was looking for, but she knew she needed to familiarize herself with her surroundings. While she sat, she looked around for the courthouse, thinking that public records would be a good place to start her inquiries. She saw only a small sign on the bank across the street that read Courthouse Inside.

As she arose to make her way there, a huge dog loped toward her, and before she could brace herself, it jumped up and put its feet on her shoulders, knocking her down on the gravel walkway. Lucy flailed her arms in panic, but the dog kept its paws on her and began to lick her face. Just as she opened her mouth to scream, she heard a loud voice yelling, "Toby, come here," and the dog left her instantly and trotted to its master. And there, flat on her back on the sidewalk, she had her first look at Pliny Burdock.

He held out his hand and helped her to her feet, apologizing over and over. "He's just a pup, despite his size," he said, motioning to the dog. "I shouldn't have let him get away from me like that. Are you hurt?"

Lucy shook her head. "I don't think so. But my goodness, he's a big one."

"I'm real sorry. My name's Pliny Burdock. Can I do anything to help you?"

Lucy shook her head again and sank down on the bench. "I'm . . . I'm glad to meet you," she stammered, and because she couldn't think what else to say, she asked, "Are you a native here?"

Pliny sat down beside her, holding the dog fast. "I reckon not," he said, "since I'm neither Mexican nor Apache."

"I meant, have you lived here since the town was settled?" Lucy felt a blush crawl up her face.

"No, ma'am. Deming got started up when the railroad came back in 1881. I was living in Iowa then. But I've been here a spell."

"I'm Lucy J. Williams," she said. "I've just arrived from Kentucky." And then she added, "I'm in real estate."

He laughed and waved his arm toward the mountains. "Well, there's a sight of that around here."

"Yes, I can see that there is. I'd like to know more about it. What does land go for here?"

"Are you looking for town lots or farming acreage?"

"I . . . I don't know, to tell the truth. What kind of farming is done here?" She looked out at the desolate terrain and wondered what would grow there.

"You'd be surprised what this climate can produce with the proper methods," Pliny said, as if reading her mind. "But most of the ranchers just run cattle."

She wondered if she could sell ranchland to her clients, but she encouraged Pliny to tell her more. For an hour, as they sat in the shade of the pine, he related the history of Luna County and the town of Deming.

"Deming was a town before Luna County was formed from parts of Grant and Dona Ana counties," he said. "The railroad from Kansas City dipped down, you see, to avoid going over the Rockies, and Deming was about halfway to San Francisco that way, so it made a natural stopover. If the railroad hadn't come through here, there's no telling whether there'd be a settlement today."

He got out his pipe and filled it while she waited for him to continue. "It was a wilderness, no doubt about it," he went on. "The first explorers were the Mexicans who were looking for a trade route between Sonora and Santa Fe. On the way, they came across the Mimbres Valley, I reckon, and scoured out all these regions. Fought the Apaches along the way. Wasn't much settlement, though, till after the Mexican War in 1846. Then armies from the States occupied New Mexico, and the soldiers made trails and 'fore long, there were paths going ever which way—all the way to California." He sucked on his pipe.

"When did the settlers begin to come?"

"Well, it was gradual for a while, but after the railroad came, it picked up. Like I said, it was natural."

"And they all ranched?"

"No no," said Pliny with a trace of exasperation in his voice. "The government was offering grants, you see, and some of the land had mining potential, so they done various things."

"What kind of mines?"

"Oh, lead and silver and a little copper."

"Is there oil here?"

"Not as I've ever heard of," said Pliny. "But I wouldn't be surprised."

They were silent for a few moments. Lucy asked him what he did for a living.

He laughed again. "I've staked me a small claim, but so far, I ain't found nothing on it but a little water."

"I should think that would be a good thing in this arid land," she said.

"Well, it waters my cows and keeps my garden from drying up, but there ain't no money in it."

The dog was getting restless, so Pliny stood up and said he guessed he'd better be going. "It's been nice to make your acquaintance, Miz Williams," he said. "And again, I apologize for the dog."

"Wait, Mr. Burdock." Lucy rose too. "Maybe you can help me. Could I hire you to drive me around the county and show me what land is available? That is, if you can spare the time."

It was obvious that Pliny had no day job, but she didn't want to insult him.

He gave her a strange look. "I reckon I could do that," he said after a moment.

Lucy wondered if he thought it unladylike to make such a suggestion. She had supposed that image would not be as much of a problem in this wild country as it was in the staid provincial town of London, but maybe she was wrong.

"Mr. Burdock" she said, "except for my children, who are now grown, I've been on my own since my husband died in 1884. I am not interested in scandalizing this community, but neither am I overly concerned with what they think of me."

"I reckon you'll fit right in here in Deming," he said.

"Good," she answered. "That's just what I want to do."

Traveling about in Pliny's old wagon wasn't comfortable, but it was interesting. He seemed liked and welcomed by everyone, and he had a real knack for knowing which properties would be most appealing to new settlers. During the next week, he showed Lucy hundreds of acres of available land and introduced her to some of Luna County's best ranchers. Some had large spreads with thousands of cows and nice ranch houses; others ran only a few cows on a few acres and lived in a shack. Pliny referred to all of them as ranchers and was as accepted by one as by the other.

Lucy soaked in everything because she wanted to know as much as possible before she committed herself or her clients to purchasing land in this strange and beautiful region.

She had arrived in Deming on a Saturday, and by the next Saturday, she had seen most of the land that was for sale within a ten-mile radius of Deming. She felt drained and told Pliny that she needed to rest. She sat and rocked on the porch of Rabb's Rooming House and tried to put her thoughts in order. There was no doubt in her mind that Deming and Luna County had a great future and that any investment she made here would be profitable. Timing would be important. Just in the week since her arrival, she had seen several families get off the train with the intention of settling in the area. They were not the poor and downtrodden, either. In fact, she was amazed at the number of lawyers, teachers, and businessmen among them. All seemed enthusiastic about the area. Her heart soared to think that she had chosen so well. She envisioned a long and worthwhile association with Luna County.

That Sunday, she spent the day writing letters to her children and her clients singing the praises of New Mexico. She wrote about the way the colors changed over the desert from morning until night, of the invigorating climate, of the quaintness of the buildings, and of the kindness of the people. She found that she could not easily express her certainty that to buy land here would be a wise decision, though. She could encourage them to come and see for themselves, but even that might be premature. She must first have something concrete on which to base her claims, and that would mean a more careful study of the laws governing land ownership and a better knowledge of the soil and what it could produce.

On Monday, she bought a quarter section of land for herself as a test site. This took almost all of the funds she had brought with her, and she debated whether she should write to the bank in London and ask them to send her more money. She decided instead to find temporary work that would allow her to stay on at Rabb's and still do the research needed to properly inform her potential clients.

As she had done in London, she wrote out a small notice and took it to the local newspaper, the *Deming Headlight*: "Wanted: A position as nurse or attendant in sickness, or general housework. Mrs. Lucy Williams, Rabb's Rooming House."

When Nannie saw her ad in the paper, she came to Lucy and said, "I know just where you can get such a job," and she introduced her to Mercy Farmington, an elderly woman who had broken her arm in a fall from her back stoop. Mercy needed someone to cook and clean for a few weeks until she could use her arm again. Lucy moved out of Rabb's and in with Mercy; and each day, when she had finished the chores Mercy couldn't do for herself, Lucy would settle the older woman in an easy chair by the window and go out in search of information.

She talked to everyone she met, and that included the cowboys who stood around outside the saloons. At first they made fun of her in a subtle way, but after they discovered she asked intelligent questions about seasons and crops and livestock, they took her more seriously.

Lucy was intrigued by the mixed society. There had been a few families of African descent in London, and though they were generally treated with kindness, it was commonly believed that they were "not like us" and were best fit for manual labor and expected to interact socially only with "their own kind." It had bothered her a great deal, but speaking out against it was like battering one's head against a wall.

It was too soon to tell if the white settlers took this attitude with the Indians and Mexicans who populated Deming. On the surface, all classes seemed to get along well, but she could not help noticing that most positions of authority were held by white Americans.

The natives, with their long history in the area, went on about their business. They could be found working on the ranches and in the stores, frequenting the bars in their own part of town on Saturday night and going to the Catholic church on Sunday. To Lucy, they were placid and agreeable, but she could not shake the feeling that they were laughing at the middle-aged woman from Kentucky who asked so many questions about things that were none of her business.

By the time Mercy was able to do her own housework, Lucy had secured options on half a dozen plots of ground, and she was anxious to go home and see who would bid on them. She had her return ticket, and so she said good-bye to Mercy and Nannie and helped Pliny load her trunk into his wagon for the short drive to the train station. She thanked him for all his help and said that when she came back, she intended to build a house and stay.

"I'm counting on it," he said.

Chapter Twenty-Nine

The first thing she did when she got back to London was to run her regular ad for local property and append a note about the Western possibilities:

. . . Good Real Estate . . .

FOR SALE

I HANDLE NO OTHER. *Farms in Laurel County, near London. Worth the price. Fine coal lands for less than their worth. Some town property that will pay 18 percent on the investment. Is this not good enough? Write or call at Catching Hotel if you want to purchase. I have the best. L. J. Williams, London, Ky.*

NEW MEXICO LANDS
IN THE MIMBRIS VALLEY—The Land of Sunshine and Promise

Here is a fortune for you. Do you want to take it? Do you want to invest a small sum and reap a fortune in a few years? If so, act at once; twelve months from now will be too late. Fine, cheap land is growing scarce. Hundreds are rushing in. In my travels I found this spot: I believe it the finest in the land today. I have my own interests there. I am out often. Come go along and look over the valley for yourself. I will assist you in selecting the best. Much reduced Railroad tickets furnished. Write or call at Catching Hotel and we will talk it over further.

Yours Truly,
L. J. Williams

Houses to let—Your Fire Insurance solicited.

Reproduction of an ad in the *Mountain Echo*, London, Kentucky, 1907

John encouraged her to get into the insurance business, saying that when a person bought property, he should have the option to buy insurance to cover his investment. This made sense to Lucy. Her son-in-law was a born salesman. With his help, she learned about insurance and made arrangements to offer it to her clients.

John and Lillian were among the first to buy land from her—a small acreage outside Deming with a house on it. They did not come to stay, though, until early in 1909 when a group that included Charles R. Baugh and Adrian Almy, Laurel County men Lucy had known and respected for a number of years, made their arrival in New Mexico. Charles was Bettie's nephew and had been a county judge; Adrian was a farmer she had met when he'd asked her to sell a piece of property for him. To this group was added several of John's friends from Virginia, including James Dymond, and two of Lucy's Jackson relatives.

Once they arrived in Deming and were ensconced at the Harvey Hotel, things happened so quickly that it took Lucy's breath away. John and Charles and James immediately formed the Dymond Insurance and Real Estate Company, and this ad appeared in the *Deming Headlight* on March 11:

> Be it well known that Chas. R. Baugh, John M. McTeer and Jas. E. Dymond are in the insurance business and are at all times ready and willing to write all kinds of insurance, esp. fire, life and accident in the largest and best companies going. They call their firm The Dymond Co. and their office is on Gold Avenue between Pine and Spruce, next door to the County offices.

Lucy was a financial investor with Dymond and Company, and she was surprised to see that her name did not appear in the ad. Once again, she was reminded of the proprietary ways of men. For Lillian's sake, she swallowed her outrage and said nothing about it to John.

Pliny had looked her up as soon as he heard that she was back in town. "I see you're moving up in the world," he said, looking around the plush lobby of the Harvey Hotel.

"It's the crowd I'm traveling with these days," Lucy said.

"Then I guess I'd best be going."

Another man heard from, she thought, but she said, "Oh, Pliny, don't be silly. I was going to look you up. I just need a day or two to get my head on straight."

"What does that mean?"

"I got this group together, and now I don't know what to do with them," she said. "I just wanted to sell them some land . . ."

"And I'm guessing you did."

It was true. The parcels she had options on had all been sold.

"It's just that . . . Well, there seems nothing left for me to do." She did not want to go into detail.

"Just keep on doing what you're doing," said Pliny. "Your friends would never have come to Luna County if you hadn't told them about it. Think of all the people that still don't know. You've got your work cut out for you."

She thought it over and decided that Pliny was right. Never mind if her name was on the ad, she would sell the idea of buying land in the great Southwest to as many people as she could.

"I guess I won't be building a house here anytime soon," she said.

"But you'll be here often," said Pliny. "And I've got a house where you could stay, if you've a mind."

She was too startled to answer. It had been a long time since a man had indicated an interest in her that didn't have to do with business. Though it was a novel sensation, she wasn't sure she liked it.

That night, she took John to task over the business arrangements he had set up. She was more than a little angry.

"I found this place, John," she said. "It's because of me that you and your friends are here. I intend to have more than a behind-the-scenes part in it."

John looked as if he would cry. "Lord, Lucy," he said, "I'm so sorry. I never meant for you to be left out."

She loved John, and she knew that he would not deliberately hurt her. She also knew that he could not change the Dymond Insurance and Real Estate Company's policies all by himself. And not for the world would she embarrass him in front of his friends.

"I have a suggestion," she said.

"Please," he said, "tell me."

"What if I devote myself to finding buyers for you? The company can pay my travel expenses and I get a percentage of the sales."

His look of relief was almost comical. "That seems like a wonderful suggestion to me," he said. "I'll talk it over with Charles and James tomorrow."

"Do more than talk it over," she said.

True to his word, he convinced his partners to install Lucy as liaison to the buying public. He drew up an official contract to that effect, and she was happy with it. Now she could travel freely between Deming and London or anywhere else the Dymond Company wanted to send her. She could tout the beauties of Luna County in her own way and at her own pace.

To her daughter's dismay, Lucy decided to move out of the hotel and back into Rabb's Rooming House. Lillian had made friends with the wives of other young businessmen who were staying at the hotel and was already involved in the town's social life, and she thought that her mother should be interested in that as well. But Lucy didn't care about parties and teas; she wanted to move in her own circles. It wasn't as if she couldn't see Lillian's family whenever she wanted to.

Lillian and John were planning to move into the old ranch house on the property they had purchased from Lucy. "I think that area has a good chance of growing into an affluent community," John said. He had great dreams. From the way he talked, it seemed to Lucy that he meant to build a whole town in what was then just weeds and sagebrush.

She settled in at Rabb's to make her plans. Pliny did not repeat his invitation to stay with him, and she was glad. Inexplicable as Pliny might find it, she really had no interest in taking their friendship to a sexual level. That part of her life had died with Henry. While she enjoyed the company of men, she could not imagine sleeping with any of them because she still loved only Henry even after all the time that had passed. It was not about morality or religious conviction but simply that she insisted on making her own choices. She knew she was considered strange, but she was at peace with it.

The first three months of 1909 were busy as they all adjusted to their new life. It did not take long for Lucy to love the desert. The sunrises and sunsets, the wild flowers, the way the shadows hung over the distant mountains awakened in her a spiritual elation like none she had ever known. She rose early so as not to miss anything, and she ended each day with a walk to the edge of town to watch the night pull its curtain over the desert. She appreciated the slower, more restful pace of Deming even with the underlying threat of dust storms and drought and bandits lurking on the Mexican border so nearby.

Daily, the trains brought new settlers. These new arrivals were anxious to have their ideas incorporated into the fabric of the community. Clubs and churches were organized and new buildings sprang up seemingly overnight. The Dymond Insurance and Mimbres Valley Real Estate Company, as it was now called, grew and flourished. By early in April, they all felt the need to stop and catch their breath. John and Lillian invited Pliny and Lucy to join them and the Almys on a visit to Faywood Hot Springs.

This resort had a long history, and Pliny loved to tell it. "I reckon them springs has been there since time began," he said. "I've heard stories about how the Spaniards come here for their health way before there was a hotel or a bathhouse. Then the Hudsons bought it—they were the first to run it as a business—but they was burned out in the '90s, I think it was. A Mr. Graham was the next owner, and when he got into financial trouble, he sold to J. C. Fay and William Lockwood, and that's why it's called Faywood."

Lucy was intrigued and wished she could know more detail. It had been a Mr. Graham who started Rockcastle Springs back home, a resort frequented by people from all over the eastern part of the country, and she wondered if it could be the same person.

Faywood's hotel was very modern. Its sixty rooms had both hot and cold running water, and its bathhouse was luxurious. Lucy and Pliny "took the waters" every day they were there. They enjoyed each other's company. Besides bathing in the mineral springs, they rode horseback around the grounds, and at night, they ate huge meals, played cards, and danced to the music of a local band. Lucy could not remember when she had last danced. Of course they were the darlings of the gossips, but that did not concern them. If Lucy had learned one thing in her life, it was that people will think what they want to and there's nothing you can do about it.

When they returned from Faywood, Jarvis was in town. Lucy couldn't believe it, but John just laughed. "I asked him to come," he said. "I wanted to surprise you and Lillian."

"So are you on vacation?" Lucy asked him when she had collected herself.

Jarvis shook his head. "I thought if the rest of you could move here, so could I," he said.

"I haven't moved here," said Lucy. "I'm going back to Kentucky in a week."

"But not for good," said Lillian. "That's what trains are for."

John and Charles were sending her back to London to find more investors. With her contacts there and others that John had in Louisville, she hoped to send out a large number of buyers by the first of June.

She transferred the land she had bought on her first visit to Jarvis because she thought it would make him feel more permanent, and she wasn't sure of his financial situation. He seemed glad to get it and began to talk of building a house there. They had a fine time that week before she went back to Kentucky. Lillian threw a party to introduce her brother to her new friends. Lucy had never seen Jarvis so animated, and she realized that he had been lonesome for his family. She wanted to stay with him longer, but her plans had been made, and at the end of the week, she went home.

In London, she found things much the same. Since she no longer had a residence there, she took a room at Ellen Brewer's boarding house and reopened her real estate business. Laura Baugh, Charles's wife, came to see her, wanting to know all about Deming and about Charles, of course.

"He says the children and I can come in June. He's renting a place for now, but he says we'll build a house as soon as I get there to help him plan it."

Lucy liked both Charles and Laura a great deal. While John had changed from the shy young man she had met in Nashville at Lillian's graduation to a forceful businessman with a somewhat ruthless air about him, Charles was the same as the boy who had spent summers working in his aunt Bettie's store and playing ball in the evenings with Jarvis and his friends. Lucy knew that he missed Laura and the children dreadfully, and she was glad to hear that he was making arrangements for his family to join him in Deming.

From her own contacts and those given her by John and James and her brother, Evan, she located as many land investors as she could from around Kentucky, Tennessee, and Virginia. To all of them, she praised the availability of land and the potential for a good living—even wealth—in the American southwest. She did not have to muster up sincerity; she believed what she was saying with all her heart. By the end of May, she had arranged for discounted tickets for two dozen men and women among her contacts who wanted to go to Deming and see the area for themselves. This included Charles's family, and Lucy was glad to be there to help Laura with the children. There were five of them: Walter, who was twelve; Frank, ten; Daniel, seven; Mary, five; and Charles Jr., only two years old.

She did not know all of those who showed up at the station, but she introduced herself as the representative of Dymond and Company, and soon they were all friends. The trip took four days, but except for crowded sleeping conditions, everyone was comfortable. Laura's children were amazed to see buffalo and Indians from the train window as they crossed the plains and antelope as they approached their destination. And of course, they were excited at the prospect of seeing their father after their long separation from him.

John and Lillian and Charles met the train when it arrived in Deming on the morning of June 8. John had arranged accommodations for the buyers at the hotel, but Charles took his family to the house he had rented for them on Spruce Street.

Before she left, Laura took Lucy's hand. "Thank you," she said. "I don't know what I would have done without your help with the children. You must be worn-out."

Lucy assured her that she was fine.

Laura looked about. "I feel like I'm in a dream," she said. "It's so beautiful here."

That day, any scene would have been beautiful to her, of course. Lucy said, "Get some rest, and when you're ready, Lillian and I will show you around."

"That would be wonderful."

"And I'm fixing supper for all of you Thursday night," Lillian said. "Come around six."

Laura said thank you again and went off arm in arm with Charles.

It was a party to remember. The weather was perfect, and Lillian had set up tables on her veranda that looked out toward the Florida Mountains, hanging lanterns from the corner posts for light. Besides the Baughs and Lucy and Jarvis, she had also invited James Dymond and the Almys, as well as Elizabeth Waddill, a young woman she had met through Deming's Women's Club.

After dinner, the adults sat talking on the veranda while the children played about the yard. John and James chatted about business, but Charles did not join in. He sat beside Laura all evening, answering her questions about the area and supporting her excited plans for building their own house in the near future. Jarvis was more involved in the general conversation than Lucy had ever seen him, and she wondered, briefly, if he was trying to impress Miss Waddill. The young woman was very pretty and poised and seemed interested in what Jarvis was saying. Finally, little Jack and Charles's children grew tired and came up onto the veranda to crawl into the laps of the adults and fall asleep, so the party ended. Jarvis and Lucy were spending the night with Lillian and John, but the others had to drive back to Deming despite the late hour.

James and the Almys had the new-fangled automobiles, but Charles still drove his horse-drawn carriage. Since coming to Deming, he had bought four horses—two to pull his carriage and two for riding purposes. Walter could not stop talking about them.

"My horse is called Starlight," Lucy heard him tell little Jack. "He's so fast he could be a racehorse."

Charles gave him an indulgent smile.

As he tucked the children in and settled Laura close to him on the front seat, he said to John, "I'll not be in tomorrow. I need to help Laura get settled, and I promised Walter we'd ride out to the gulch late in the day when it's not so hot."

"Of course," John said.

Lucy could have gone back to town with John as he went to work the following morning, but she wanted a good visit with Lillian, so she waited until Jarvis went back in the late afternoon and rode with him. He was expecting to start work at Bolich's Department Store on the following Monday, and she had offered to help him move his things from the hotel to Rabb's Rooming House.

As they approached the town, they heard shouts and screams and running feet. Even before they came in sight, Lucy knew that some tragedy had occurred. She saw the doctor and John, and she realized that the screams were coming from Laura Baugh, who stood clinging to the hitching post in front of her house.

"Stop," Lucy said to Jarvis, and climbing down from the wagon as fast as she could, she ran to Laura.

The other woman clung to her while in the background Lucy saw the wide-eyed faces of the children.

"It's Charles, oh, Lucy, it's Charles," Laura moaned.

"Help me," Lucy said to Jarvis, who had come up.

Together they eased Laura onto the front steps.

"Now," Lucy said, "tell me what has happened."

Laura could barely speak. "Charles and Walter went riding after supper. Charles's horse ran away, and he was thrown. He's unconscious and the doctor . . . the doctor says there is no hope he'll recover." She buried her head in her hands and wailed.

"See to the children," Lucy whispered to Jarvis, and he went to where Walter had gathered his siblings around him, picked up the baby, and motioned for the others to follow him inside. The smaller children did not seem to grasp the situation, but from the look on his face, Lucy could tell that Walter knew the worst. Had he and his father been racing their horses when the accident occurred? Whatever had happened, he would never forget what he had witnessed that day. Her heart went out to him.

Charles lingered, unconscious, from the day after the welcoming party, which was a Friday, until the following Tuesday. Laura never left his side, but he did not know she was there. Lucy and Mary Almy took care of the children while John and James handled the many legal and business issues that arose, which, of course, Laura was in no condition to address.

On Wednesday, they laid Charles to rest at the Deming Cemetery. Lucy and Lillian stood one on either side of Laura during the burial. She was calm now, but pale and listless. "I wish I could have taken him back to London," she said. They could only hold her close and offer their sympathy.

In Thursday's edition of the *Deming Graphic*, the town's second newspaper, there was a long obituary, which Lucy cut out and sent to the papers in London:

MR. C.R. BAUGH DEAD

A pall of sorrow and regret overspreads Deming by the sad and lamentable death of one of her leading and most highly respected citizens, Mr. Chas. R. Baugh, who was thrown from a runaway horse last Friday evening a little after seven o'clock and died from the injuries received at 9:20 Tuesday morning, having never regained consciousness.

On the day of the fatal accident Mr. Baugh and his young son rode out horseback to his claim a few miles east of town, where he was having a house built with the view of moving his family on the place in the near future. On the way back the horse Mr. Baugh was riding ran away and got beyond his control, and when it reached the S. P. crossing at the smelter, it ran into a barbed wire fence. The awful comtact with the animal going at breakneck speed threw the rider some forty feet over its head. The unfortunate man struck with terrible force on the side of his head, concussion of the brain being caused, which baffled the best medical aid that could be summoned, and he lingered in an unconscious condition until he passed away.

Mr. W. J. Clifford was at the smelter at the time of the accident and quickly ran to Mr. Baugh's assistance. Realizing he was badly hurt he phoned for Dr. Steed, who hurried to the scene in company with F. C. Peterson and J. M. McTeer. The injured man was removed to his home, where he remained until Monday morning, when he was taken to the Ladies' Hospital and an operation performed by a specialist from El Paso with the last hope of saving his life. However, as soon as the brain was exposed to view it was seen at once that the case was hopeless, the doctors realizing that a few hours at best of life was all that could be hoped for.

Deceased is a member of the Mimbres Valley Realty Co., a leading land firm in Deming, and while he had been identified with our little city but some six months, yet in that brief time it would have been difficult for a man to have gained a higher plane of standing in any community.

Chas. R. Baugh was the soul of honor, charitable in all relations with his fellow man and in the daily walks of life he was impervious to temptation and true to his God. He was a prominent and devout member of the Christian Church and his worth was beautifully portrayed in his religious work. His life was an influence for all that was noble and uplifting, and truly the world is better that he lived.

Deceased was born in London, Ky., 42 years of age, and remained a citizen of that place until he came to Deming. He was frequently honored in his home town with positions of trust and enjoyed the greatest confidence and esteem of his home people, people who had learned him through the passing of the years and admired him for his high principles and noble character.

A loving wife, who is bowed in deepest grief over the sudden and heartrending bereavement that has overtaken her, and five small children—four boys and one little girl—are left to mourn the loss of one of the kindest and most devoted husbands and fathers who doubtless ever lived.

To this afflicted family the sympathy and prayers of a sorrowing community is extended in its entirety.

The funeral was held yesterday afternoon at the residence, Rev. Z. Moore, of the Christian Church, officiating at the last sad rites. The remains were buried in the cemetery here.

The shock of Charles's sudden death took its toll on all of them. Besides the loss of his friendship, they had counted on him to provide the wisdom to make their business enterprises profitable. Just before his death, the four of them—John, James, Charles, and Lucy—had agreed to separate Dymond Insurance from Mimbres Valley Real Estate Company with John and James running the insurance section and Charles and Lucy the real estate. Now Lucy felt at a loss. Clearly, she could not travel and stay in the office of Mimbres Valley Real Estate at the same time, but she did not want to give up either function. In the end, she left the office in John's hands and went back to Kentucky sooner than she had intended in order to accommodate Laura, who was moving back to Kentucky and needed her help with the children.

And so it was that she was back in Laurel County in time to be recorded there in the 1910 census.

Chapter Thirty

Lucy did not go back to Deming for any length of time for nearly a year though she made one or two quick visits. In Kentucky, she sold the last of her real estate properties, spent time with friends and family, and took stock of her financial situation. She was pleased with where she stood in that regard, but not being one to rest on her laurels, she soon began a systematic effort to find new investors in land in the Mimbres Valley among friends, relatives, and acquaintances in Kentucky, Tennessee, and Virginia.

Meanwhile, John took on a new partner, C. H. Hon, and they hired another Kentucky man, O. H. Cooper, to handle publicity for their firm. Jarvis left Bolich's and went into business with John as well. He sent Lucy a clipping from the *Deming Graphic*.

> Mr. H. J. Williams has resigned his position in N. A. Bolich's store and will take charge of the Western Brokerage Co., formerly conducted by Hon and McTeer. Mr. Williams, since coming to Deming, has proved that he is a young man who will do to tie to, as it were, and his many friends here wish him every success.

He also sent a copy of the advertisement he'd placed in the Graphic:

H. J. Williams

Commission Merchant

Dealer in Alfalfa, Grain, and all kinds of feedstuffs in carload lots

Lowest market quotations furnished daily

Deming, New Mexico

Reproduction of an ad in the *Deming Graphic*, 1910

By the summer of 1910, she was back in Deming with plans to stay for several months. Jarvis now did the paperwork for the real estate business while John turned his attention to a new venture, the Southwest Immigration Company, and also worked full-time for Missouri Life Insurance. He and Lillian had a busy social life as well. Lucy worried that John wore too many hats.

Jarvis seemed to be doing well. Lucy was glad for him to have a more substantial job than selling clothes at Bolich's and to know that he had made new friends. He held official positions in a club for men and several other local organizations. Everywhere she went, she heard about her children and how they enhanced Deming society, and she felt a mother's pride in them. Lillian seemed to find the pace harrowing at times, but Jarvis was serene.

"I think Jarvis will ask Elizabeth to marry him," Lillian said as they sat drinking coffee on her porch one morning, soon after Lucy's return.

Her heart caught. "Are you sure?"

"Why not? They see a lot of each other, and socially they are equals."

Lillian and the other young matrons who had come to Deming were determined to establish a class system like that in the East—especially now that statehood for New Mexico had become a big issue. They wanted everything done "properly." The older she got, the less Lucy cared for any of that. She had no doubt that statehood would come and she supported it, but she loved the frontier nature of Deming and hoped it wouldn't change too much too soon.

"Do you think Elizabeth's in love with Jarvis?" she asked.

"I don't know, but she likes him. I can tell."

"Unless there's love between them, it wouldn't work out," Lucy said.

"Oh, I don't know," Lillian said. "Sometimes it's enough to have similar values and dreams."

Lucy didn't argue, but she didn't agree. Like her mother, Lillian was a woman of strong opinions though sometimes Lucy felt she wasted that strength on superficial issues. At Lillian's age, she had just been beginning her long struggle to prove that a woman alone could make a good life for herself and her children. With John's success, Lillian would be spared that struggle, and Lucy was glad, but when she thought of her daughter's musical talent, now barely used, she felt a pang of regret that such a gift should go unrecognized. The talent that had brought her and John together now seemed irrelevant to both of them. That morning, she asked her daughter what she planned to do with her music.

"I don't know what you mean," said Lillian. "I practice every day, I play for church on Sunday..."

"You could have a concert career," Lucy said.

"You were the one who wanted me to get married." Lillian laughed. "And now there's Jack."

"So marriage wasn't what you wanted?"

"I didn't say that. I just said it changes things."

"Well, of course, but music has been a part of your life longer than John and the baby have, and it still could be."

"And it is, Mother. Just on a smaller scale."

They drank their coffee in silence for a few minutes. Lucy reminded herself that Lillian now made her own decisions, and she was free to take what she'd learned about a woman's independence and use it or not as she chose.

Lillian reached across the table and touched Lucy's hand. "I'm fine, Mother. I'm happy. And I haven't lost my music—not at all."

"I know," Lucy said. "Don't pay any attention to me. When you get old, you turn into a meddler, I guess."

Jack came in from his play and climbed into Lillian's lap. She hugged him close. "How can you not meddle in your children's lives?" she said. "I can't imagine it."

That fall, Lucy let John do the traveling, and she stayed in Deming, riding out on horseback with Pliny to inspect the properties of Mimbres Valley Real Estate, helping Jarvis outfit the new house he had built and spending time with her grandson. Lillian and John were also building a new house, this time in town, and Lillian was busy all day with that and her other social duties. Elizabeth Waddill was usually a guest when the family went on outings of any kind.

The Florida Mountains—Lucy had been surprised to find that Florida was pronounced FLOREEDA, with the emphasis on the middle syllable, and not like the state of Florida—drew people from all around on camping trips. Lillian loved to organize these excursions, and though John was rarely free to accompany them, she would gather other of her friends, plus Jarvis and Lucy, and they would go and spend a night or two in the quiet and beautiful atmosphere of the mountain foothills. This was not an easy task, but it was a pleasant experience. Just after Lucy got back to Deming that year, Lillian asked Elizabeth and her father and a friend of his from Kansas, along with Jarvis and a Mr. Rutherford, to go on such a trip, and they had a lot of fun. Lucy paid close attention to Jarvis and Elizabeth, but she could not sense anything special between them. They did not wander off together in the evenings but sat with the everyone else around the campfire, talking and playing games. They returned to Deming tired and dirty, but in excellent spirits.

The *Headlight* and the *Graphic* took pride in covering everyday events, and in fact, John's movements seemed to get special attention.

The *Deming Headlight*, October 1910: *J.M. McTeer, a local real estate dealer, left a few days ago for Louisville, Ky, with the view of sending a number of people here to locate in the Mimbres Valley.*

The *Deming Headlight*, January 1911: *John M. McTeer returned Monday night from Louisville where he had been for the last two months on business.*

The *Deming Graphic*, January 13, 1911: *John M. McTeer is home from Kentucky and is mighty glad of it. He says, "There's nothing to it but the sunshine state," and intimates that a good many Kentucky people are beginning to think so.*

When John returned from this trip, he was excited. "Lucy," he said, "I need you to go to Kentucky and arrange for another trainload of buyers to come out here. I've got a list of names, and I know most of them will want to get in on this."

She agreed to go, leaving the sunny weather in Deming to return to a cold and snowy Kentucky. In her role as liaison for the Southwest Immigration Company, she contacted the people on John's list and chartered a special train to take them from Louisville to Deming. Her job was to act as hostess for the journey. Most of the passengers were men, but a few had brought along their wives and even their children, so Lucy was busy all day and most of the night answering questions and seeing to the comfort of the group.

The *Graphic* wrote,

KENTUCKIANS COME IN STANDARD PULLMAN
Big Business Men of Louisville Join Deming's Progressive Boosters
OTHERS COMING SOON
Mimbres Valley Extends Glad Hand of Welcome to these Good People

It is with a feeling of justifiable pride that the Graphic has frequently called attention to the superb quality of citizenship that has been coming as a steady stream into the Mimbres Valley for many months, but we want to stop a minute to take off our hats to the fine crowd of business men and farmers who arrived Friday morning from Louisville, Kentucky, the party of twenty coming through in a special Pullman, under personal escort of Dr. Smith, passenger agent of the Missouri Pacific, and under the especial leadership of that prince of boosters, O. H. Cooper, one of the livest wires of the Bluegrass State, representing the hustling real estate firm of Cooper & McTeer, who are to be credited with this big Kentucky business. It will be remembered that J. M. McTeer but recently returned from that region.

That there is some class to the party is evidenced by the fact that one of the members, E. E. Sutton, is president of the American Skirt Manufacturing Co., another, B. F. Pearcy, is special agent of the Fidelity and Casualty Co. of Louisville, Mr. O. H. Cooper, whose family has already come to Deming and settled in one of the Baker ranch homes, southwest of the city, is one of the big rustlers of Northern Kentucky, and Albert Ernst, whose family is likewise here to stay, is one of the solid Kentucky farmers, who made a big success there and will make a bigger success here. Robert H. Simmons is another successful young farmer who thinks the sunshine state superior to the bluegrass country.

Mrs. L. J. Williams, who gave additional prestige to the party, was accompanied by Mrs. Simmons, mother of Robert H., and who couldn't resist a good land investment, and last but not least Mrs. Wm. E. Blackburn., one of Kentucky's bright women writers and a close relative of the famous "Joe" Blackburn, who belongs to the whole South. Mrs. Blackburn is a guest at the home of Mr. and Mrs. J. M. McTeer.

Kentucky is giving the Great Mimbres Valley some of her best people and we are more than delighted to extend them the glad hand of welcome.

Mrs. Blackburn (Lucy never learned her first name) had been unwell on the train, and Lucy had invited her to stay with her at Lillian's house rather than going to the hotel. As soon as she was able, Lucy took her around to see the properties in which she'd expressed an interest. The *Graphic* reported it: "Mrs. Blackburn of Kentucky has purchased a ten-acre plot south of the city . . . and Mrs. L. J. Williams couldn't resist the temptation to take ten acres for herself."

Mrs. Blackburn was a poet, and she would sit for hours on Lillian's veranda writing in a little notebook. She became fond of Jack, and one night, she presented Lillian with a poem in his honor. Lillian was so proud of it that she showed it to the editor of the *Graphic*, who, of course, printed it:

To Master Jack McTeer

Far up in the land of Heaven—
This side of the Palace of day;
The dear little angels were playing
In the fields near the Milky Way.

They raced with the flying meteors—
Played hide, 'mongst the stars so bright—
They climbed to the top of the rainbow,
To coast down its sides of light.

They took some of all its bright colors
And mixed them with starlight and dew,
And then, through a hollow sun-beam,
The most beautiful bubbles they blew.

One dear little fellow grew tired,
And lay down on a cloud to rest;
He fell asleep, as he floated along,
On its downy, billowy, breast.

There Love, the Heaven-born, found him,
And lifting him whispered, "he's worth
All else that I have, I will take him
To brighten a home on the earth."

In a basket Love laid him—a basket
Made of moonlight and dreams—then furled
A pearly cloud closely 'round them,
And floated away to the world.

Away to the world—to our doorway,
Where he found, oh the wonder of things!
There lay in the basket a baby—
The angel had dropped its wings.

You, sweet, were that angel-baby
Love brought to us from the skies;
Heaven's music is sweet in your voice—
Its light softly beams in your eyes.

And when you smile in your slumber,
"The angels are whispering," we say,
"To our lad of the Heaven he came from
And the fields where they used to play."

Mrs. Wm. E. Blackburn

Mrs. Blackburn soon left Deming, and Lucy never met up with her again, but her tribute to Jack, who was the joy of all their lives, would make her ever dear to them. Lillian bought extra copies of the newspaper and cut out several copies of the poem for framing. Lucy hung hers on her wall with pride.

That summer of 1911, Lucy traveled a great deal, ending up back in Deming in time for the big July party Lillian gave in honor of Elizabeth and Jarvis. The notice in the paper did not call it an engagement party, but they all assumed that Jarvis would use the opportunity to make an announcement to that effect. He did not, and Lucy worried. When he came to sit beside her later in the evening, he asked her if she would be interested in taking a vacation with him to the Blue Ridge Mountains.

Lucy was surprised, to say the least, but she told him she would. "What about your work?" she asked.

In addition to his duties for John, Jarvis was also working with C. J. Laughren, another one of John's associates, to improve the local Water Works Plant with an eye to managing it when the improvements were completed.

"I think I can get away," he said. "I haven't been back East for a long time, and I'm homesick."

If he had other reasons to want to get away, he did not tell his mother. They left at the beginning of August. The reporter from the *Graphic* was at the train station to ask questions and write a story about their trip. When Lucy read the notice on her return, she was pleased to see that Jarvis and his accomplishments had been the focus of the piece:

H. Jarvis Williams, the very efficient office manager at Laughren's, secretary of the Adelphia Club, assistant secretary of the Board of Education, and handy man anywhere, is enjoying a three-week vacation with his mother in the Blue Ridge Mountains of Tennessee.

Jarvis had become a man of prominence in Deming, but he said little of business while on their travels. They visited with Lucy's brother and his family in Tennessee and then hired a car to drive into the mountains. Lucy was still uncomfortable with automobiles, but Jarvis was a good driver. He took charge of their itinerary, and she was grateful not to have to make arrangements for passage or accommodations as she did with her real estate clients. If he missed Elizabeth, Jarvis did not show it. Lucy tried to broach the subject of his future once or twice, but she got nowhere. He was determined to have a good time, to show her the greatest respect and concern, but he had no intention of talking about himself. For the first time, she recognized his father in her son's quiet but efficient manner. She talked to him about Henry on that trip, and in the end, they traveled on to London to put flowers on Henry's grave and to have a short visit with a frail and dying Martha.

On their last day there, Lucy went to see Poca. She was thin and taut as a piano string. "What is the matter, Poca?" Lucy asked her. "Are you ill?"

Poca didn't answer directly but said, with her brittle laugh, "I envy you with all the traveling you do. It must be so much fun."

Lucy thought of the long train rides in smoke-filled cars, the querulous people she had to placate, and she shook her head. "Surely you and Mac travel," she said.

"Mac used to travel," said Poca, and her look made it clear that the subject was closed. She talked about her children and other members of her family whom Lucy had known in years past, but she made no further mention of her husband. With reluctance, Lucy said good-bye. She knew she would never see Poca again.

In January 1912, New Mexico became the forty-eighth state, and everyone joined in the celebration. It was a wild time, but lots of fun. Living in Kentucky, which had been a state since 1792, Lucy had never thought to be in on such an occasion. Music and speeches and a big parade filled the day, fireworks and dancing the night. A huge flag with forty-eight stars was raised over the Adelphia Club, and Mayor Corbett issued a proclamation, saying, "Whereas the Congress of the United States has granted unto us the priceless boon of statehood, the President having issued his final proclamation this 6th day of January, 1912; therefore, be it resolved, that we bow in grateful appreciation to the Giver of every good and perfect gift for the rich and manifold blessings He has bestowed upon this favored region in giving us the purest water, the purest air and the richest soil in America. Be it further resolved: that each and every one of us are mighty glad we're here. We hereby renew our united allegiance to the best city in the best part of the best State in the Union."

There was nothing modest about Demingites. As she listened to the speeches recalling the history of the territory and the campaign for statehood, Lucy heard over and over how glorious a place was this desert land and how, at last, the rest of the country had acknowledged it. The hardships suffered in reaching statehood were as if they had never happened.

In February of 1912, Lucy's niece, Margaret Moore, came for a visit, and Lillian arranged another camping trip to the Floridas. The *Headlight* proclaimed, "A two-day picnic to the Florida Mountains for Mr. & Mrs. John McTeer, Miss Elizabeth Waddill, Miss Margaret Moore and H. J. Williams."

Lucy begged off, but she was glad that Jarvis could get away. She expected to hear that he and Elizabeth were engaged on their return, but nothing was said. Jarvis's face was grim as the vehicles were being unloaded. Lillian invited Elizabeth to spend the night, but she declined, saying the trip had worn her out and she needed to get home. Jarvis offered to drive her, and she agreed, but the two of them seemed ill at ease with each other.

When they were alone, Lucy asked Lillian what had happened.

Lillian shrugged. "I don't know. Everything seemed fine until this morning. They went for a walk, and when they came back, Jarvis looked like death, and I could tell Elizabeth had been crying. They tried to put a good face on it, but it looks like they've broken up."

"But she let him take her home," Lucy said.

"What else could she do? He was going that way, and she had no other ride."

Lucy assumed that she might never know the straight of the situation, but to her surprise, Jarvis came to her the following day and told her about it. He said that he loved Elizabeth and had asked her to marry him, but she had refused. He was stoic, and Lucy didn't dare try to put her arms around him.

"Did she give you a reason?" she asked.

"She has found someone else," he said.

"But surely . . ."

"No, Mother. She will not change her mind. That was plain."

She did try to hug him then, but he gently pushed her away. "I want you to know that I never intend to talk about this again," he said.

"I'm so sorry, Jarvis."

He nodded and left. A few weeks later, Lucy saw a brief announcement of Elizabeth's marriage to Thom Rutherford in the newspaper, and she remembered the young man who had gone on the first camping trip with them.

"How cruel of her not to tell Jarvis of her attraction to Rutherford, to let him hope," she said to Lillian.

"I thought I knew her, but I guess I didn't," Lillian answered. "It turns out that she and Thom were neighbors in Virginia, but she thought she had lost him until they met again here and discovered they had always been in love."

Lucy and Lillian did their best to fill the gap in Jarvis's life, but with little success. He threw himself into his job at the Water Works Plant, but he had lost his joy and vigor, and only with his nephew, Jack, did he retain his fun-loving attitude.

Chapter Thirty-One

Mimbres Valley Real Estate owned many town lots, which John and Mr. Hon organized into the Hondale Townsite Company. Their land clients got first choice of these lots and, indeed, were urged to buy one of them rather than purchasing acreages outside the city limits. Lucy was not happy with this arrangement, for she had made it clear to her clients that she would help them find the land they wanted, wherever it might be. John and his partner saw it differently, of course, and rather than make trouble, she sold her part of the real estate company to them and moved in another direction. She had always worked better on her own.

She began corresponding with Philip Ward, an oilman she had met in Oklahoma a few years before when she was there on real estate business. He told her what to look for when deciding whether or not to drill for oil, how to go about the drilling, and what marketing options were available. He loaned her books on the subject and put her in touch with agencies in New Mexico where she could get more specific information.

Because she preferred her own space, Lucy stayed in town at Rabb's, and over the next year, she dedicated herself to learning all she could about the oil business. She and Pliny rode out on horseback to a dozen or more sites where they applied soil tests according to what Lucy had learned.

They found the most promising signs on the Pecos River just south of Artesia, near Dayton, a tiny town established by J. C. Day in 1902, and named for him. Lucy immediately bought up as much of the land in that area as she could afford—several hundred acres—with an eye to selling it to those who wanted to invest in oil property. She did nothing in haste. With Pliny's help, she set out to test the soil at every likely spot within her holdings, and that was not an easy task. They loaded his wagon with food and bedrolls and tents and prepared to stay on the land for months, if necessary.

Once again, Lucy was in business for herself. How much she had missed that autonomy! She felt invigorated and so full of plans that Pliny became concerned.

"Whoa, Lucy," he said. "You don't know that there's one speck of oil down there." He pointed to the ground where we had just taken a soil sample.

"But there has to be," she told him. "All the signs point to it."

One of those signs was that other oil prospectors had also begun to test in the area. The newspapers wrote about the Dayton oil field as if hundreds of wells had already come in there. Lucy believed, with all her heart, that there was oil to be discovered, but she thought the news reports were premature and that they were more harmful than helpful.

As she had done with her real estate business, she set up a company to develop her property and began a campaign to enlist her friends and acquaintances as investors. There was a lot of enthusiasm. John and Jarvis and Pliny bought in, along with a dozen others in both Deming and London. Lucy explained that such a business venture was risky, that should oil not be found on the property, they had no legal recourse, but none of the buyers seemed to be the least concerned about that.

Then just as the last lot had been sold, Pliny found the first real evidence of oil on her land, near the river, and she put down a well. The *Headlight* wrote,

> Mrs. Williams has large interests in the oil fields at Dayton, New
> Mexico, having formed a company to develop her holdings in that
> locality when oil was discovered there. The well has been drilled to
> a depth of 600 ft. and the flow of artesian water is being cased off.
> The indications are very promising for a good flow of oil.

It felt like the old days, and Lucy was having the time of her life. With the money she made from the sale of her lots, she purchased drilling equipment and hired workmen with Pliny as overseer. Other companies moved in, and soon, the whole area was filled with the noise of the drilling machines and the sight of workers' tents. Lucy put up a tent for herself and spent most of her time on site.

They were now into their second year in the oil field. The first had been spent in obtaining buyers and equipment and putting down the well. Since then, they had expected to strike oil with each new day, but they did not.

Pliny mingled with the other prospectors and brought her all the news. "How would you like to sell your holdings, Lucy?" he asked one day.

"Why would I want to do that?"

"You could make a lot of money."

"Who says?"

"I keep my ears open. If you sell out now, you can make a big profit on the land."

"But not as big as I'll make when the well comes in."

"What if the well don't come in?"

"We're only down to 1,500 feet."

"I'm just saying that sometimes . . ."

"Pliny, I'm not a 'take the money and run' kind of person. We haven't given this a real chance yet," she said, but she was worried.

She had trusted Pliny with the knowledge of everything she did and had assumed that his frequent visits to the other drillers' sites had been to spy on them, but now she wondered if he had his own agenda.

"What is it you're not telling me?"

"Oh, nobody can tell you anything, Lucy. You know it all."

"Pliny, what is the matter with you?"

"I'm just trying to help you."

"I'm not interested in selling," she said. "I owe it to my investors to see this through."

Pliny stalked off in a huff.

Meanwhile, things were changing for John and Lillian. John was working full-time for the Missouri State Insurance Company and had been appointed district manager. He left most of his other projects to his partners or to Jarvis. On the occasions when she went into Deming, Lucy found him frantically working to maintain the level of activity in which he had involved himself.

"Am I making any money in the oil fields, Lucy?" John asked.

"Not yet," she said, "but you will."

"I'm beginning to wonder. Pliny tells me that the Dooley Oil Company offered to buy you out, but you wouldn't sell."

"Well, Pliny should keep his mouth shut," Lucy said.

John took her hand. "Lucy," he said, "I think the world of you and I don't want to see you get hurt."

"What makes you think I'm going to?"

"I'm hearing that there isn't any oil up there on your land."

"Then why would Dooley want to buy me out?"

"I don't know, but I think you should accept their offer and repay your investors before you lose everything."

"And I think that someone at Dooley knows we're going to make a strike, and they want to get their hands on all the land in the area before that happens."

John sighed. "Maybe it's just gossip," he said.

Lucy had rarely known John to make a bad business decision, so she thought long and hard about what he had said. Then looking back at her own career, it seemed to her that she had made good decisions too, so she decided to wait for further developments before accepting Dooley's offer.

Pliny was not as conciliatory as John had been. "Lucy, you've done give this well enough time. It ain't going to come in, and as an investor, I'm asking you to sell out."

Most of her investors had gone on about their lives, expecting Lucy to see to it that they did not lose the money they had entrusted to her.

"I don't hear anyone else complaining," she said.

"What do you think John was doing?"

"You and John seem to have gotten pretty close lately."

Pliny had the grace to blush. "I'm sorry I went behind your back, Lucy," he said. "But I'm worried about you, and I didn't know who else to talk to about it."

"I was taking care of myself before I ever met you or John, and I can take care of myself now."

"You are the stubbornest woman I ever knew," Pliny said.

"I've had to be," Lucy answered.

She and Pliny had never quarreled before, and it shook her. As she had so often done, she sat on the porch at Rabb's and thought about her situation. In the end, she took John and Pliny's advise and offered to sell to Dooley Inc. The company spokesperson, a Mr. Flynn, listened to her without expression, and when she had finished, he said, "If you had come to me a month ago, I could have helped you, but Dooley is closing its operation here for the time being."

"Why?"

"We've come to believe that the wells we've drilled are not going to be productive," he said. "We're no longer interested in further investments in the area."

That afternoon, Lucy wrote letters to all her investors telling them that there would be no oil well and that she had spent all their money on land and equipment. She told them that the land would be put up for sale and that any money she got from that and the sale of the equipment would be divided among all the investors. There was no way they would get back the full amount they had entrusted to her. Fortunately, no one sued, but Lucy's sense of failure was almost more than she could bear.

She advertized the land for sale, but there were no takers. Pliny offered to see about getting rid of the equipment, but she told him she would do it. She contacted Phillip Ward and asked him to recommend a market for the drilling rig. By the end of 1914, she had sold all of the equipment to wildcatters at a third of its value. Finally, Dooley agreed to buy the land because it joined their own holdings, but they refused to meet Lucy's price. By this time, she only wanted to be free of it. She took what she could get, divided it among her investors as an act of good faith, and retired to Rabb's to lick her wounds.

Her funds were dangerously low but worse than that was the depth of her standing in the Deming community. People she had called her friends now found excuses not to talk to her, and this made life hard, not only for her but for her children as well.

John arranged to be transferred to Missouri State Insurance's office in Albuquerque, and though he came back and forth to Deming for some months as he wound up affairs with his other companies, he never again took an active part in the community. Lucy's heart went out to Lillian, who, having been one of the leading ladies of Deming, now had to find a niche in a much larger society.

Lucy made plans to leave, and she asked Jarvis to come with her.

"I have responsibilities here, Mother," he said. His job at the Water Works did not seem to be in danger.

"But what if people hold my mistakes against you?" she asked.

"Mother, haven't you learned by now that what others think of you doesn't matter?"

His straightforward evaluation of the situation raised her spirits. "You know, Jarvis, you're absolutely right. I can't believe that I forgot that, even for a moment."

"So why don't you stay here?"

She shook her head. "Throughout my life, whenever things got hard, I just backed up and started over. That's what I'll do now."

"So you'll go back to London?"

"Oh no. There's nothing for me there. I think I'll go to California."

Chapter Thirty-Two

Once more, Lucy took the train toward a new adventure. For the next five years, she lived in Burbank, working in the business she knew best—real estate. It was a good time for it, and she was able to buy a small house where she took in boarders to supplement the income from her listings. Not since the first years after Henry's death had she lived so frugally. She made few friends, for she had grown wary of alliances, but she enjoyed the California weather and being her own person once again. She heard that Pliny was in San Diego, but she did not try to contact him.

Her greatest concern was Jarvis. His letters were always cheerful, and she could detect no sense of ostracism from his neighbors for which she was thankful. He worked hard and talked of going into business for himself.

She subscribed to the *Headlight* so she could keep up with all that was happening. The newspaper was full of the unrest in Mexico. Being so near the border of that country, adverse events were sure to affect the peace in Deming. In 1916, when Pancho Villa marched across the border and invaded the little town of Columbus, New Mexico, so near Deming, Lucy could not sleep for fear that Jarvis would be hurt. As it turned out, Deming was relatively unaffected by Villa's raid, but she could imagine the tension among the Americans and their Mexican counterparts.

She had no doubt that the threat of war contributed to Jarvis's decision to join the navy in the spring of 1917. Lucy found this announcement in the *Headlight* of May 18, 1917: "H. Jarvis Williams was entertained at a number of informal dinners by his friends in Deming before his departure for the Presidio at San Francisco where he expects to take up training for a position in the officer's reserve corps."

She was proud of Jarvis for staying in Deming when the rest of them had run away. He had proven something to himself, if nothing else. Elizabeth and her husband had moved back to Virginia, so at least he did not have to meet her at every turn. His decision to join the military probably had more to do with making a change in his life than with any patriotic duty, but Lucy admired him for enlisting. His job as utility clerk on a naval vessel that moved troops between the United States and Europe was often lonely and boring, but it was rarely dangerous.

Lucy was sixty-three and glad that the pace of her life had slowed. When the census taker for 1920 called on her at her home in Burbank, she gave her age and occupation with thankfulness that she had survived another ten years. She had no idea what would ultimately happen to such records, but she hoped the government would take good care of them and make them available to the public. It pleased her to imagine some future descendant being able to trace her movements across the country by reading the census reports.

Her Burbank friends were casual, at best. They lived a busy life that included lots of parties to which she was often invited, but rarely attended. One evening, she did go to a reception for a local politician where William Wrigley Jr. was holding everyone spellbound with his descriptions of the beauty of Santa Catalina Island, which he had just purchased, off the coast of California. "I plan to find buyers for the houses and bring in all sorts of improvements," he said. "But mostly, I want to preserve it for future generations."

Lucy could not forget his words. The old longing to try something new begin to crawl into her mind. To move to Catalina would mean another big change in her life, and she argued with herself over whether it was advisable at her age, but the idea would not go away. After trying to ignore this inner voice for nearly a year, she shut down her business, sold her house in Burbank, and moved to Catalina.

There she bought a house on Sumner Avenue that had four cottages attached to it—cottages she could rent to people who came to the island for business or recreation. Since new people came in daily on the ferry from the mainland, she soon had tenants in all her rooms. That income helped her keep body and soul together while she embraced the challenge of starting yet another real estate company.

A devastating fire had destroyed nearly half of Avalon, the only city on Santa Catalina Island, in 1915, and there were still many unsightly places when Lucy arrived. This meant that some of the lots in the main part of town were for sale, and she listed as many of them as she could. Then she spent hours of her own time cleaning up the debris and making those lots sellable again.

Her children were dubious about her chances of being successful, but Lucy's confidence in herself had returned, and she knew her decision was a wise one. Mr. Wrigley had been right about everything. Catalina was a world of infinite possibilities. The ugly scars left from the fire began to disappear, replaced by more modern homes and stores. The Wrigleys, who were great conservationists, brought in hundreds of trees and flowers and donated them to the rebuilding project. By the summer of 1922, Avalon bloomed, tourists poured in, and Lucy began to make money again.

Never had she done such satisfying work in such a perfect setting. As she had loved the lush foliage in London and the colors of the desert in Deming, she was now captivated by the ocean. How had she had ever lived without it? On her evening walks, she stopped on the pier to savor the vastness of the sea. Los Angeles seemed thousands of miles away instead of only twenty-six. Lights from ships on the horizon and the yachts of the rich nearer to shore twinkled as darkness fell. As she listened to the peaceful whisper of the sea breeze, Lucy felt complete.

Epilogue

CATALINA ISLAND, CALIFORNIA
APRIL 18, 1925

I cannot believe that I've spent Saturday, my one free day, just sitting on the porch of my cottage, remembering. Not that I think the time was wasted; memories need to be taken out at times and examined as a way of evaluating one's life. The sad memories are difficult, though . . . like the last time I saw Poca, that year Jarvis and I went back to Kentucky . . . Why didn't she tell me that Mac was in prison for embezzling funds from the bank? Did she think I would hold it against her? Now she is gone, and I can never tell her how sorry I am that she had to bear such a burden or how proud I am of her strength. I'll say one thing for Poca: As long as I knew her, she kept her head up and faced life with courage and determination. I miss her to this day.

Some bad memories have happy endings, though. I read in the Deming Headlight that the Dooley Company struck oil on the very land where I put down my well and on many of their adjoining fields too. They had to go down to around six thousand feet to find it. My equipment would never have drilled that far down, so I was destined to fail. But at least my instincts were right.

I had meant to do other things today. I owe both Lillian and Jarvis a letter, and there is a house that I need to get ready for showing. I am pleased with the business opportunities here. Someday, Catalina will be a place where wealthy people come on holiday. Of course, it is already that, to some extent, but it can be much more. The possibilities make my mind whirl.

If only Jarvis could see his way clear to move here, but he is not interested in real estate. He has never found his place since the war, and I worry about him. Lillian's life is full with her husband and Jack, but Jarvis has a "lost soul" quality about him that breaks my heart. I must invite him to visit as soon as the weather is more stable. There is no place like Catalina in the early summer.

I have had some dizzy spells these past few weeks, but when I write to the children, I will not tell them that. What good would it do? They are so far away. I think I will take Mrs. Byrd's advice, though, and make an appointment with the new doctor. It can't hurt. And speaking of my neighbor, Mrs. Byrd, I seem to remember that I promised to meet her for dinner at the Busy Bee Café this evening. I'm really not up to it, but perhaps if I take a short nap, I'll feel better.

Afterword

On the evening of April 18, 1925, Lucy J. Williams was taken to the hospital on Santa Catalina Island where she died the following Wednesday, April 22. No one knows on whom she called for help that night, but it may have been a neighbor. The *Catalina Islander* reported that she was ill with a "general breakdown," but her death certificate from the California Department of Vital Statistics lists cause of death as "chronic myocarditis and arteriosclerosis complicated by a traumatic brain concussion caused by a fall at her home." Her children were contacted, but Lucy died before they could make the long journey from their homes on the mainland. Her body was taken to Los Angeles, where it was held until Lillian and Jarvis arrived, and then buried on April 27 at Forest Lawn Cemetery, Glendale, California.

A memorial stone for Lucy, similar to the one at Forest Lawn, was placed beside Henry's grave in what is now the A. R. Dyche Memorial Cemetery in London, Kentucky.

Jarvis, who died in 1947, is also buried there. Lillian outlived both her mother and her brother, as well as her husband and son. She died in Marin County, California, in 1970.

Edwards Brothers Malloy
Thorofare, NJ USA
April 1, 2016